ANYWHERE IN TIME

MAGIC OF TIME SERIES
Book Two

Melissa Mayhue

Published by Melissa Mayhue
Copyright © 2015 Melissa Mayhue
Last Updated - 10/2015
Cover art by Inspire Creative Services
Edited by Editing 720
All rights reserved.

Print Edition ISBNs:
ISBN-10:1519150822
ISBN-13:978-1519150820

Ebook Edition ISBNs:
ISBN-10: 09898272
ISBN-13: 978-0-9898272-6-3

DEDICATION

This book is dedicated to all the wonderful readers whose interest in the series keeps me motivated to write the next book.

Special mention goes out to all the very special ladies at The Magic of Time Facebook Group! Thank you all for being there when I need to complain about the characters or share my excitement when the writing goes well!

Other Books by Melissa Mayhue:

~ Magic of Time Series ~
(Time Travel and Highlanders Romance)

1 - All the Time You Need (2014)
2 - Anywhere In Time (2015)

~Chance, Colorado Series~
(Contemporary Romance)

1 - Take a Chance (2013)
2 - Second Chance at Love (Coming 2016)

Daughters of the Glen Series ~
(Time Travel and Highlanders Romance)

1 - Thirty Nights with a Highland Husband (2007)
2 - Highland Guardian (2007)
3 - Soul of a Highlander (2008)
4 - A Highlander of Her Own (2009)
5 - A Highlander's Destiny (2010)
6 - A Highlander's Homecoming (2010)
7 - Healing the Highlander (2011)
8 - Highlander's Curse (2011)

~ Warriors Series ~
(Time Travel and Highlanders Romance)

1- Warrior's Redemption (2012
2 - Warrior's Last Gift (2012)(Novella/e-book)
3 - Warrior Reborn (2012)
4 - Warrior Untamed (2013)

PROLOGUE

Highlands of Scotland
1295

"I thought I'd find you out here."

Startled, Syrie turned to find Patrick MacDowylt striding toward her. As always, he moved confidently, though his every step was silent. Everything about the man, from his long black hair to the glint in his deep blue eyes, struck her as somehow lethal, reminding her of an enormous cat of prey. Truly, he was a man born to be a warrior of the highest grade.

"I enjoy the evenings out here in the garden," she said as he stopped at her side.

It was no lie, though it wasn't her real reason for being in the garden tonight. With yesterday's wedding behind her, Syrie had no doubt but that the Goddess would be contacting her to relay her displeasure with Syrie's careless fit of anger. Here, in the open glory of nature, would be the most likely spot for the Goddess to speak to her. It was also far enough from the keep that, should the Goddess see fit to discipline her, the other inhabitants of Castle MacGahan would be safe.

"I should miss this place so very much were I to..." But this wasn't something she needed to share with Patrick, so she changed what she'd been about to say. "I take it you were looking for me?" she asked. "Am I needed in the keep?"

"No," he answered, his usual grin lifting one corner of his mouth. "Not in the keep. I sought you out to say my farewell in private."

"What?" Her voice cracked on the word. How could he possibly know about—

"I wanted to tell you that I'll be leaving at first light. I'm leading the company that will escort Chase and Christiana on their return to Tordenet. Now that Torquil has been vanquished, my sister and her husband can begin the next phase in their lives together. I've agreed to assist them in setting things to rights as they settle in."

"Oh." Of course, he hadn't known about her situation. How could he possibly? "Now that I think on it, I believe I did hear Christiana speaking of their plan to return to her home after Hall and Bridget were wed. She even might have mentioned that you were going with them."

She'd heard the news and had chosen to ignore it. Or, more accurately, she'd heard and hoped it was untrue. Castle MacGahan without Patrick would be a much less interesting place.

"And here I'd hoped to be the one to tell you." Again that infectious grin lit his face. "Still, I could hardly leave without saying farewell to our resident Elf."

"You know well enough, Patrick MacDowylt, I'm not an Elf—"

"But a Faerie," he finished for her, laughter underlying his words. "Yes, I believe I've heard you make mention of that very thing a time or two."

In spite of his incessant teasing, the thought of his leaving turned her stomach sour and filled her with an emptiness she was at a loss to explain.

"You'll take care in your travels, will you not? And send word, now and then. For…for your brother's sake, that is. He'll worry himself over your safety, I'm sure. And should you decide not to return—"

The catch in her own voice caught her by surprise. How foolish she was! No man, especially no mere mortal, could ever be worth her shedding a tear. And yet, as she prepared to say farewell to Patrick, she found her throat pulling tight and her eyes misting over.

"Aye," he said, moving so close to her that she almost forgot how to take her next breath. "But you've no cause to fash yerself over my absence, sweet Elf. It's no' like I could stay away from this place forever. No' this place and definitely no' you."

Before she could respond, before she could even think of how to respond, his lips were on hers, and she found herself unable to think at all. She felt as if she'd been transported, lighter than air, to a place far away where only the two of them existed. It was as if her very soul sprang to life, filling her with an unimaginable joy.

When his mouth broke away from hers, she sucked in a shaky breath. Her fingertips untangled from the silken mass of his hair where they had mysteriously found their way, and rose to cover the lips that now felt bereft of the exquisite physical touch they'd just experienced.

"I," she began, her mind reeling with thoughts she couldn't quite seem to form into coherent utterances. "You…"

"Apologies," he murmured, so close his breath fanned over her. "I doona ken why I—apologies for my mistake, my lady."

Abruptly, Patrick turned and strode away, leaving her more confused than she'd ever felt in her very long life.

Through her confusion, one thing became quite clear in her thoughts. That kiss…whatever else it might have been, it was certainly no mistake.

CHAPTER ONE

Highlands of Scotland
1295

Three months.

Elesyria Aí Byrn brushed a stray lock of hair from her face and stared out into the distance. Three months had passed since the wedding of Halldor O'Donar and Bridget MacCulloch. Three months and one day had passed since she'd lost her temper and so rashly used her Magic in a manner strictly forbidden to her.

Three months.

A long enough time that any normal person might be lulled into a sense of safety under the false belief that the Goddess had chosen to ignore her transgression.

But Syrie wasn't any normal person. She was Faerie. And she knew that three months meant nothing to her people. Time passed differently for the nearly immortal race of Fae than it did for other, more short-lived creatures like the Mortals with whom she had chosen to live.

Regardless of how they viewed time, her people had an intense intolerance for disobedience. And the visit she'd had just this morning from the Tinkler, Editha Faas, confirmed that the Fae were well-aware of her indiscretion. Well-aware of it and preparing to take action.

Unable to stand still any longer, Syrie began to pace, making a circle around the parapet, taking in the scenery of the surrounding countryside, bathed in the glow of the setting sun.

She would miss the beauty of this world. She would miss the people here who had become so dear to her.

She would miss one person in particular more than all the others.

No doubt her punishment would entail her returning to Wyddecol, the Faerie home world. At best, she could expect to spend the next few centuries serving the Goddess in her Temple, lowest of the low in the order of Danu's Maidens. One did not disobey the Earth Mother and expect to go unpunished.

But for her, a sentence of centuries might as well be a lifetime. Though she would age little, *his* life would be over before she could return.

With a sigh, she stopped and pressed her back against the outer wall. Life had rarely been fair to her, but feeling sorry for herself would hardly help. It never had. There was nothing to be gained from wallowing in this bout of self-pity. She was merely wasting what little time she had left here in this world. She had always prided herself in being able to find something positive in any situation, no matter how dark. This situation was no exception. Now, more than ever, she needed to reach for the light and find some small positive to hold on to.

Confinement to Wyddecol, to the Temple, would allow her to reunite with her friend, Nalindria Ré Alyn. Sweet, shy Nally, a woman so devoted to the Goddess she'd chosen permanent service at the Temple as the course for her life. Syrie couldn't count the times she'd hoped some of Nally's devotion and meek acceptance of life would rub off on her. She also couldn't count the times she'd berated that same friend to be more assertive, more self-serving.

Seeing Nally again would be good. Life in the Temple would be good. Everything would be good, if not for the mess she'd made for herself.

She scrubbed her hands over her face before staring up at the darkening sky, her heart filled with a longing stronger than any she'd ever felt before.

If only *he* were here now. If only she'd controlled her temper better. If only she hadn't used her Magic so rashly.

But she had. And though what she'd done was strictly forbidden, she couldn't regret the act itself. Using her Magic to bring together all those souls who were meant to be together might be the single most important thing she'd ever accomplished in the whole of her life, even if it was forbidden for her to have done it.

Too late to worry over the consequences now. She'd done what she'd done and now the flow of events was set in motion and far beyond her ability to control or change.

Her one big regret was that they'd likely come for her before Patrick returned to Castle MacGahan.

There were so many things she would like to have said to him before he'd gone north to help his sister and brother-in-law settle in at Tordenet. But, as too often had been the case in her life, foolish pride had kept her from

7

speaking up once she'd realized what feelings she carried for the big warrior. Foolish pride and fear that he'd likely not hold the same feelings for her as she held for him. Especially not after the way he'd reacted to that unexpected kiss.

His *mistake*, he'd called it.

Now, as she felt her time here slipping away from her, she deeply regretted not having confronted her feelings for him sooner. Regretted not having confronted him as to his feelings, if any, for her.

Patrick MacDowylt was hardheadedly stubborn, unrelentingly sure of himself, and easily the most annoying male she had ever met, Faerie or Mortal. But he was also thoughtful and kind, and handsome in a way that had wormed his very essence securely into her heart. The thought of never seeing him again carried with it a bitter pain that lodged deeply in her chest, threatening at times like this to steal away her ability to breathe.

"What will be, will be," she murmured into the rising breeze. "It is as the Goddess wills."

"We are surprised to hear you still acknowledge that little fact, Elesyria, based on how you've repeatedly ignored the will of the Goddess."

Syrie pressed her back against the large wooden door, scanning the parapet for the owner of the disembodied voices ringing in her ears. Though she was alone, the voices continued, a murmur from somewhere behind her ears, deep inside her head.

"The time has come for you to pay penance for your disobedience."

As she had known it would. If only-

8

Her thoughts were cut short as a wall of emerald-green light descended in front of her. Slowly, the wall began to part, like a curtain being pulled back, and the scenery before her eyes split and wrinkled, revealing the blinding green vista of Wyddecol.

Regret pounded in her heart like the blood pulsing through her veins and she turned her head for one final glimpse of the Mortal world as she stepped through the opening, leaving that which she held dearest behind her.

CHAPTER TWO

Now what?

Patrick MacDowylt masked his impatience, pasting a smile on his face to greet his sister's hurried approach. It wasn't Christiana's fault that his leaving Tordenet had been delayed so many times. It wasn't the fault of any one being he could point to. The delays had just seemed to keep coming, especially after he realized why he was so anxious to return to Castle MacGahan.

"Thank the Fates I caught you, Paddy," Christiana said breathlessly, using the old endearment he'd rarely heard since their childhood.

She laid her hand on his arm as she reached him, her tension seeping into his skin as if it were a living thing.

"What troubles you, little sister?"

"Orabilis," she answered. "I've a feeling something has gone wrong on her journey back to her cottage. It's as if…" She paused, shaking her head, her eyes filled with worry. "It's as if I can hear her calling out to me for help."

If the old witch who'd raised his sister after their mother's death were to be in need of help, Patrick had little doubt but that it would be Christiana who would be in her thoughts. And, considering Christiana's *Gifts*, he could hardly discount her concern.

"What would you have of me?"

"I ken yer anxious to be on yer way, brother, and I'd ask this of Chase if he hadn't already left with the herdsmen to inspect the condition of the winter grazing pastures."

"And?" Patrick encouraged, biting back on his need to speed her along in the explanations so that he might find out what fresh new delay the Fates had in store for him.

"Could you check upon her for me? Please? It should be no great deviation from your own route, as you'll be traveling along the same roads she took." Christiana dipped her head before casting a glance up at him. "More or less."

Exactly as he'd feared. The delay hid itself in the *more or less* portion of his sister's rationalization. In truth, the path he'd take would follow Orabilis' own only for a few miles before he'd need to break to the south.

Not that he would deny Christiana the assistance she sought, not when she'd asked so little of him over the years. And most especially not when her husband was away doing exactly what Patrick had advised him to do to prepare for the coming winter.

"Very well," he said, smiling down at her. "Though I've little doubt that yer old witch is perfectly fine, I'll see to her well-being, myself."

"Oh, Paddy," Christiana squealed, throwing her arms around his neck and hugging him tightly. "Yer such a fine brother. I'm going to miss you, you ken? Yer always welcome here at Tordenet. It is, after all, yer home as much as it is mine."

"My thanks, little sister," he said, gently removing her arms from around his neck so that he could straighten up. "Now, doona you fash yer pretty head over Orabilis for one more moment, aye?"

"Aye," she agreed, backing away as he mounted the big, black horse he favored.

A slight pressure on the reins and he trotted toward the portcullis, turning only once to lift his hand in farewell before passing through the gates and out onto the road.

The creaking of chains sounded as the iron grate slid shut behind him and, for the first time in many days, he felt as if he could draw the breath of a free man.

He loved his little sister and had nothing but admiration for the man she'd married. Christiana and Chase had gone above and beyond in their efforts to make him feel welcome during his stay. But since that night out on the parapet, he'd wanted nothing so much as to be gone from this place. On that night, alone in the glow of the setting sun, he'd realized that the happiness he saw his sister and her new husband sharing could well be his own. All he'd needed was to accept his feelings for the woman he'd left behind at Castle MacGahan. If she felt for him as he felt for her? Well, then, everything else be damned. They'd find a way to make it work.

He licked his lips and could well imagine the taste of her lingered there still, even though it had been over three months since he'd been compelled to steal the kiss that had changed his life.

A smile spread over his face as he anticipated his future for perhaps the first time since his childhood. As the third son of the MacDowylt laird, his lot in life had never been to marry well and settle into a home of his own. As third son, the best he could hope for was a trusted place in his brother's home.

But all of that had changed the night he'd dared to rashly give in to his desire to kiss Syrie. From that moment, the need to be with her had taken root. The root had spread as he'd spent time with Christiana and Chase. If ever there had been a love story that shouldn't have been, their story was it. If they could find their happiness, then there was a chance for him to find his, as well.

It wouldn't be long now. A few hours' delay, at most, as he checked on Orabilis and then he'd ride like the wind, determined to reach Castle MacGahan in record time. The stars in his life were aligning at last.

His optimism lasted no more than an hour, dying a sudden death as, in the distance, he spotted the wagon Orabilis had been driving when she'd left Tordenet the day before. From all appearances, his sister had been right in her worries. The wagon lay tipped on its side, the horses and their rigging nowhere in sight.

For a moment Patrick considered that Orabilis might have continued on her journey home with the missing animals. But when the bundle of cloth beside the wagon began to move, he knew he'd been wrong.

Urging his mount to speed, he reached the wagon in a matter of seconds and jumped from his horse's back to kneel beside the old woman.

"Tell me where yer hurt, Orabilis," he said, praying she'd open her eyes. When she did, he slid his hand over her forehead. "Can you speak to me?"

"Of course I can speak, whelp," she growled, though not with her usual vigor.

For a fact, she actually smiled, in spite of her words.

"Can you stand?"

She shook her head. "No' on my own, I fear. My knee fair twisted under me when the wagon sent me for a tumble. Save that, I could have walked home by now."

Patrick lifted her in his arms, ignoring her little squeak of surprise when he stood.

"Here now, lad, what do you think yer about? Put me down."

He ignored her protests, climbing up on his horse while doing his best not to jostle her too much. "We'll get you back to Tordenet where Christiana can have a look at you."

"Oh, no, you willna," the old woman protested. "You'll take me to my own cottage, where I belong. I can see to my own healing, thank you very much."

"I'm sure you can," he said quietly, continuing on the course he'd already set. "But we'll no' take a chance on that for now."

"Do you have any idea what I could do to you for yer disobedience, lad?" she protested, actually putting some strength into her struggles this time, though it wasn't enough to deter him.

"I've an idea," he answered, urging the horse to move more quickly. "But I'm also well aware of what my wee sister is capable of when she's riled. That being the case, we'll give her a go at you first. Then, when she gives us leave, you've my word that I'll personally see you home safely. Now quiet yer fussing before you make that knee worse than it already is."

As if mollified by his promise, the old woman stilled in his arms and seemed to relax.

They rode in silence for close to an hour before she spoke again.

"Was it by accident you found me?" she asked.

"Only if you'd consider Christiana's concerns for you an accident," he responded, grinning down at her.

"I see," she murmured, as if considering what to say next. "I take it that means you detoured from yer travels back to Castle MacGahan to check on me."

"Aye," he responded. "It was the only way to soothe my sister's fears. Well-founded fears, I might add, considering yer plight when I came upon you."

Again they rode in silence, this time until the white walls of Tordenet shone in the distance. As they approached the big gate, Orabilis spoke once again.

"You always were a good brother to Christiana, Patrick MacDowylt, and I can see you've grown into a fine man, as well. Though you rescued me for the sake of yer sister, you still rescued me, all the same. For that rescue, I'm in yer debt." The old woman was quiet for a moment, then she turned her face up to him, a wide smile stretching her thin lips. "And let me assure you, lad, there are far worse things than having old Orabilis owe you a favor, aye?"

"Aye," he agreed, returning her smile. "I'd well suppose there are."

Who could say? Though he couldn't for the life of him imagine a need arising, one day he just might want to call on her for that favor.

CHAPTER THREE

Wyddecol
Land of the Faerie

"Do you deny any of the charges for which you stand accused?"

Deny the charges? No, she could not. But Syrie fairly ached to explain why she'd done each of the things the Reader of Complaints had enumerated.

Instead, she gritted her teeth together to keep herself from speaking. Explanations would do her no good here. While the Mortal world functioned in shades of gray, the world of Faerie consisted of only black and white when it came to their laws. In this place, in front of the High Council, there existed only right and wrong, guilty and innocent, with no room in between for explanations or reasons.

That had always been Syrie's problem. Her mind and her heart functioned best in that nebulous in-between, in the gray world of contradictions. Perhaps that was why she'd always felt so comfortable in the Mortal world. She knew right from wrong as well as the next person, but, sometimes, obeying the rules felt more wrong than treading into the waters of the forbidden.

"Surely you must have realized the risk the Earth Mother took on your behalf when she, herself, broke the rules to allow you to cross through the veil between worlds with your Magic fully intact. And yet, in spite of the risk to you and to her, you disobeyed her instructions and used that Magic whenever you saw fit, without regard to the rules so meticulously crafted by the Lawgivers of Wyddecol. You disobeyed even after warnings were sent to you. Repeated warnings, I might add." The Supreme Leader of the High Council peered over the top of the scroll she held in her hands, her disapproving eyes shifting from Syrie to the Earth Mother and back again. "At this time, we enter into the record all the individual instances where your lack of control and good judgment led you down the wrong path. It is not our task to judge you as a good or bad being, Elesyria Aĺ Byrn. It is our task to see to it that you are held responsible for the rules you have broken. As a result, we are in unanimous agreement that you must pay for your repeated willful disobedience, and your punishment has been determined to see that you do exactly that."

Keeping her head bowed, Syrie cast a covert glance toward the Earth Mother, as if there might be some reprieve coming from that direction. She should have known better. The Goddess sat in her chair, back ramrod straight, any emotions she might have felt securely hidden, except for her oddly pursed lips.

No help would be coming from that quarter.

Perhaps the Council would be lenient. Perhaps they wouldn't sentence her to anything as severe as living out her days in the Earth Mother's Temple. Perhaps, if anything, they'd choose to exile her to the Mortal world, to live out her days without her Magic, as if she were but a regular Mortal.

Her heart quickened at the thought. While it would surely seem a harsh punishment to the Council, it wouldn't really be so bad. Not for her, anyway. The loss of her Magic would pain her deeply, but she could be with Patrick. Exile was the most severe punishment she'd ever heard meted out by the High Council, and then only for the most serious of offenses. Surely, the things she'd done could hardly be considered among the most serious.

And yet one look at the faces of the Council members assured her that they must consider her transgressions among the worst they'd ever encountered.

The Council members rose from their seats as one and slowly made their way, single file, to the chamber floor where Syrie stood. They stopped only after they'd formed a circle, with her in the center.

Once again, the Supreme Leader of the Council spoke, this time without her scroll in front of her.

"Exile is your Judgment, Elesyria Aí Byrn. Exile to the Mortal Plain."

The Mortal Plain! Once again Syrie struggled to keep her eyes downcast. It was exactly as she'd hoped.

"Through the River of Time," the Supreme Leader continued, her voice droning on without any trace of emotion. "Stripped of your Magic and your memory."

"What?" Syrie exclaimed, her head snapping up so that she might meet the eyes of her judges.

"Surely service in my Temple—" the Goddess said from behind her, but any protest was cut short.

"Service as one of your handmaidens did nothing to prevent the transgressions for which she stands accused," the Leader said. "If anything, her relationship to you only emboldened her disobedience."

"I see nothing in this punishment that will aid in her reform," the Earth Mother said.

"As we made no attempt to judge this woman as good or bad, so we make no attempt to reform her. Our judgment is that she be punished for what she did wrong. Punishment we mete out now."

The Council members joined hands and the first flicker of soul-searing pain racked through Syrie's body. Like bolt after bolt of lightning, the pain burned through her body and her mind until she lost her ability to stand under her own strength and was held upright only by the strength of the power that continued to assault her.

Wave after wave the attack continued, bringing a merciful blackness to close in around her, obliterating all thought. All thought except for the picture she held in her mind of Patrick's face, the feel of his lips on hers, clinging to his image as if she could sear her memory of him so deeply into her soul it could never be taken away from her.

Brave, strong Patrick. He would have withstood this, she had no doubt. For him, for her love of him, she struggled to hold on until, at last, even that one precious image dissolved, ripping a scream from her throat as the void took her, body and soul.

* * *

Being a Goddess was never easy. Especially not when the beings who'd raised you to the level of Deity put so much effort into stealing the power they'd bestowed upon you in the first place.

The Earth Mother studied the members of the High Council circled around her handmaiden, wondering at their audacity. Didn't they realize she could feel how they economized on the power they put into the Magic racking poor Elesyria's body? Didn't they realize she'd know what they plotted?

Though, in their favor, she had been slow to recognize their intent until it was too late to prevent what they had so obviously planned. Even now she could feel the tendrils of their power winding around her body, encasing her, ensnaring her, sealing her away from her own power.

Careless of her, really.

This particular group of Fae, more than any in a very long time, was excessively power-hungry. From the time they'd deposed the royal family and banished the queen from Wyddecol, she'd suspected their ultimate intent. Oh, they said all the right things, did all the right things, held to all the proper rituals.

But she'd known this day was coming. In her heart she'd known. It had been only a matter of time.

Little doubt now that one of her trusted handmaidens was a traitor, loyal to the High Council rather than to the Goddess. She searched her memory, struggling to identify who it had been that had brought the High Council's summon to this trial.

In the center of the circle, Elesyria screamed, Magic sparkling and sizzling as her being faded and, after several long, agonizing moments, disappeared completely.

If nothing else, the Earth Mother could be certain that Elesyria was not the traitor. Though the knowledge was of little use, it did give her some comfort. Elesyria had long been one of her favorites, as much for the depth of her raw abilities as for her wild and passionate nature. It was good to know that one such as she had not betrayed her Goddess.

It was also good to know that through their choice of which handmaiden to sacrifice and how they had gone about the process, the High Council had unwittingly given the Goddess a potential weapon to use in regaining her own freedom.

She might have thought it odd that this august group had opted to seal off the handmaiden's Magic rather than strip it from her as they'd declared they would. Perhaps they didn't remember the dangers of their actions. Perhaps they'd never known. More likely, their only thoughts had been for the preservation of their own powers so that, together, their circle of nine might imprison their Goddess. Only by combining their powers were they strong enough to accomplish such a thing.

"True Love," she whispered on a hiss of air, just before the tendrils of the High Council's Magic thickened around her, encasing her in a semi-transparent tomb of pulsing silver light.

"You know now, don't you, Goddess?" the Supreme Leader asked. "Your Temple has been sealed, separating you from the Ether of your Magic. You are powerless now. A prisoner as much as your unfortunate handmaiden. We have won and Wyddecol is ours, without the need for a single hand lifted in violence." A broad smile covered the woman's face before she turned her back to make her way from the chamber, followed by the other eight members of the High Council.

Yes, she knew well enough now. She knew of their treachery and something else, as well. The High Council had seriously miscalculated what had just happened here today. All was not lost for the Goddess. Though the nine usurpers may well have won this battle, the war was far from over. They might have sealed away the source of her power, but not before she'd released a weapon of her own. The most powerful Magic possible was loosed in the world, seeking a way to right the wrongs of this day. A Magic that, once set in motion, could never be defeated.

The Magic of True Love.

CHAPTER FOUR

Highlands of Scotland
1295

The oft-delayed homecoming was so close, Patrick could almost hear the greetings of his family ringing in his ears. Anticipation pulsed in his chest, causing an unfamiliar bubble of discomfort to writhe deep in his belly. Perhaps it was excitement that had taken him captive.

Castle MacGahan rose above him in the distance, growing closer with each long stride his mount took.

Dampened reins slid through his fingers as he readjusted his cramped grip, and the serpent in his belly reared its head more forcefully.

At last he recognized the emotion tormenting him. Not anticipation. Not excitement.

Fear.

Given a name, the unfamiliar emotion blossomed in his gut.

Ridiculous!

It wasn't as if he were riding headlong into battle. He bore no bad news, no evil tidings. There was no reason for this feeling. He couldn't think of one single possibility. Nothing.

Nothing, that is, except…

Syrie.

She loomed large in his thoughts as he lifted an arm to greet the guard on the wall. Her sparkling eyes, her unruly red curls, her sharp tongue, everything about her that was so familiar. So dear. Equally large was a vision of her shocked expression when he announced to her his feelings for her. So real was the fear of her possible rejection that he could almost hear her laughter in the recesses of his mind.

He must be losing his sanity.

"Fate of the lonely warrior," he muttered as he hurried through the tunnel and out into open bailey.

"Patrick!" His brother, Malcolm, called to him from across the bailey, his steps picking up speed as he trotted toward Patrick.

When they drew close to one another, Patrick halted his horse and dismounted, just in time for his older brother's warm embrace.

"So good to have you returned home, brother," Malcolm said, grinning as he stepped back. "We were beginning to fear you'd decided to stay with Christiana and Chase."

"Little enough danger of that, Colm," Patrick answered.

Though they'd been born and raised within the walls of Tordenet, the castle held far too many painful memories for either of them to ever willingly call it home again.

"Good." Malcolm nodded in agreement, as if he could hear Patrick's unspoken thoughts, before laying an arm around Patrick's shoulders. "Though it's selfish enough of me, I'm more than pleased to have the captain of my guard back where he belongs. Let's get you inside. You'll want food and drink after a long journey such as yers."

"Aye," Patrick agreed, following his brother's lead as one of the stable boys led his exhausted mount toward the stable.

Food and drink was what they both needed. Food and drink, and, for him, a moment alone with Syrie.

At the thought of her, his eyes were drawn upward to the high parapet, long a favorite retreat of the Faerie's. No sign of her there likely meant he'd find her in the gardens. If she wasn't one place, she usually could be found in the other. Either that or creeping up behind him when he least expected it.

He repressed the smile tickling at the corner of his lips. It was far too soon for him to allow himself to relax. He'd reserve that luxury until after he'd spoken to her, after he knew what her feelings for him were.

As they came through the great door, he heard his sister-in-law approaching. Two steps from the bottom of the staircase, Dani caught sight of him. Squealing in delight she launched herself to the bottom of the stairs, running toward him, arms outstretched.

"You're home!" she proclaimed laughingly as she hugged him tight. "We missed you. Malcolm's been beside himself since you've been gone."

Next to him, his brother's face wrinkled in displeasure. "So you think that's a wise thing for you to be doing, wife?

Throwing yerself from the stairs like that? What if you were to fall, eh?"

Dani rolled her eyes, grinning as she stepped back from Patrick to turn her attention to her husband. "But I didn't fall, did I?"

"But you could have," he insisted, reaching out to tuck her protectively under one arm. "You need to be ever mindful of yer condition, wife."

"Condition?" Patrick echoed, stopping to study the couple moving ahead of him toward the Great Hall. "What's wrong with you? Has something happened since I've been gone?"

She looked fine to him. Her cheeks glowed healthy and pink. If anything, she appeared a bit more filled out than the last time he'd seen her.

"Nothing at all is wrong with me," she called over her shoulder. "Malcolm's just being a fuss-butt, like always nowadays. I told you, didn't I? He missed you. And thank goodness you're back so you can be the one to fuss with him. I'm going ahead to get Cook started on something wonderful to celebrate Patrick's homecoming. You two go on in and have a seat. After so long a time, I'm sure you have all sorts of things to catch up on, don't you, Malcolm?"

"Yer a fuss-butt now, is it?" Patrick turned a questioning look in his brother's direction. "Whatever that is, I can only imagine. Well? I'd have an answer. What's going on here?"

Malcolm grinned, a smile so large, Patrick wasn't sure he could remember seeing the like of it on his brother's face since they were children, except for, possibly, the day of his marriage to Dani.

"Damnation! I'd planned to wait to share the news until I could pour us a wee drop, but it would seem I've ruined that now." Malcolm slapped him on the back, urging him into the Great Hall and toward the table at the front. "Congratulations are in order, brother. Yer going to be an uncle."

"Uncle?" Patrick shook his head in wonder. "Well, I'll be. Of all the things I should have guessed, that one never came to mind."

"Aye," Malcolm said, still grinning. "I'll admit to having been fair surprised, meself. But now that I've grown used to the idea, I find I'm quite pleased. Now, if I could only get that woman to do as I say and use more caution."

There was an idea that made Patrick smile. Dani had never been one to quietly do as she was told. But her independence was no more than his brother should have expected when he chose to marry a woman born and raised in a future time, sent to him by the power of the Fae. Well, the power of one Fae in particular. And thinking of that particular Faerie, he'd be willing to bet Syrie had plenty to say on the subject of the impending birth, too.

"Where is—" he began, cutting off his question as Dani hurried into the room, followed closely by Cook and two of her helpers, all bearing trays laden with tempting fare for a man who hadn't eaten since the evening before.

"Here we go," Dani said, sliding in to sit next to her husband, not looking nearly so happy as she had when she'd left them. "Now that you've had some time alone, I assume you've told him?"

"He did," Patrick answered for his brother. "Any more of that stair-jumping, lass, and you'll be answering to me, as much as to our laird. And to the Elf as well, I'd imagine. Where is she, by the by?"

He hoped the question had fit into the conversation as naturally as it had popped out of his mouth, though he doubted it had from the troubled look that passed between Malcolm and his wife.

"So you didn't tell him," she said flatly. Her voice carried no question, only a touch of disappointment.

"Tell me what?" Patrick asked, a small tendril of dread curling in his stomach.

"Syrie is missing," Dani said. "For over a week now."

"Missing?" His voice sounded strangled, even to his own ears.

"Likely it's nothing to fash ourselves over," Malcolm reasoned. "You ken how she is. It's no' like she'd take the time to tell us where she was going if she took it into her head to pop back to…well, to her own home."

Malcolm was wrong. Patrick could imagine nothing else. Syrie well might have chosen to return to the Land of the Fae but, based on the little things she'd said here and there about her home world, he doubted it. At least he doubted she would have returned willingly.

He was on his feet, at a run, taking the stairs to the floor above, to reach Syrie's chamber. He burst through the door, coming to an abrupt halt just inside, his heart beating as if he'd been in a daylong battle.

The chamber sang with an echo of the woman who had claimed it as her own. Covers on her bed were neatly drawn up and straightened, though her nightgown lay across the foot of the bed as if she'd tossed it there to await her return at end of day.

He crossed to the center of the room, breathing in the air that still held the delicate herbal scent he associated with Syrie. He scanned the room more thoroughly, searching for any little detail out of place that might serve as a clue to her whereabouts. After a moment or two, he was drawn to a chest standing under the one high window. On its top lay a hair comb.

Her comb.

Patrick ran his fingers over the wooden tool, brushing against one long red hair tangled in its teeth. If she had left at a time of her own choosing, she wouldn't have left such a personal item behind.

His fingers closed around the comb and he dropped the item into his sporran just as he heard his brother and sister-in-law enter the room behind him.

"She disappeared the same day the Tinklers left, so…" Malcolm shrugged, his meaning clear enough.

"But you and I both know she didn't go with them," Dani argued, her voice leaving little doubt that she and Malcolm had discussed this line of reasoning more than once. "She was still here hours after they left. I talked to her myself because she seemed so upset, so I know for a fact she didn't go with them."

"You searched for her?" Patrick asked, unable to get more of his thoughts into words.

Malcolm nodded. "Everywhere. I even sent riders out, but they found no sign of her."

"Then I'll find her myself," Patrick growled. "Which way were the Tinklers heading when they left?"

"I think Editha mentioned Inverness as their next destination," Dani told him. "I'll have a bag of food packed for you by the time you have your horse ready."

With a nod of thanks to his sister-in-law, Patrick strode from the room. There was no doubt left in his mind. Wherever Syrie had gone, it was not at a place or a time of her own choosing.

"Have you a plan?" Malcolm asked when he'd caught up with Patrick. "Any idea at all as to where you'll begin yer search?"

"I know exactly where I'll go," he answered, breaking into a trot.

He didn't want to talk about it. He only wanted to be on his way. Fear knotted his stomach and dried his tongue. Though he teased the woman at every opportunity about being an Elf, he knew what she really was. He knew who her people really were. And because of that, he recognized the danger she faced. The Fae were a powerful race in this world. In their own, they were without match.

He forced his mind away from the danger and back to the woman herself until all he could think of was his driving need to find Syrie and bring her back where she belonged.

Did he have a destination and a plan in mind? Indeed he did. To discover where Syrie had gone and to see her safely home at Castle MacGahan.

And the best way to discover where Syrie had gone appeared to be to find the Tinklers.

CHAPTER FIVE

Ft. Collins, Colorado 1968

"Miss?"

Floating in a fuzzy blanket of endless black, Syrie tried to ignore the irritating noise that threatened to pierce her slumber.

"Time to wake up."

Some unknown instinct warned against leaving this comforting cocoon, but the outside world, in the form of a vague male voice, grew increasingly insistent.

"C'mon, honey, up and at 'em. The city isn't running a hotel out here." A different, deeper voice this time.

Something nudged Syrie's arm and, like glass tapped with a hammer, the dark world sheltering her cracked and shattered, forcing her to open her eyes.

"That's a good girl," the deeper voice that had awakened her encouraged. "Let's sit you up, okay? Are you hurt?"

Syrie managed to shake her head in response to the question. Blinking against the glare of the light coming from a tube in the man's hand, she tried to focus on him rather than on the light.

"Think we have one of the frats to thank for this?" the second man asked. "Must have been some party, from the looks of that outfit."

"Could be," the deeper voice answered. "What's your name, hon?"

Her throat was drier than she could ever remember, and it took two tries before she could make her mouth form the words to respond.

"Syrie," she croaked at last. "Elesyria Aĺ Byrn, but I'm called Syrie."

At least she was pretty sure she was called that, and by someone important to her, too. She could almost, just almost, hear her name being spoken by someone…but no, the memory was gone before it could ever be fully recalled.

"Well, Syrie Alburn, how'd you end up out here in the park tonight?" The man with the deep voice squatted beside her, one arm behind her, lending gentle support to her back as she sat.

Syrie stared into Deep Voice's expressive eyes and knew he was someone she could trust. She couldn't say how she knew, any more than she could remember how she got to this place. Or even where this place was. A second man stood a few feet away, one hand resting on an object strapped around his waist. Both of them were dressed identically, so she could only suppose they wore uniforms of some sort. It appeared as though these men held some authority here.

"I don't know," she answered at last.

Deep Voice nodded slowly, his eyes never leaving her face. "Then maybe we should just get you home for now and worry about how you got here later." He stood as he spoke, helping her to her feet, as well. "Where do you live?"

Where did she live? Syrie lifted her fingers to her temple, and stared at her feet, stalling for time. Where *did* she live?

She had not the slightest idea.

"I…I don't know."

"Well, what do you know?" the second man asked, his voice tinged with impatience. "Drugs, you think? I didn't smell any alcohol."

"No," Deep Voice responded. "I don't think that's it. Trauma, maybe. What's the last thing you do remember?"

Syrie searched for a memory of any kind, but found nothing but a dense, prickly black void, as if she were bumping up against a wall of invisible thorns. "Waking up here. With you."

"Should we take her down to the station? Let them deal with it?" the second asked.

"*Them?*" Deep Voice repeated. "I'm senior officer tonight, in case you forgot that. *Them* is me. No, I have a better idea. We're not too far from Ellie's."

"Your sister's place?"

Deep Voice nodded, his hand at Syrie's back, urging her forward. "I know this must be upsetting, but you're okay now. I'm Sergeant MacKail and this is Officer Stevens. We'll get you someplace where you'll be safe for tonight."

They walked across an open stretch of land and stopped at a black and white object, easily large enough for all of them to fit inside.

Sergeant MacKail opened a door and encouraged her to step inside. "Have a seat in the car," he said. "Watch your head."

Syrie waited quietly as the two men also entered, using different doors. She bit back a scream of fear when the *car*, as he'd called it, roared to life and began to move. By the time they came to a stop, fear had been replaced with total awe for the power of this amazing conveyance.

The door opened again and Sergeant MacKail assisted her out. The house they walked up to was large, with a light burning outside. Her companion knocked on the door and, after a few minutes, it opened to reveal a sleepy young woman.

"Danny? Is something wrong?"

"Not exactly," he said, pulling on Syrie's arm to bring her up beside him. "This is Syrie Alburn. We found her unconscious in the park. She can't seem to remember anything except her name. I thought maybe this would be a better place for her tonight than down at the station."

"Absolutely it is," the young woman said, holding the door open wide in a clear invitation to enter. "You're more than welcome to stay here, Syrie. Come on in."

"Thanks, Ellie," Sergeant MacKail said, backing away from the door as if relieved to hand over his charge. "We'll check with campus police tomorrow morning to see if they have any missing reports that fit our little lady here. Until then, just give me a holler if you need anything, okay?"

"Go on back to work, Danny. I got this."

The woman closed the door and then turned to face Syrie, shaking her head. "Sounds like you're having a real bad day, Syrie. But don't you worry about a thing. You're going to be just fine now. Let's get you a bedroom and then we'll figure out everything else."

"You're called Ellie?" Syrie asked, following the woman toward a large staircase.

"Ellen," her hostess corrected. "Ellen MacKail. My brother's the only one that calls me Ellie, and I still hate it from when I was little and he called me Ellie Bellie just to make me crazy." Ellen smiled, and started up the stairs.

There was something in the woman's eyes that reminded Syrie of the brother who'd left only moments earlier. A goodness she couldn't quite put her finger on.

"He's your older brother?" she asked, realizing as she compared the two that there appeared to be a big difference in their ages.

Ellen nodded as she stopped in front of a door midway down the upstairs hallway. "Older by fifteen years. I think he was supposed to be an only child, but my parents got a little careless and next thing you know, there I was. Danny always says Mom and Dad only had me to make his life more difficult."

She grinned, her expression making her look even younger than she had before, and she pulled open the door to allow Syrie to step inside.

"The house is old and built mostly by my great-grandfather in a wonky kind of way. For some reason, he thought doors should open out into hallways rather than in to the rooms. But it's comfortable and, having pretty much grown up here, I do love this old place."

Syrie might not remember anything about where she came from, but she knew lovely when she saw it. "This is wonderful. I'm to stay here?"

"Yes," Ellen said. "We'll deal with clothes and stuff tomorrow. You're a good six inches shorter than me, I'd guess, but I doubt having a nightgown that's too long will matter all that much. Tomorrow, when Rosella gets up, we'll see if she has any regular clothes you can wear. She's closer to your height than I am."

"No need to wait until tomorrow." The young woman who stood in the doorway grinned. "I heard voices and thought I'd come see what was going on."

"I'm sorry we woke you, Rose," Ellen said. "I was trying to be quiet."

"Oh, don't worry. You didn't wake me." Again the other woman grinned. "I was up late reading and I heard the door. I waited as long as I could stand it before coming out. Who's our guest?"

"Syrie Alburn, this is my tenant and best friend, Rosella MacKeon. Syrie's going to be staying with us while she works her way through a bit of a rough patch."

"Welcome, Syrie," Rosie said, casting a quizzical glance toward Ellen. "Family troubles?"

Syrie smiled in acknowledgment of the introduction and then tried to be as inconspicuous as possible while Ellen recounted Syrie's troubles to her friend.

A bit of a rough patch, Ellen had labeled her situation. That hardly sounded awful enough to encompass just how lost she actually felt. Somewhere in the recesses of her mind, she remembered hearing someone speak of amnesia, and this certainly seemed to fit the bill for what she suffered. Still, she could hardly have imagined that amnesia could mean that everything and everyone she'd ever known was suddenly hidden away from her. Not even the everyday things that these people took for granted seemed the least bit familiar to her.

"Syrie? You okay?"

Syrie jerked her attention back to her companions to find them both staring at her with concern.

"I'm fine. Just tired, I guess."

Tired and confused and feeling so far out of her element, she couldn't even remember what her element was.

"Well, of course you are. What should we expect for three in the morning?" Ellen shook her head as if annoyed with herself. "And here I am, keeping you up when I should have gotten you right into bed. Your bathroom is through this door. It's shared with the attached bedroom, but nobody is staying there right now, so it's all yours."

Ellen pushed open a door and slid her hand along the wall, causing the room to come to life with light before stepping inside.

Syrie followed, her chest tightening with amazement. Maybe this was simply a side effect of having no memory, but everything here seemed so absolutely revolutionary. A room dedicated just to bathing? And...oh!

Ellen twisted a metal handle and water began to flow into a small basin underneath.

"Just wanted to check that the hot water is okay," she said. "It's a really old house, so you can never be too sure about the plumbing. The toilet is all new, though. We just replaced that last month," she added with a grin, pressing her hand against another handle, sending the water swirling away down a second basin.

As she and Ellen had entered the wonderful bathing room, Rosella had slipped out the door, but now she returned, carrying a soft-looking bundle of cloth.

"Here's a nightie and a robe, Syrie. We'll find other stuff tomorrow. When you get up, just come on downstairs and one of us will be there, likely hanging out by the coffeepot."

"If you need anything, just yell," Ellen said as both of them left the room. "I'm right across the hall and I'm a light sleeper, so don't even have a concern about bothering me. Try not to worry too much. Danny's real good at his job. I'm sure he'll find out where you belong by morning. You get some sleep now, okay? Good night!"

When the two women had left her alone, Syrie sank to the bed. Her earlier claim of being tired was suddenly more fact than excuse. She slipped the long, silky green dress she wore over her head and replaced it with the nightie Rosella had brought her. The thing barely reached her knees, but she was too tired to worry over it for now. She pulled back the covers and crawled into the bed, realizing only after she'd burrowed under those covers that she'd left the light turned on. No matter. If she'd managed to survive all the host of other bizarre things she'd seen tonight, a little extra light certainly wasn't going to keep her awake.

And tomorrow? Unless her memory miraculously returned as she slept, tomorrow promised to bring a whole new set of surprises.

CHAPTER SIX

Highlands of Scotland
1295

It had taken two days of hard riding, but Patrick had caught up with the Tinkler wagons at last.

"Where is Elesyria?" he asked as soon as he pulled even with the lead wagon.

He chose to ignore the look that passed between Editha Faas and her husband as he posed his question. He also chose to ignore the pity brimming in the Tinkler woman's eyes when she turned her gaze in his direction.

"I'm afraid she is beyond your reach, warrior," Editha answered.

"Explain yerself," he demanded, his impatience growing with the typical Tinkler answers.

This woman who stood before him didn't understand the depth of his feelings. Nor did she understand what he would do to find the woman he loved. No place was beyond his reach. There was nowhere in the world he wouldn't go to find Syrie.

"She's not in this world, I'm afraid," Editha said with a shake of her head, responding to him as if she'd heard his thoughts.

"Then where is she?" he asked, fear and anger bubbling together in his chest. "I ken that you spoke to her before she disappeared. You spoke to her, leaving her visibly upset. Within hours after that, she was gone. I'd have you tell me what you said to her and where she's gone to."

Editha climbed down from her perch on the wagon and clasped her hands in front of her, clearly signaling that she waited for Patrick to join her.

Tinklers and the Fae. They might as well be one and the same. Perhaps that was why some claimed they *were* one and the same.

"I merely carried warning to Elesyria of what was to come. She had angered the powers that be in her home world and they intended that she should return to them to answer for her offenses."

"Offenses be damned," Patrick said. "Wherever she is, I plan to bring her home. You've but to point me in the right direction and I'll do the rest."

Again Editha and her husband exchanged a pointed look.

"It's no' so easy as that. She's been taken to Wyddecol, a place no uninitiated man can reach unaided."

The Faerie home world. He should have guessed as much.

"Then aid me. Or initiate me. Whatever it takes to get me to her."

"I'm afraid I have no way to—"

"Orabilis?" her husband suggested, his voice little more than a hiss of air.

"She does have the power," Editha said with a hint of a shrug. "Though perhaps no' the desire."

Patrick's heart pounded in his chest, his fears lifting at the possibility those words opened for him. The old witch had the power to get him to Syrie.

"Orabilis it is, then," he said, his foot already lifted to his stirrup.

"Wait!" Editha ordered, her voice carrying an authority that stopped him where he stood. "You canna go to her alone. We'll go with you to assist."

With an effort, Patrick shook off the invisible hands that held him and lifted himself onto the back of his mount.

"You'll only slow me down, Tinkler. In this part of my quest, I've no need for yer assistance."

Editha snorted, turning her back to climb up onto her perch on the wagon. "The assistance we offer is no' to you, warrior, but to Orabilis herself. There's much she'll need to hear before she can set about helping you. Assuming she has the desire to help you at all."

"Suit yerself," Patrick muttered, turning his horse in the direction he'd traveled from only days earlier.

In spite of what the Tinkler woman believed, the desires of the old witch who'd all but raised his sister were of little matter in this situation. After all, Orabilis had already declared herself to be in his debt, and the time had come for him to collect on what she owed.

CHAPTER SEVEN

Ft. Collins, Colorado
1968

"Nothing." Dan MacKail stood in the middle of his sister's kitchen, his hands lifted helplessly. "No match on any register for the fingerprints, no missing person reports. Not one single damn thing to give us even the slightest clue as to who Syrie is or where she came from. I know we're just a small-town department, but I even spoke with the Denver PD and they can't find anything either. It's like she dropped in from another planet. I'm sorry, but there it is. We haven't been able to find out anything about who you are."

Syrie nodded, not surprised that her missing past was still a mystery. A feeling of irrecoverable loss had plagued her every waking moment since she'd been here, as if somehow she'd known that neither Dan nor all the resources at his beck and call would find where she belonged. This just confirmed that she was truly adrift in the world.

"So, what now?" she asked at last, praying they wouldn't kick her out of the house to fend for herself now that she was truly on her own.

It was the question that had nagged at her for the past week since she'd awakened in that park with Dan at her side.

"Don't you worry about it," Ellen said, sitting down next to her at the table, one hand protectively on Syrie's shoulder. "Your past doesn't matter. You'll stay here with us. This is your home now."

"A job would probably be a good idea," Dan suggested, his voice hesitant, as if he expected her to refuse.

"That's a great idea," Syrie agreed. "I don't want to be a burden to anyone."

If there was one thing she'd already learned about her life now, it was that everyone needed to pull their own weight, and she felt as if she was far from doing that.

"Okay. Good. What can you do?" Dan asked as he headed over to the sink, his voice a little more skeptical than Syrie would have liked.

Still, she could hardly blame him. What *could* she do? So many things she encountered daily were items she couldn't remember ever having seen before, let alone have any knowledge of how to use them.

"Careful with the faucet, Danny. One wrong turn and it'll have water all over the kitchen," Ellen warned before turning her attention back to Syrie's situation. "First of all, you're not a burden, so don't even let yourself go there. As to what she can do, secretary is out of the question. My typewriter completely confounded her."

43

"Phone, too," Rosella added as she strolled into the kitchen. "Probably rules out receptionist."

"How about waiting tables?" Dan looked around expectantly. "At least for now. If you're open to that, I can ask around at some of the restaurants where I know people. Maybe we can find something like that for you."

"Yes, please." Syrie nodded enthusiastically. "I'm more than willing to give it a try."

It seemed the least she could do. Ellen had been so wonderful to her, taking her in and making her feel as if she belonged here. Her being able to pay her own way was even more important to her after she'd heard Ellen speaking to her fiancé last night.

Syrie hadn't intended to eavesdrop, but her bedroom window had been open and the young couple had been sitting in lawn chairs almost directly below. Robert's voice had attracted her attention first, strident in his efforts to convince Ellen to do what he thought was best for her.

"Look, El, I stood behind you in wanting to keep this house as long as you could make a go of it. I know you love this place. But you can't keep it up if you're just going to go further and further into debt. You can't keep running this place like some government-supported charity."

"I know," Ellen had responded. "But I can hardly ask Rosella to pay more. She can barely afford what she's paying now and still be able to save up for her wedding."

"Well, if that's how you feel, the only way you're going to make this work is to take in more boarders." He'd snorted then and lowered his voice, but not by much. "And not freeloader boarders like this charity case Danny brought to you. You have to put your foot down, Ellen. You can't save the whole world. I'm serious about this.

Either this house starts paying its own way or you need to give up this whole crazy idea."

"Saving the home my grandmother grew up in isn't a crazy idea. Keeping it in the family isn't a crazy idea. Neither is providing low-cost housing for students. And before you even think to say another word, you can leave Syrie out of this. She'll be self-supporting soon enough. She's just got to have a little time to get her life on track." Ellen paused just long enough to catch her breath. "Besides, what else would you have me do? Give up the house I love? Move into an apartment and pay someone else rent?"

"We've talked about this before, El. There's no good reason for us to wait until next June to get married. We can get married right now. You move into my place with me, put this house on the market and stop hemorrhaging money every month. At this rate, you're going to go through every red cent that your grandparents left you."

"Oh, right." Ellen's laugh sounded almost like a sob. "I can just see that. Your mother, deprived of her social event wedding of the century? Your parents already think I'm not good enough for you. If we did something like that, she'd never let me live it down. No, Robby. That isn't an option and you know it as well as I do."

They'd lowered their voices then so that Syrie couldn't hear any more of their conversation, but it hadn't mattered. She had heard all she'd needed to hear. If Dan could find a job for her, any kind of job, she was taking it. Ellen had already done so much for her, it seemed that the least she could do was begin to repay her new friend's kindness with a little cold, hard cash.

"Are you sure you're okay with this? Waitressing is hard work, dealing with all the different personalities, and it's long hours on your feet. But, if you end up in the right place, it can earn you good money in tips."

Syrie jerked her attention back to the moment as Ellen spoke to her, realizing only now that everyone else had gone, leaving just the two of them. "I'm not one to fear hard work."

"No, I know that. I really appreciate how you've pitched in around here to help with cleaning and all. It's just that..." Ellen tipped her head to one side, her brow wrinkled with concern. "It's just that, since Danny suggested a job for you, well, you just seem kind of troubled today."

"Troubled," Syrie repeated, all but biting her tongue to keep from laughing. Or was it tears that threatened? She couldn't be sure, but whichever it was, she breathed deeply, stuffing all emotion back in the box where it belonged before saying more. "My troubles have nothing to do with your brother's suggestion. For a fact, I'm grateful to him. I need something to do with myself. Something that doesn't allow me to sit and brood as I have been. With each passing day, I feel more and more as if I've misplaced something. Something important. Something I don't want to go on without. Does that make sense?"

"Oh, Syrie." Ellen leaned into her, capturing Syrie within a big hug. "Of course it does, my friend. You've lost everything, everyone who was dear to you. Your whole life is a blank slate. I can't imagine how I'd bear up under similar circumstances. But don't you worry. You have a home here with me. Rosella and I are your family now. We'll find you a job and, I promise you, Syrie, things will get better for you. Once you start to rebuild your new life and make more friends, that *something* you fear you've lost won't haunt you the way it does now."

ALL THE TIME YOU NEED

Syrie hoped Ellen was right. She hoped it would all get easier. She hoped Dan would find her a job quickly. Keeping her hands and her mind active might help to keep at bay this awful, nagging sense of loss that threatened to engulf her every time she let her thoughts drift to what— or who—she might have left behind when she lost her memory.

CHAPTER EIGHT

Highlands of Scotland
1295

"They only blocked her powers, you say? And yer sure of that? Sure that her powers were no' stripped from her when they exiled her in time? I canna begin to imagine why they would take such an enormous risk."

Patrick stared from one woman to the other in disbelief as they discussed the fate of his Syrie as if it were no more than simple gossip about some crofter's wife in the next town. Orabilis seemed almost giddy as she asked her questions, while Editha nodded her response, her eyes wide.

"Perhaps they dinna ken the danger they created for themselves. I've no doubt as to the truth of it. The Goddess herself witnessed their—"

"What is wrong with the two of you?" Patrick interrupted when he could stand it no longer. "The Magic be damned! Whether she has powers or no' is of no concern to me. It's Syrie herself who's important, no' her

Faerie abilities. From what yer saying, she's lost somewhere in the future, with no' even her own memories to guide her. We have to do something to bring her home right now."

"Be still with yer blether, Patrick," Orabilis admonished, not even giving him the courtesy of her attention. "We are both well aware of the challenges facing Elesyria. But until we can get this right, until I can understand exactly what we are dealing with, we canna bring her home, aye? So summon yer patience, lad. Lock yer lips and allow us to do our work."

She spoke to him as she had when he was no more than a boy demanding her attention. When he thought on it, it wouldn't surprise him if she still considered him as such.

He growled his displeasure, not bothering to form the words. She was right, of course. No matter how powerful Orabilis might really be, not even she could afford to rush into an encounter with Faerie Magic without the armament of knowledge. He'd have to force himself to wait. At least now he could take solace in knowing that she intended to help, a fact she hadn't shared before this very moment.

"That little twist changes everything," Orabilis muttered, her forefinger tapping her upper lip thoughtfully as she stared up at the ceiling. "As I'm sure the Goddess realized when she sent word. Well then. It would appear there's naught left to be done but to go to a source of power if we're to follow her."

"No!" Editha protested, the word expelled on a burst of air. "You ken it's no' safe for you to return to Wyddecol. Especially no' now with the Council embroiled in a full-on grab for control."

49

"Do I look the fool to you?" Orabilis asked, her laughter tinkling around the room. "No need to fash yerself over my considering such an unwise move, little one. No, the place I have in mind is in this world, but with an opening to the other. A place where the powers of Wyddecol leak through into the Mortal world."

"The glen," Editha whispered. "That's where yer thinking of going, is it no'? You intend to take yer leave from there."

"That is the only spot I can see someone using to begin a journey such as we discuss," Orabilis said with a chuckle, turning her gaze toward Patrick.

He did his best to ignore the shivers prickling up his spine, fear for Syrie urging him on, stoking the fire of his anger yet again. Delays and more delays, it was what these people knew best.

"Why must we waste more time, traveling to yet another place? Yer supposed to be the one with the Magic to bring Syrie home. Why can you no' just do it here and now?"

"Do it here and now?" Orabilis asked, her voice rising in pitch. "What is it you think I'm to do, lad? Toss some herbs into the fire and pull Elesyria from the rising smoke? You've no idea how difficult a task you've set for me, nor the price to be paid for accomplishing it. No' even my powers are strong enough to simply undo what the High Council of Wyddecol has set in motion. I need to touch upon the Magic of Wyddecol itself to have any chance in fighting this battle."

Why the Fae could never take the simple path baffled him. His father had always claimed they were a race more convoluted in their thinking than even the old gods of

Asgard. It all seemed clear enough to him. But if she insisted that she needed to touch upon the power of Wyddecol, so be it. Simple enough.

"Then we go to Wyddecol," he said. "Go to the source and eliminate the need to travel to this glen of yers."

Orabilis exchanged a look with Editha and sighed, a sound clearly intended to convey her irritation with having to school him yet again. "There were once many entry points connecting your world with Wyddecol. But, as you'd know if you'd listened to any of yer mother's stories, most of those doorways were destroyed many ages ago to keep out those who should never return to the Land of the Fae."

Stories. The Fae did love their stories. But stories were for children and people with nothing else to do. He had no time for stories, not even those Orabilis would tell. Syrie's very life could depend on his forcing this old woman to move quickly. Orabilis and the Tinkler woman might well be descended from the Fae, but his lineage stretched back to Odin. He would not be denied that which he wanted more than life itself.

"I willna be stopped in my quest to save Elesyria. I'll rend an opening between the worlds with my own two hands if I have to."

"You do try my patience, young warrior, but that foolhardy streak may yet serve you well." Orabilis shook her head as she approached him, close enough to lay a hand on his shoulder. "I said *most* of the openings had been destroyed. Not *all*. It is one of those openings that we seek in the Faerie Glen. From there I can access the power we need to enable you to save her, all with no rending on yer part required."

In that case, there was only one thing left that he needed to know.

"How soon can we go?" he asked, hoping against hope that she didn't think she was going to leave him behind when she made her way to this special glen of hers with its rare opening to the Faerie home world.

"As soon as you and William can get the wagons ready," she answered, her gaze unwavering as she stared at him. "Editha and I will gather a few things to take along and meet you outside."

"Finally," he muttered, turning his back and heading out of the little cabin and into the fresh air to find William.

At last he felt as if rescuing Syrie might actually be within his reach.

CHAPTER NINE

Ft. Collins, Colorado
1968

"What in the world is going on in here?"

Syrie waited in the doorway of the kitchen, surveying the disaster area laid out before her. Every conceivable flat surface in the room was covered with dishes, all of them either filled with food or dirty from the preparation of that food. In the center of the room stood Ellen, obviously the source of all the upheaval. Her apron heavily spotted with the evidence of her handiwork, she raised a hand to brush back a lock of hair that had escaped her neat bun.

"You're home already?" she asked, a trail of flour now marking the spot her hand had touched a moment before. "I can't believe it's so late. I still have so much to do to get ready for tomorrow."

Ellen's celebration of two new tenants signing their leases. Their rent, along with what Syrie was now able to pay, would finally mean that Ellen's boarding house was no longer losing money. She had announced the news to

Syrie and Rosella four days ago and had immediately decided it was, in her words, a party-worthy event.

"I can help." Syrie chuckled at the skeptical look on her friend's face. "I may not be able to cook worth a darn, but dishes I can do."

"Are you sure?" Ellen asked, her voice carefully modulated even though her expression gave her away. "You just got off work. You must be exhausted."

Syrie was exhausted, but she wasn't about to admit that to Ellen. Not now. After working the late shift last night and then both the breakfast rush and the lunch rush at the restaurant, the only thing that had gotten Syrie home was the thought of a late-afternoon nap. But there was no way she was going to dash the hope she saw glowing in Ellen's eyes when she'd offered her help. She'd fit that nap in once the work here was finished.

"I've still got plenty of life left in me. After all the hard work you've put in, I think a little cleaning is the least I can do. After all, we're all looking forward to your party."

"*Our* party," Ellen corrected, flashing a smile in her direction before turning back to the little cakes she was frosting. "I'm celebrating financial independence, Rosella is celebrating Clint's homecoming, and you're going out on your first real date since you've been here. I think that means we all own a piece of this little shindig."

Syrie's stomach did a little flip at the reminder of the upcoming date. Why she'd allowed herself to get talked into it, she didn't know. Well, in truth, she did know. She had agreed to it because she wanted to fit in. After all these weeks of feeling like a fish out of water, she desperately wanted to be like everyone else. Young women her age had boyfriends. Commitments. A sense of who they were.

She didn't have any of that. But, according to everyone she talked to and all the programs she saw on the television, if she wanted those things, she'd need to find a man. And to do that, she had to start by dating.

Even if she found the idea to be less than appealing.

"What are you sighing about over there?" Ellen looked over from her spot at the kitchen table, clearly determined to wait for an answer.

"I didn't realize I was sighing," Syrie answered truthfully. "I was just thinking."

"About?"

"Nothing. Everything. Life in general."

Ellen laughed and dusted her hands off on her apron as she crossed to the sink where Syrie had begun drawing water to wash the dishes. "Other people might fall for those lovely evasive answers of yours, Syrie Alburn, but you're not fooling me for one minute. So, tell me, what specific thing is it that's distressing you enough to drag those heartfelt sighs out into the open? Is it your job? Are you hating it?"

"Not at all." Syrie hurried to deny even the idea of hating her job. She might not love it all the time, but it gave her a paycheck and it made her feel like she was doing her part to help out around here. "It's just that…"

"Just what?" Ellen encouraged as she picked up a dishtowel and began to dry the dishes Syrie laid out to drain.

"This whole date thing," Syrie admitted. "I'm not comfortable with it. I feel like I'm doing something I shouldn't. Like I'm cheating, or something. Like, maybe I left someone behind and I'm being unfaithful to him."

There, she'd done it. She'd voiced her fears aloud at last. Maybe exposed to the scrutiny of rational people, those itchy little feelings plaguing her would shrivel and die a natural death.

"You can't live like that, Syrie. You'll never be happy that way. Always worrying about what unknowns lurk in your past isn't the way to go forward. You have to look at your life as a blank slate. Let go of everything that's back there. Anyone special in your life? Well, not anymore, there's not. They're gone. All the good stuff is gone. I hate to be the one to say that out loud, but it's true. On the flip side, though, all the bad stuff is gone, too. Any mistakes you made? They might as well have never even happened. You get the extraordinary chance to start all over. Fresh. You need to carry on as if nothing ever happened to you before the night you showed up at my front door. For you, nothing and no one existed before that night. You have to accept your reality." Ellen gripped Syrie's shoulders and turned her so that they were staring into one another's eyes. "Listen to me on this. If you don't let go of the past you can't remember, you'll make yourself crazy with worry. Letting all of that go is your only way forward."

"I know you're right," Syrie said at last, following up with another deep sigh. "But doing is much harder than knowing."

"I can't even imagine how hard it must be, to have to give up a whole lifetime. But there really are positives. You get to create a whole new life. You just have to give yourself permission to do that. There are lots of people roaming the world who would love the chance to start over, to explore a new life." Ellen paused and looked as though she might be about to say more, but the kettle she'd placed on the stove a little earlier began to squeal out its readiness. "Water's hot. Let's have ourselves some tea. Get off our feet and take a little break in the front parlor. How's that sound?"

After the hours Syrie had put in on her feet today, the suggestion sounded like sheer heaven.

They carried their steaming cups to the front of the house and settled into their favorite spots before Syrie pursued the question that Ellen's suggestion had planted in her mind.

"Are you one of those people, Ellen? One who'd like to explore a whole new life?"

"I don't know. Sometimes I am, I guess."

The admission surprised Syrie. Not that she hadn't guessed that her friend wasn't completely happy with her life. She had. She was simply surprised that Ellen felt safe enough to admit that to her. It meant their friendship had grown to a whole new level.

"You always tell me that I don't have to do anything that I don't want to do. You know that goes for you, as well, right?" Syrie watched her friend closely over the rim of her cup.

"Of course I know that."

"So, you know that you don't have to marry Robert if you don't want to, right? I mean, just because he asked and you said yes, that doesn't mean you can't still change your mind. You know that, too, right?"

"I do." Ellen smiled, running her finger around the edge of her china cup. "I have every intention of marrying Robert. It's only that, sometimes, I doubt my ability to fit into his family's world."

Insecurities? From Ellen? The very idea was something foreign to Syrie.

"Do you love him?"

"I guess so." Ellen nodded absently as she spoke. "I mean, yeah. I do. Although do any of us really recognize what love is when we first bump into it? I'm not talking about attraction or desire or that physical mojo that happens. I'm talking about the kind of love that begins with a bone-deep connection, way down in your soul, you know?"

Syrie nodded. There was a whole lot she didn't know. A whole lot she might never have known and even more that she couldn't remember ever having known. But the kind of love Ellen spoke about was something that had to have been imprinted in the depths of her being. It was the one thing she longed for more than anything else. It was the one thing she feared more than anything else that she might have lost when she lost her memories.

Ellen shrugged and smiled again before taking a sip of her tea. "Who's to say? I guess there's no way to ever know for sure, is there? There's only making your best guess at it all and then taking a shot and forging ahead."

They might have pursued the subject more deeply, but Rosella's feet sounded on the stairs, and within a moment, she appeared in the room, hair done up in curls and a bright smile on her face.

"And where might you be off to?" Ellen asked. "All decked out in your brand-new dress? Must be someplace wonderful."

"Clint's going to be here any minute. He's taking me out to see the property he's made an offer on. The place where he wants to build his ranching kingdom." She giggled as she said the last, rolling her eyes. "He thinks he's such a cowboy."

"Must be some nice place he's getting ready to buy, considering the way you're all dressed up."

Rosella's cheeks took on a rosy glow as the smile on her face grew. "Not at all. In fact, it's plain old raw ground, out in the sticks over toward Estes."

"Then why aren't you wearing something more sensible?" Syrie asked.

If ever Syrie had seen attire wholly inappropriate for the task at hand, what Rosella wore now certainly fell into that category.

"Syrie has a good point. That brand-new miniskirt of yours hardly seems—" Ellen suddenly stopped speaking, a silly smile of her own adorning her face. "Never mind. I get it now."

"Get what?" Syrie asked, truly puzzled.

Rosella always struck her as such a practical young woman, but the outfit she wore was in no way practical for hiking around a large tract of empty land.

"First time you've seen your cowboy since he got back from his summer training, right?" Ellen sent an exaggerated wink in Syrie's direction before turning back to Rosella. "I'm guessing she doesn't want him to see her looking like she's ready to work in the yard."

"You got that right." Rosella nodded, the flush on her cheeks growing more pronounced. "Longest six weeks of my life, I swear. I could easily hate that darn ROTC unit and their stupid summer training if it weren't for the fact that they're paying his way through school. Besides, I think tonight is going to be special."

"Really? You planning something you haven't told us about?"

The smile disappeared from Rosella's face, giving way to a pensive expression. "No, nothing like that. I just have this odd feeling about going out to look at the property. And if there's one thing I've learned over the years, it's that my weird feelings are never wrong."

"Never?" Syrie asked, a tingle filling her body as if the words rattled at some locked door in the recesses of her mind.

"Never," Rosella confirmed. "In fact, I remember this one time when—" She stopped speaking and tipped her head to the side before hurrying over to look out the window. "Oops. He's here. End of story time. Do I look okay?"

"You look outta sight," Ellen said, though there was a good chance that Rosella didn't hear, since she was already through the front door.

"See that? That's exactly what I was talking about earlier," Ellen said softly, staring at the empty doorway where Rosella had stood only moments before.

"What do you mean?" Syrie asked.

"Her," Ellen answered, turning a broad smile in Syrie's direction. "That girl hasn't one single doubt about having found the love of her life. She knows to the depths of her heart that Clint Coryell is the one man meant for her. Now, if that wannabe cowboy would just get off the pot and pop the big question, Rosie's life would be perfect."

"Pop the big question?" Syrie echoed the words, not sure of their meaning.

"Ask her to marry him. Give her a ring to seal the deal. He hasn't done that yet, you know."

Ellen's answer surprised Syrie.

"But I thought you said she'd be moving to Denver after graduation when they married."

"Yes indeedy, that's her current plan." Ellen chuckled softly, rising to her feet and heading back to the kitchen. "I just hope Clint is planning the same thing. I'd hate to have to tear him a new one for breaking her heart."

"I can almost see you doing exactly that," Syrie said, chuckling as she picked up her empty cup and followed along behind.

"There's no *almost* to it. You and Rosella are like family to me now, as much as Danny is. And woe unto anyone who thinks to mess with my family."

Ellen spoke with a smile, but there was a glint in her eye that assured Syrie her friend was completely serious. The sentiment sent a wave of warmth through her heart, filling her again with wonder at her good fortune in ending up here with Ellen. One day, she would find a way to make all of this up to her friend. One day, she vowed, she would prove herself as good a friend to Ellen as Ellen was to her.

* * *

Highlands of Scotland 1295

"We're close now."

Patrick nodded his acknowledgment of the words Orabilis spoke, reaching around her to hold back a thick branch so that she might continue unimpeded along the path they walked.

As if drawn forward by a power outside herself, she kept moving at the same steady pace she had set for them more than an hour earlier when she had announced that the remainder of their journey would best be accomplished on foot. Leaving the wagons, horses and their companions behind, Orabilis had led him into a dense forest, following some hidden path only she appeared to be able to see.

At least he hoped they followed a path. The very thought of wasting more time lost in the trees and copious undergrowth of this forest galled him. He'd already wasted more time than he could have imagined when he first set out from Castle MacGahan to find Syrie.

As had become his recent habit when he thought her name, he saw her face in his mind and his chest tightened. Wherever she was, *whenever* she was, he prayed that she'd found safety and comfort. The very idea of her being alone and lost haunted him. He couldn't bear to think of her frightened and in danger. Or worse. If anything happened to her before he could reach her—

"Very close." The words Orabilis murmured drew him from his waking nightmare. Her steps drew to a halt as she spoke, and she turned to face him, her green eyes glittering when she captured him with a hard look. "Can you feel it?"

He could hardly claim he felt nothing. To do so would be a lie. But neither could he find the words to describe the odd sensations coursing through his body and nibbling at the back of his thoughts.

Whatever lay ahead, it indeed held an unusual power of some sort.

"Ever the silent, determined warrior, eh? We'll see about that shortly." She muttered the last, stepping back to allow Patrick to shove aside the thicket ahead of them to reveal that they'd arrived at their destination.

One look and he had no doubt this was the glen they had sought. It was exactly as he had pictured it in his mind. A large green pool of water, surrounded by a forest of trees. At the backside of the glen the land rose as if a small, rocky mountain had chosen that exact spot to break through the earth and reach up toward the sky. From its heights, a waterfall plunged down into the pool, rippling the waters in a sound that reminded him of laughter.

Syrie's laughter sounded exactly like that. A tinkling, melodious sound that echoed in the back of his mind as her face floated into his thoughts. Her face, with those eyes that danced with mischief whenever she spoke. Or darkened with emotion in moments like the one they'd shared when he kissed her in the garden. It was that moment—

"Stop yer vagaries and pay attention to the task at hand, Patrick."

He started, as if waking from a dream, when the old woman spoke. He'd been so far into his own thoughts, he hadn't even noticed when she'd moved to the water's edge and squatted down, though, clearly, she now waited for him to join her.

Hurrying to her side, he knelt down next to her, still struggling to wipe from his thoughts the visions of Syrie that assailed him.

"We've made it to yer glen, just as you insisted we must," he said, covering his discomfort with annoyance. "What now? Will you travel to Wyddecol?"

The breeze swirled around him, and he could almost swear he heard the startled protests of hundreds of wispy voices carried on the air.

A trick of his imagination, no doubt, spurred on by his already raw emotions.

"Doona fash yerselves so!" Orabilis hissed. "Well enough I remember the dangers that lurk along such a path. It's no' as if I've gone brainsick."

Patrick wasn't so sure about that. "Yer words make no sense, witch."

Orabilis jerked around to look at him, chuckling as a smile tipped one corner of her mouth. "They make plenty of sense to the ones I answer, lad."

The ones she answered?

He cocked his head to one side and strained to hear whatever it was that she seemed to be listening to, but the only sounds reaching his ears were those of nature: the waterfall splashing into the pool and the breeze rustling through the leaves.

Orabilis, meanwhile, had turned back to the pool, her gaze fixed on the water. Once again she turned back toward him.

"The time has come for you to know the truth of the task ahead. Time for you to decide if yer truly willing to risk all to bring Elesyria home."

"There is nothing to decide," Patrick answered, knowing he would risk anything for Syrie.

"Do you love her that much? Truly love her?" Orabilis asked. "Does she return those feelings?"

"I…"

How could he bring himself to admit to this woman that which he had only come to accept for himself so recently? And certainly there was no way he could speak for Syrie. That was the question he'd planned to have answered when he'd returned to Castle MacGahan and found her gone.

"Well? Do you?" she asked again, more harshly this time. "Because if yer answer is no, then our journey has come to a close."

He opened his mouth to tell her again that nothing would keep him from going after Syrie, but she stopped him with a raised hand.

"They have the right of it. Asking a commitment of you without telling you what you face is wrong of me."

"Though it will make no difference, say what you need to say."

As long as she didn't take too long. He'd wasted more than enough time already.

"There's a war brewing in Wyddecol," she began, but he stopped her.

"I doona care about the political unrest in yer home world, Orabilis. I care only for Syrie and her safe return. I want only to know how to find her and bring her back."

"Yes, Patrick. That's what we all want." Orabilis patted his shoulder as she might approach an unhappy child. "But to do that, you must understand what has happened to her. The sooner we get through this, the sooner you can be on yer way, aye? Are you prepared to listen?"

He nodded, feeling more than a little foolish for having interrupted in the first place.

"The Goddess insists upon our people following the law of the land. The High Council seeks total control to do as they please. To do that, they have no choice but to overthrow the Goddess."

"How does one even begin to—"

An upraised eyebrow from Orabilis had him quickly silencing his question. He had agreed to listen, and that was what he would do.

"It would appear the High Council chose to utilize Syrie's punishment as a cover for doing exactly that. Though their judgment was that her memories and Magic would be stripped, it appears they didn't remove anything. They only locked them away in the recesses of her mind. It is only due to this negligence on their part that we are allowed a chance to bring her back."

"But why would they—" Again he caught himself and stopped talking.

Orabilis shrugged, shaking her head. "I canna know the reason for sure. But I suspect they were rationing their own strength in order to turn on the Goddess. Completely removing the memories and Magic from a Faerie is no' an easy task. The energy required to accomplish that would have been immense. But, whatever their reasons, they did what they did, leaving an opportunity for us. Or, better said, for you, should you choose to take it."

Should he choose to? He'd already told her no risk was too great.

"What must I do?"

"I will send you as close to where she is as I can. You've but to reawaken her memories. Specifically, you must awaken her memories of you. Once that happens, she'll be able to return the two of you to yer own time."

He rubbed a hand across his face, stalling until he could force himself to confront the question that had troubled him for more than a month.

"And if she canna remember me?"

It was as close as he could come to voicing his real fear. What if she did not love him?

"Then you'll both be stranded in that time with no way home. I willna be able to help you. Knowing this, do you still choose to go?"

"Aye."

It was no hardship to choose. His time, Syrie's time, anywhere in time, none of it mattered if he couldn't bring Syrie home safely.

CHAPTER TEN

"There are those in this world whose powers are very special, even among my people." Orabilis paused, as if debating how much to say. Her obvious internal battle at an end, she sighed heavily and then continued. "They are called Sensors. They unconsciously draw the Faerie Magic to themselves. Where you find an amazing coincidence, there you will find a Sensor."

Patrick knew that Orabilis was sharing something important with him. Something she likely never shared with mere Mortals. "Am I to assume that these special people play some part in what I am about to do?" he asked.

"A very large part. When you arrive in the time that Elesyria has traveled to, you will need to find one of these Sensors in order to locate her." The old woman frowned, an uncharacteristic look of concern wrinkling her features. "If only we had a personal belonging of Elesyria's, we could set yer arrival more accurately."

A personal belonging?

"Would a comb do?" Patrick asked, opening his sporran and digging inside as he spoke.

"Perfect!" Orabilis squealed as she snatched the comb from his hands. She then tore a strip of cloth from the end of her skirt and wound it around the comb's teeth before handing it all back to him. "That in yer hands when you travel will ensure that the first person you meet will be the Sensor nearest to Elesyria."

He liked the sound of that. At last it seemed as though the dice were falling in his favor. "And have you any suggestions on how I should approach this Sensor? I'd imagine my popping in out of thin air and saying I'm from their past might be difficult to take all in one swallow."

Another deep sigh met his question, as if the answering of it would again force the old Fae to share more than she really wanted to reveal.

"Most Sensors, and definitely those of my bloodline, will have heard my name. You've no' a need to look so surprised, my wee warrior. I've no' always been as weak and helpless as you see me now."

Patrick blanked his expression, irritated that he'd allowed the surprise of her words show on his face. "Go on," he said, making sure his voice didn't betray his feelings. "Though I must tell you in truth, witch, I've no' ever made the mistake of thinking of you as either weak or helpless."

"That's only as it should be, lad," she said, a smile spreading across the old woman's face before she wiped it away. "Because you were raised properly. But back to the business at hand. When you meet the Sensor, you must tell her right off that Orabilis has sent you into her keeping. Tell her that the Faerie home world is rife with turmoil and revolt and that I am asking a boon of her to help in locating one of our own who's been exiled to her place and time. Explain why you've come and who you seek. Without her knowing all of that, yer no' likely to get the help you need in a timely fashion. You must remember what I've said and do exactly as I've told you."

"I will," he answered, anxious to be on his way. Anxious to find Syrie and bring her home where she belonged. "I'm ready."

"No' so fast, lad. There's a bit more you need to understand if yer to find success in yer quest. I've already told you of the danger you face in failing. There are Fae who, once they realize what yer attempting, will do everything in their power to stop you. Everything. They will not hold back, and the Magic they wield is mighty in both reach and effect."

His mother had told him stories of Faerie Magic when he was but a lad. Stories that had disturbed his dreams for months afterward. If the old witch thought to dissuade him from his quest, she'd certainly chosen a strong argument.

Though not strong enough. Nothing was strong enough to keep him from trying to reach Syrie.

"How am I to defeat Magic such as this? I am but a mere mortal."

Orabilis snorted, shaking her head as she leaned closer to him. "Yer no more a mere mortal than I am, son of Asgard. Son of Deandrea. The blood of two powerful lines of beings mingles in yer veins. Never forget that. You may not have the Gifts of yer sister, but you've Gifts of yer own, even if you've no' seen them yet."

In spite of what Orabilis said, Patrick knew better. He had no Gift of any kind. No talents for Magic or the Sight. He had no special powers at all, only the power of his own two hands.

He did have determination, though, and, as his family had mentioned more than once, a stubbornness unmatched by any. He had that on his side. That and the love he carried in his heart. He would battle the greatest armies to save Syrie. That would have to be enough to see him through.

"Patience and cunning, my young warrior," Orabilis said. "You've that on yer side, as well. And honesty. A virtue you'll need to exercise as you work with she who will help you. Because the Sensor also faces a danger. But, whereas yer danger comes with yer failure, hers comes with yer succeeding in yer quest. There are powerful Fae who will be angered by what they will see as her interference. And yers. She must be warned of this. As for yer dealings with the Sensor, Patrick, doona forget this: Anything less than complete honesty in all things and you've lost her help before you even begin."

"I'll tell her all I can," he answered. "With honesty. You've my oath on it."

"Good." Orabilis nodded as if his answer had satisfied her. "Now, equally important, I'd hear what you intend to say to Elesyria when you first lay eyes upon her?"

Say to her? He hadn't thought so far ahead as to the moment he saw her again. And he certainly hadn't thought of what he'd say. He'd only imagined himself gathering her in his arms and holding her until she couldn't do anything else other than to remember him.

"It's as I feared," Orabilis said, shaking her head as if she'd heard his thoughts. "Syrie's memory will only return with time. If you think you've no need to prepare because you'll simply force her to remember by telling her who she is and what has happened, yer no' recognizing the depth of the Magic you face. Doing such as that could lock her into her new reality forever. For a fact, I'd imagine you'll find yerself unable to say the words that would share her history at all until you've done what you need to do. You'll have to win her heart again, Patrick. Just as you did in this time. Only then will her memory break free of the chains that bind her. It's part and parcel of the Magic sent out by the Goddess. There are no short paths to yer quest."

All good and fine for her to say. Just make the stubborn Elf fall in love with him again. Sounded so easy as the words came from her mouth. But there were problems with that path. Problems like the possibility that he hadn't yet won Syrie's heart in this time. He had no way of knowing what her feelings for him really were. It might be only him that fancied himself in love.

"Doona fash yerself over it, lad. You can only do what you can do, aye?"

His panic must have shown through in his expression. Either that or the old witch really was reading his mind.

He nodded his acceptance of this latest twist to his quest. "Do you have any other advice for me as to what I should do or say?"

A fitting question, since Orabilis seemed full of advice.

"Only that you should be guided by the Sensor who finds you first. That is yer best course of action. She will ken the ways of the time in which you find yerself. Are you ready?"

Again he nodded, holding very still as waves of green sparkles appeared to course out of the water and began to circle his body. A noise filled his ears, like the buzzing of angry insects getting closer and closer. Only as the sparkles turned into dazzling multicolored lights, diving haphazardly around him, did he think to question the actual process of sending him through time.

"Yer sure this will work?" he yelled over the din of the buzzing. "That I'll end up where Syrie is?"

"Of course I'm sure," Orabilis yelled back, putting distance between her and him.

The lights grew more dense and their movement more frantic until they seemed to melt into a shimmering bubble of green surrounding him. The earth itself trembled under his feet and he fell, endlessly, into a huge black void.

He'd known the fear of battle and the fear of loss, but this? This was a new beast altogether, made even more disconcerting when he heard Orabilis' voice again as if she stood next to him.

"At least, I think it will work."

Perfect. Even as the last shreds of his world faded away, he was still subject to the perverse vagaries of Faerie humor.

If it *was* humor and not true concern.

"Please let it be humor," he muttered, his last thoughts before he gave in to the forces that stole all conscious thought and tossed him helplessly through the void.

* * *

Syrie knew this place, though she had no memory of ever having been here before. Perhaps it was only from the legends that she recognized it.

Whatever the reason, she hadn't a single doubt about where she stood. This place was the Void and *that*, only steps ahead of her, was the River of Time.

Slowly, she moved toward the river and stopped to kneel when she reached the bank's edge to hold her fingers only inches away from the enticing waters. Here, at the bank, the waters eddied and circled, deceptively calm and inviting. Farther out, near the center, they showed their true nature, churning and writhing in a riotous shower of color and sound.

The spray generated by their tumult cast a fine mist of liquid color across her hand, like a dusting of living glitter. To dip her fingers into the crystalline blue water would be a mistake. To step inside would be beyond forbidden.

And yet that was exactly what she was drawn to do.

Rising to stand, she lifted one bare foot and tentatively dipped her toes into the gently lapping water. A toe and then her whole foot. Before she allowed herself the time to consider the potential consequences of her actions, she found herself waist deep, unable to turn back to the shore. The path she followed led only forward, leaving her no options but to continue on.

Somewhere near the center of the river, with the waters raging around her, buffeting her body from every direction, she found *him*.

He stood there, head bowed, unaffected by the tumult around him, impervious to it, as if the waters feared to touch him. Tall and strong, he stood as if waiting, with his dark hair splayed over his shoulders like a curtain of black silk.

That silken curtain parted as he lifted his head, long, shimmery strands of hair caught up by the blowing wind to reveal blue eyes so mesmerizing Syrie couldn't have looked away even if her life had depended upon it.

"Elf," he murmured, his deep voice spreading over her soul like a long-absent balm.

When he opened his arms to her, she stepped in close, allowing him to enclose her in his embrace as if she were coming home to a place where she belonged.

"I've missed you so," she whispered, not realizing the truth of her words until they reached her ears.

He made a noise low in his throat, primal and possessive, as his lips trailed a slow, heated path down her cheek, across her jawline, to settle near the base of her neck.

"Mine," he growled, his kisses trailing lower until his mouth covered one hardened nipple.

Had he not held her so tightly, she would have fallen. She would have been swept away by the furious torrents crashing around them. But he held her, close to his body, wrapped in an embrace that told her more than any words ever could have just how safe she was with him.

She ran a hand through his hair, brushing long strands back as he lifted his head to meet her eyes.

"I feared I'd lost you forever," he said, his voice breaking with emotion.

"It's not possible for you to lose me," she answered, fighting against the waters that suddenly buffeted them, threatening to pull them apart. "I'm here. You're here."

"No." He shook his head, pain and sorrow battling in his eyes. "Soon, but not yet."

As if the water were a living creature, waves rose up, tearing them from one another, tossing them to opposite banks of the massive river.

"Remember me, Elesyria," he called, as much a command as a plea.

And then he simply disappeared. There one instant and gone the next, like a candle flame snuffed out.

"Come back!" she demanded, shouting to be heard over the roar of the river. But it was no use. The sound of the water gradually faded away, leaving only her own desperate voice to echo in the empty void as tears filled her eyes and ran down her cheeks.

Remember him? How could she do anything other than remember him? He was as the night to her day, as much a part of her as her own heart. She could scarcely forget her own heart, so certainly she couldn't forget someone who...

The void began to swirl around her, its inky black slowly giving way to a soft yellow glow.

Once, twice, a third time she blinked, only then coming fully awake.

Her shoulder cramped from the crumpled position in which she'd slept, and her feet tangled in the afghan she'd draped over them when she'd first lain down for her nap. Her pillow was uncomfortably damp and not until she sat up did she realize her whole face was wet.

"That was one awful nightmare," she said, pulling herself off the bed to make her way to the bathroom.

Switching on the light, she glanced in the mirror to discover her makeup was smeared and her eyes were as red and swollen as her nose felt. One awful nightmare, indeed. So awful, it had brought her to tears, and yet all she could remember of it was an overwhelming sense of loss and something about a pair of blue eyes that had the power to bring her to her knees.

Like everything else that had happened in her life prior to the night she came to this house, the dream was a memory she couldn't recover.

CHAPTER ELEVEN

"It'll take a lot of work, that's sure enough. But I feel like this is the place where I'm supposed to be." Clint Coryell ducked his head, a shy grin lifting one corner of his mouth. "Even though I'd be the first one to claim how silly that sounds."

"Not silly at all."

Rosella MacKeon felt a matching grin form on her face as the man beside her spoke, his gaze firmly fixed on the horizon. On the future. Their future.

He reached down to clasp her hand in his, and the smile she wore spread through her whole body.

With all her heart, she knew that Clint was her True Love, the one she would spend her life with. That he hadn't actually popped the question yet was only a small technicality, to her way of thinking. And technicalities didn't matter when you stood next to your SoulMate.

At least, they *shouldn't* matter.

From the time of her first memories, Rosella had heard the stories of SoulMates. Both her mother and her grandmother had filled her head with their family legends of Magic and Faeries and, most important of all, True Love. She'd known even before she'd hit grade school that finding your SoulMate, your one True Love, was more rare than snow falling in July at the equator. Rare, but, for those lucky few among them, it happened. As it had happened for her.

Knowing all that, believing all that, why was it that one small technicality like Clint's not yet having proposed marriage—which shouldn't matter at all—mattered so much?

Maybe it mattered because there was a chance that those stories she'd been raised to believe were just that: stories. And even if they were true, after all the centuries that had passed, her bloodline would have to be diluted, making her as much Mortal as Faerie. Maybe even more Mortal than Fae.

No wonder his lack of a proposal mattered.

With each passing day, the doubt loomed larger, more real. It had reached a point where sometimes she caught herself wondering whether he even—

"Rosie!"

Startled, she jerked her attention back to Clint.

"Sorry," she mumbled, loath to think he might suspect what had been going through her thoughts.

"Wherever you were, it sure wasn't here," he said, squeezing her hand.

"Miles away, I guess," she answered, her face heating with embarrassment.

More like years than miles, actually. Years into the future, daydreaming about all the things they'd spoken of wanting one day. A home, a family, a life together.

Or had the *together* part been something only she'd wanted?

"Well, wherever you drifted off to, I need you back here with me. See that rise out there? The one with the tuft of trees lining it?" Without dropping her hand, he draped his other arm around her shoulders, hugging her close to his side. "That's where I plan to build our home."

Her heart skipped a beat and her breath caught in her throat. "*Our* home?"

"Yup," he said quietly, taking an audibly deep breath before turning her in his arms to face him. "I'm no romantic, Rosella. I'll be the first to admit that. You deserve a man who can come up with all the pretty words and do just the right thing to sweep you off your feet. But that sure isn't me."

If she'd thought her heart had skipped a beat moments before, this time she felt as if it had stopped beating altogether.

"Clint—"

He stopped her with two fingers placed gently against her lips.

"Hear me out. I can never be the kind of man that women dream about, Rosie. I'm just a plain ol' cowboy at heart. I don't imagine a future filled with fame and fortune. When I look into the future, I see a home right out there on that rise. A home filled with a loving wife and a brood of kids. I can't offer more than that. But I can promise you that I will always love you more than anyone else ever could. I will always be there for you. I'm just hoping that's good enough."

As he stopped speaking, he reached into his pocket, pulled out a small black box and popped open the lid.

Nestled inside lay the most beautiful diamond ring Rosella had ever seen. It wasn't a big stone by any stretch of the imagination. Its beauty lay in the fact that Clint had picked it out just for her.

She wanted to say something perfect for the moment. Something about what a liar he was about not being a romantic. Something about how they both dreamed of the same future. But the tears clouding her eyes somehow seemed to clog up her throat, too. So, instead, she threw her arms around his neck and hugged him for all she was worth.

"I sure hope that's a yes," he whispered into her ear as he held her against his big, warm chest.

"It's definitely a yes," she said when she was finally able to speak.

"Sweet!" Clint laughed, and stepped back, catching up both her hands to pull her along with him. "Come on. Let's go have a look at the view from where I'm going to build our front porch."

The sun had started its descent, a big, fiery ball sinking behind the mountains, casting a warm orange glow over the landscape. As they drew closer to the rise where Clint planned to build their home, pockets of shadow formed and deepened around trees and the outcroppings of rock that dotted the land.

It was as they passed one such outcropping that Clint suddenly stopped, tugging Rosella's hand to pull her behind him.

"Did you hear that?" he asked, his body tense and alert in a way she hadn't seen before. "Listen!"

Rosella stilled, straining to hear something beyond the birds and the rustle of the wind blowing through the tufts of weeds covering the land. Her mind quickly filed through everything Clint had told her on their way out here today. At the time, the idea of a ranch filled with everything from rattlers and elk to coyotes and bear had sounded exotic and wonderful.

It sounded a whole lot less wonderful now, standing in the middle of that wilderness, so far from the safety of Clint's old pickup.

"There it is again," Clint said, his voice hushed and urgent.

This time she did hear the noise. A groan, low and unmistakably human.

"That doesn't sound like any animal I've ever heard," she said, unconsciously matching Clint's whisper.

"No four-legged one, anyway," he answered, moving toward the large outcropping. "You stay there. Anything but me comes out from behind those rocks, you run like hell, you understand?"

She nodded her understanding, but followed him as soon as he turned his back. No way was she crossing all that open land by herself. Especially not wearing a miniskirt and heels.

Rounding the stones, they spotted him. A large man lay on the ground as if he'd been tossed there by some giant hand. Clint hurried to him and knelt at his side, two fingers on the man's neck.

"Pulse and breathing are fine, but he's out cold," Clint said. "I'm going to go get the pickup. I think there's enough clearance for me to make it out here without busting an axle. Carrying somebody his size isn't something I'd particularly want to do."

"I'll wait here with him," Rosella said, dropping to her knees at his side.

"You sure?" Clint asked, indecision painting his features.

"I'm sure. Go on. It's not like I can't see you from here." Even if he would appear the size of a pea by the time he got to the truck. "But hurry up, okay?"

"No worries about that," he said. "I'm not leaving you here alone with that guy one second longer than I have to."

With a quick kiss to her forehead, Clint was on his feet and off toward the pickup at a dead run.

Only after she was alone did she have any time to wonder about the stranger. How badly was he hurt? How did he get here? Where had he come from? With his long black hair and his odd choice of clothing, he looked as if he were some strange mixture of the original people who had roamed this land and some wild highlander, both of them straight out of ancient history. And, more important, neither of them belonging here in this place and this time. The comb clutched tightly in his fist only added to the mystery.

"If nothing else, you should have one heck of a story to tell when you wake up," she muttered, standing up to track Clint's progress toward the pickup.

He was nearing the truck and still running at full speed.

The man at her feet groaned, and Rosella dropped to her knees again to place a hand on his forehead. Her hand froze when, without opening his eyes, he spoke.

"Remember me, Elesyria," he whispered.

Rosella's life had been filled with coincidence on more occasions than most people would believe. It had happened to her so often, she'd learned to ignore them for the most part. But this stranger speaking Syrie's name was simply too much of a coincidence for even her to ignore. The name was far too unusual. Maybe this man was the key to unlocking the mystery of their guest with no memory.

As Rosella watched, the stranger opened his eyes.

"Are you okay?" she asked, feeling foolish the moment the words were out of her mouth.

Of course he wasn't okay. If he was, he wouldn't be lying out here unconscious, in the middle of nowhere, dressed like someone who belonged in one of the historical romance stories she loved so much.

"Orabilis sent me," he said, struggling to form the words as if his mouth wasn't quite ready to be awake yet.

Orabilis! It was a name she'd heard often enough on the lips of both her mother and grandmother, usually uttered in hushed tones of reverence. Rosella had always thought it the name of a creature straight out of a Faerie tale. But if that were true, then her Faerie tale had just come to life.

* * *

The young woman sitting on the ground next to Patrick flinched as if she'd been struck when he spoke the old witch's name as Orabilis had insisted he must do. Quickly he ran through those final instructions in his memory, hoping he hadn't made some horrible mistake.

But no, he'd done as he was told. He'd spoken to the first woman he'd set eyes on in this time. He'd told her who sent him.

"Yer the Sensor, are you no'?"

Again she flinched, scrambling to put some distance between them.

In truth, she seemed stranger to him than any Faerie who'd ever crossed his path. The clothing she wore covered so little of her body, he'd felt the need to sit up and search for the stream where she must have been bathing when he appeared.

If he could control his muscles well enough to sit up straight, that is, a feat he doubted his ability to accomplish at the moment.

"Am I in trouble?" she asked, one hand fluttering up protectively to her throat.

Women. In any time, in any place, they were all the same.

"It's no' about you." He stopped and sighed, shaking his head in frustration. "I've a speech I'm supposed to give you. Something about there being turmoil and revolt in the home world. About how Orabilis is asking a boon of you to help me in finding one of her own who's been sent to this place and time."

"Thank the Goddess," the young woman murmured, the pink of her cheeks quickly fading.

"Who are you?" a man asked as he rounded the outcropping of rock, taking a protective stance behind the woman. "And what are you doing out here?"

"My name is Patrick MacDowylt. Before I can say more, I'm bid to warn you that by helping me, you risk the

85

wrath of powerful Fae who won't look kindly on yer interference in this matter."

"Powerful what?" the man exclaimed.

"From the stories I've been told, I guess I'd have to expect something like that," the woman responded, sitting up straighter, as if to indicate she'd not be intimidated by such threats. "My name is Rosella MacKeon and this is Clint Coryell. If Orabilis herself has sent you to my keeping, then whatever you need, I'll do my best to help you with it. It won't fall on my shoulders to be the one who lets Orabilis down. Now, what does she want me to do?"

"Who is this Orabilis you're talking about?" the one called Clint asked. "Do you actually know this guy, Rosie?"

"No, I don't. I'll explain everything later," she said, absently allowing him to help her to her feet. "Does this have something to do with Syrie?"

In the process of pulling himself up to sit, hearing the name of the woman Patrick had come here to find wiped from his mind any thoughts of how weak he felt. "It does," he said. "So, Orabilis was right. You do know her. Do you know where I can find her?"

Rosella nodded slowly, her eyes narrowing before she spoke. "I do. But I should warn you, Syrie is my friend. Whatever it is you want with her, you need to understand one thing. Although I will do my best to help you, I won't do anything that would bring harm to her in any way. I won't let you hurt her, either, so maybe you better start by telling me exactly why you're the one who's come to find her."

"Nobody is hurting anybody around here. You better get that straight right from the start," Clint growled, inserting himself in front of Rosella.

Had the silly woman not been listening? Irritation warred with frustration in this odd place where women flaunted their bare legs and their men seemed not to notice. As he tried to move, Patrick felt as though each of his limbs weighed more than a full-grown horse, and his vision blurred just enough that he didn't dare trust his legs to hold him if he stood. And on top of that, he'd found the one Sensor who couldn't seem to understand what it was she needed to do for him. He'd told her why he was there. He'd told her who had sent him.

"I already told you of my quest. I've been sent to this time to find Syrie, to take her home where she belongs," he said, making little effort to keep the suffering he felt from coloring his voice. "Orabilis said you would help."

Across from him, Rosella shrugged. "I understand what you want to do. But none of that answers the question I just asked. Why is it that *you* are the one who's come for her? And, equally important, is it possible she doesn't want to go with you?"

"She will go with me without hesitation once her memory is restored."

If he could restore her memory.

"Did I hear him right?" Clint asked, his head turning as he looked from one of them to the other. "Did he say he'd been sent to this time? What the hell is that supposed to mean?"

"In a minute," Rosella said to Clint before turning her attention back to Patrick. "By what Magic do you propose to restore her memory?"

"Magic?" Clint choked out. "What kind of crazy bullshit is this, anyway? What's going on here, Rosie?"

"Hush," Rosella said absently, her gaze still focused on Patrick.

"No Magic," Patrick said. "I just need to make her fall in love with me again."

If he could make her fall in love with him again. Assuming, of course, she'd ever been in love with him before.

"I see," Rosella said.

"Well, I sure as hell don't," Clint protested. "None of this is making any sense at all to me."

"Will you help me?" Patrick asked.

"I will," Rosella said, before reaching out to clasp Clint's hand in hers. "We will."

"Not without some kind of an explanation, we won't," Clint said, but he didn't pull his hand from Rosella's.

"I come from a long line of people," Rosella said, looking up at Clint as she placed her hand on his cheek. "A line that extends back to a time when one of our ancestors was Faerie."

As Clint began a sputtering response to Rosella's disclosure, Patrick closed his eyes and leaned his head back against the big rock. He had no interest in the argument ongoing between the two people who had found him. All he cared about was that the Sensor had agreed to help him, bringing him one step closer to finding the woman he loved. Finding her and enticing her to fall in love with him all over again.

Or, perhaps, for the first time.

CHAPTER TWELVE

"Thank you so much, Ellen. I swear I'll find a way to pay you back for this. This and everything else you've done for me. Clint will bring him when he comes to the party this afternoon."

"Bring who?" Syrie asked, entering the kitchen to looks of surprise from Rosella and Ellen.

"I thought you'd still be sleeping," Ellen said, rising from her chair to refill her coffee. "It's not even seven yet."

"Nightmares," Syrie answered, shuddering as she crossed to the cabinet to retrieve a cup and fill it with hot water from the kettle on the stove. With teabag in hand, she joined her friends at the table. "Who is Clint bringing?"

"My cousin," Rosella said, concentrating on the cup in front of her. "Patrick. He arrived last night. From Scotland."

A look Syrie couldn't quite interpret passed between Ellen and Rosella before both of them once again turned their focus to the fascinating cups in front of them.

"What's going on here that you're not telling me?" Syrie asked.

After all this time, she knew the two of them well enough to recognize strange behavior when she saw it.

"Ellen has agreed to allow Patrick to stay here," Rosella said, lifting her eyes for the first time. "For a while, anyway."

"Rosie is worried that you might be uncomfortable with him living here with us, since, you know, he's a guy and the only open room is on the other side of your bathroom."

A man living in their all-female household? And on her floor? Syrie sipped her tea and considered the prospect.

"Men have to live somewhere, too. And he is your cousin." She took another sip and lifted her eyes to meet the oddly anxious gazes of her friends. "It really makes no difference to me if your cousin moves in with us. Is he awful or something?"

"Oh, no. Not at all," Rosella denied quickly. "He's just...different. You know. A little strange, him being a foreigner and all."

"And tell her your good news," Ellen chimed in, almost as if to change the subject. "Show her!"

"Show me what?" Syrie asked.

Rosella held out her left hand, her cheeks coloring an even brighter pink than they already were. "Clint popped the question yesterday. It's official now. We're getting married!"

Staring at Rosella's hand, Syrie realized this bauble she wore on her hand must be the "ring to seal the deal" that

Ellen had spoken of the day before. "It's lovely. I'm so happy for you."

Easy to be happy for her dear friend when she could see how very happy Rosella was.

"Thanks," Rosella said, allowing her hand to drop back to her cup. "But I've been so into myself the past week getting ready for Clint to get back, I feel like I've missed everything that's going on around here. So, update me, ladies. Ellen tells me you're bringing a guy to the party today. I want to hear all about him."

What was there to say? Ellen had told her to bring someone she found interesting, and Gino was a fascinating young man.

"There's not much to tell. He's one of the waiters where I work."

"And…" Rosella countered, trailing out the word as if she clearly expected more.

"Details," Ellen added, her face breaking into a smile. "Tall or short, dark hair or light, skinny or fat? You know, all the juicy details we love so much."

"Tall, dark hair, medium build, I suppose. Neither skinny nor fat. Unique eyes."

It was his eyes that had first drawn Syrie's attention. So dark they were almost impenetrable, and yet still they shone with his every emotion. Old eyes, her intuition told her. Old eyes, old soul. And, even without remembering anything about who she used to be, she knew in her heart that she'd always had a fascination with old souls, as if she had spent her whole life searching for one particular soul.

One particular soul that she had no doubt belonged to the eyes she'd seen in her nightmare.

Her breath hitched in her chest and she stood up quickly, moving to the sink to rinse out her cup to hide the tears that so inconveniently clouded her vision.

How silly of her.

No matter how hard she tried, the dream she'd had was little more than a blur of impressions, so why she insisted on thinking of it as a nightmare she could only guess. And that guess centered around her fear that the eyes floating in her hazy memory of the dream belonged to the soul she'd sought her whole life. Eyes that belonged to a man she'd found after a lifelong search. Found and then lost again when she'd lost her memory.

Nightmare, indeed.

* * *

Patrick stood in the middle of Clint's room, feeling like a prime sheep awaiting the inspection of a buyer on market day.

He wore a tight, finely knitted garment Clint had called a sweater and a pair of pants called khakis. They felt restrictive and completely foreign. He couldn't remember ever having been so uncomfortable in the whole of his life.

"I'd prefer to wear my plaid," Patrick grumbled.

Though he'd intended the complaint only for his own ears, he'd obviously not been successful in his attempt.

"Not a chance," Clint said with a chuckle, continuing to circle around him, inspecting from all angles. "It'll be hard enough to explain all that long hair. No way I'm going to try to justify you showing up at that party with a blanket wrapped around you. We'll have to get to the store tomorrow for some shirts that fit. For now, that sweater will have to work. Maybe shove up the sleeves if it gets too hot."

Shoving up the sleeves might provide some relief for his arms, but what about the rest of him? He still felt as if he had been shackled within the constrictive garments.

A knock on the door drew Clint's attention, leaving Patrick uncomfortably waiting to see what new torture device would come next.

"I knew I had these stuck back somewhere," the young man entering the room said as he thrust something into Clint's arms. "My brother left them here when he came to visit last year. They're too big for me, so maybe they'll work for your friend."

"Sweet," Clint said, lifting two separate objects up for inspection. "Thanks, Greg. I appreciate your help."

"No biggie." Greg started out the door, but turned at the last minute and sighed. "There is one thing, though, you should know. Some dickweed tipped off Professor Hudson that you had someone staying in your dorm room. I heard he went ape over it and is headed your way this afternoon, ready to go all establishment on your ass."

"I can't say I'm surprised. Being in ROTC hasn't made me real popular with some of the people around here, so I'm sure they've been waiting to catch me doing something they could jump on. But no worries. We're bugging out of here as soon as we can get Patrick put together, and these cowboy boots are the last piece of what we needed. He'll be staying over at Rosella's place from here on, so Hudson won't have anything to have a beef with by the time I see him. But thanks anyway, Greg. For the boots and for the warning."

"He's a good friend of yers?" Patrick asked as soon as the door closed behind their visitor.

"He's a friend," Clint answered, handing over the boots. "I guess I don't trust anyone enough to claim them as good friends."

Patrick nodded, understanding such a feeling all too well. As he tugged the strange footwear onto his feet, another thought struck him.

"If there are known enemies here, why haven't you dealt with them? Why would you leave them to skulk about and bring you troubles?"

Leaving his enemies to roam free sounded all too much like some political move his brother Malcolm would have suggested.

Clint chuckled, his face breaking into perhaps the first genuine smile Patrick had seen.

"You sound like my grandmother now. She always told me if someone was giving me a hard time, I should just sock 'em a good one."

Sock them? Patrick shook his head, frustrated at his own ignorance. Orabilis had told him that somehow the Magic would allow him to communicate with people in this time. What she hadn't told him was how much of that communication still would be a mystery to him. He understood the words, but not always what was meant by the words.

"Why would you use footwear on yer enemies?" he asked, hating to look foolish, but hating worse not to understand.

"Footwear?" Now it was Clint who looked confused.

"Yer grandmother's advice to sock yer enemies." Patrick stood up to test the feel of the boots, surprised at a degree of comfort he hadn't expected. "I canna see how giving them yer socks would change their behavior."

"Give them my socks?" Clint's grin turned into a full-fledged laugh before he caught himself. "Yeah, you're right. Socks are something you wear on your feet. But sock is also a word people my grandmother's age use when they mean to hit someone. You sock them. You hit them. Same thing. Make more sense now?"

Patrick nodded slowly, beginning to realize that he might never truly understand this strange place and time.

"Try not to be so literal, Patrick," Clint advised as he walked over to open the door. "To fit in, you're going to need to be more laid-back. And to win over this Syrie chick, you're going to need to fit in. Try to follow along with what people say. Just go with the flow."

Patrick nodded again, his mind occupied with the vagaries of this language as he followed Clint outside and across the lawn toward the metal beast that would carry him to see Syrie. Clint was correct, of course. To have any chance of success in his quest, he needed to fit in. He wasn't sure how lying on his back might help, but he did understand the concept of going along with things, of doing what he was told. After all, a good warrior almost always did as he was told by his leader. If that was what it took to win Syrie's heart, he could do whatever anyone in this strange place told him to do.

No matter how much he might want to do otherwise.

To prove to himself he could do this, he climbed into the belly of the beast Clint called his *truck,* and did his best to lie back.

.

CHAPTER THIRTEEN

Syrie stared at her reflection in the mirror a moment longer before heading back into her bedroom and straight to the closet. Though both Ellen and Rosella had assured her the plaid miniskirt and white boots were perfect for the party, she just couldn't make herself walk down those stairs wearing this outfit.

The young man from work she'd invited to the party had been acting strange enough since she'd extended the invitation. Some little voice in the back of her head told her that this particular outfit would definitely be sending the wrong message when he arrived, and that was a complication she could do without.

She slipped out of the tiny scrap of material and chose instead a pair of white pants with large, flowing legs. Perhaps not as festive as the skirt, but they made her feel much better about herself.

After one last check in the mirror, she headed downstairs to find Ellen waiting in the living room.

"What happened to the skirt and boots? You looked so good in them."

"The boots are here," Syrie said, lifting the hem of one pant leg. "The skirt just didn't feel right for today."

"You're such a prude," Ellen said, her grin taking any sting from the words. "But I do understand. You have to do what feels right for you. I would want nothing else."

"Looks like our first arrivals are here," Rosella said from her spot at the window. "Three cars all coming at once. But not my guys yet." She turned from the window, chewing her bottom lip. "I'm so nervous about you guys meeting my cousin. How dumb is that?"

"Pretty dumb," Ellen agreed. "Syrie, you get the door. Rosie, you hit the music. I'm going to start bringing the munchies out to the table."

Syrie glanced out the window at the laughing people heading up their sidewalk. Most were people she'd met only once or twice. A few were totally new faces. Only one was someone she saw every day.

The guest she'd invited stood away from the others, at the curb, waiting.

Though his chin thrust out in his usual belligerent manner, Syrie saw more in his stance. Uncertainty? Definitely. Fear? Most likely. Her coworker broadcast a swagger, an indifference that never quite reached his eyes. It was these complex layers that had first drawn her attention to Gino Williams. Clearly, he was a man in need of a friend. And she was determined to be that friend, no matter how difficult he made it for her.

At this moment, how difficult he was making it was all too plain. He'd dressed in the most outlandish, garish clothing she could imagine. A tight, long-sleeved shirt adorned with a pattern of huge flowers in eye-piercingly unnatural shades of pink, green and yellow. The legs of his pants rivaled hers in their width, and in his bushy hair he'd stuck something that, from this distance, appeared to be a small leaf rake.

With a long-suffering sigh, she opened the door to greet their guests, and then made her way down the sidewalk to the spot where Eugene waited.

"Aren't you coming in?" she asked when she reached his side.

Eugene's mask of indifference slipped for a second as he turned wounded eyes in her direction. "Why did you ask me here? I saw those other people. You and I both know I'm not going to fit in with this crowd."

"I asked you because I'm your friend," she answered immediately. "And I want you to meet my friends. Come on."

Looping her arm through his, she urged him forward toward the lovely old house she'd come to think of as home. As they stepped inside the door, she spotted Ellen and Rosella, and led her guest in their direction.

"Ellen, Rosella, this is the young man I told you about, Eugene—"

"Whoa, little mama," her guest interrupted, his public face and loud, aggressive manner securely back in place like a suit of armor. "It's Gino. Gino Williams."

"Gino," she repeated, adding emphasis to the name. How careless of her! She should have remembered how upset he'd become when their shift supervisor at the restaurant had used his real name.

"Eugene is a bummer, baby," he told her as they walked away, his voice little more than an uncharacteristic whisper. "Totally brings me down."

"Why is that?" she asked, sincerely at a loss to understand his dislike of his own name.

Once again, Gino lowered his defenses, allowing her to see behind the mask he wore. What she saw in his eyes was raw emotion.

"Because Gino is one cool badass. But Eugene? Eugene is some science-loving square."

Again he'd lost her.

"But why do you want to be a badass?" She rolled the unfamiliar word off her tongue, having only a vague sense of what he meant in its use. "You told me you were studying science, didn't you? I thought it was something you really enjoyed."

For a fact, the one time she'd gotten him to open up about his studies, he'd gone on for longer than she'd ever heard him speak, on a topic about which she could understand only a little.

"Most people aren't like you, Syrie. They don't accept me in the way you do." He shook his head and stared out the window. "There are maybe seven others like me at this university. Eight tops. I've learned that people respect what they understand and fear what they don't. For the most part, they leave alone those they either respect or fear. I earned my way in here by working hard for grades, but people out in the world don't have much respect for brains. So, if I can't have their respect, I'll settle for their fear. Whatever gets them to leave me alone."

"But you don't want to be left alone, really," she said, as perplexed as ever. "You want friends. That's why you agreed to come with me today, isn't it?"

"You are one crazy-assed little white mama, for sure. With one rose-colored view of the world. That's a fact."

The man seemed obsessed with asses.

"As far as I know, I am mother to no one," she said. "Little or otherwise."

Gino's laughter was authentic, but his emotional mask was back in place and Syrie doubted she'd have another opportunity to see on the other side of it any time soon.

It was a discussion Syrie wanted to continue anyway, to try to understand this odd man. But Rosella called out her name, and when she turned in her friend's direction, all thoughts of her curiosity to learn more about what motivated Gino fled her mind.

Rosella stood just inside the front door, her hand clasped within the grasp of a man who could only be her beloved Clint. That alone, though interesting, wouldn't have kept Syrie from her pursuit of information about Gino. No. It was the man standing just behind Clint. A stranger. A stranger with eyes so blue they seemed to fix upon Syrie and draw her toward their owner.

"Syrie, I have someone I want you to meet. This is my Clint," Rosella said, a smile spreading over her face. "And this is Patrick MacDowylt. My cousin. From Scotland. The one I was talking about earlier who's going to be staying here with us."

Nothing in the world could have torn her gaze from Patrick's. Without conscious thought, she lifted her hand and he clasped it within his own, bending his head until his lips brushed lightly against her skin, sending a frisson of electricity tingling up her arm and down her spine.

"Do I know you?" she asked, her voice as breathless as if she'd been running.

He straightened back up to his full height, his gaze keeping her pinned to the spot, her hand still held by his. "I canna say, my lady. *Do* you know me?"

His voice, deep and smooth, rolled over her like a blanket of soft, fuzzy wool, his accent at once foreign and familiar and completely captivating.

"I don't..." She paused, words failing her as she continued to stare into his eyes.

"Hey, man," Gino said, arriving at her side to physically disentangle her hand from Patrick's grip before casually draping his own arm around her shoulders. "What's your bag, anyway? You some longhair, draft-dodging peacenik or what?"

"He's asking what you do," Clint said quietly as if translating from a foreign language. "He wants to know what your occupation is."

"My occupation," Patrick repeated thoughtfully. "I'm a warrior."

He made the statement as if what he said should have been clear to anyone without their having to ask. For some reason, Syrie wasn't the least bit surprised.

Gino snorted, a sound unmistakably filled with contempt. "You don't look like any soldier I ever saw. Not with all that hair. The army buzzes you short, man. They don't go for that look."

Her gaze freed with the release of her hand, Syrie allowed herself the luxury of studying Rosella's cousin. The hair that Gino mentioned was definitely something most people would notice right away.

Right after they were able to get past his eyes, that is.

Long, straight and black, it would likely have hung to the middle of his back if it hadn't been caught up with a tie at his neck. As it was, his leaning over her hand had brought the whole of it cascading over his shoulder, where it lay now, caressing his chest in a way she found herself wanting to emulate.

"You've a piece of something caught in yer hair," Patrick said, his voice lowered as if he hoped to avoid attracting attention when he spoke to Gino.

"What is with you?" Gino asked, his face crinkled in disbelief. "That's my comb, man. You don't know that? You just land on this planet or something?"

"Patrick isn't from around here." Clint didn't make a move physically, but something in his voice made him appear closer, larger than he had a moment before, almost protective of the man standing at his side. "You might be surprised at the differences you can find around the world, if you take the time to look."

"I don't find too many real surprises in the world. Or in its people," Gino replied, his arm tightening on Syrie's shoulder.

"I should introduce my friend," Syrie began, hoping to fill the uncomfortable silence that followed the initial exchange. "Gino Williams."

"Nice to meet you, Gino. This is Clint Coryell and Patrick MacDowylt," Rosella said, finishing the introduction as she lifted a hand to indicate each man. "Syrie told us that you work with her and that you're a student at the university. Clint's also going to school there."

"You at one of the houses on campus?" Gino asked.

"Could you help me in the kitchen, Syrie?" Ellen leaned in close to ask her question, having arrived silently sometime during the earlier introductions. "They're eating us out of house and home over there. Everything needs refilling and I'm short a couple of hands."

Syrie nodded, reluctant to leave Rosella's fascinating cousin, but not willing to ignore her friend's request. She dipped a shoulder to move out of Gino's grasp and followed her friend.

They'd been in the kitchen pulling containers out of the refrigerator for only a few minutes before Ellen spoke again.

"I have to admit, Syrie, I'm a little surprised you'd bring someone like Gino to the party as your date," Ellen said, arching her eyebrow as she spoke. "He's not at all what I expected."

"Why is that?" Syrie asked. "Because his skin is a different color?"

It was something she had heard Gino claim repeatedly after confrontations at the restaurant. Though she hadn't noticed it, apparently people always judged him differently because of his skin color.

"Not at all," Ellen denied quickly before she paused, tipping her head to one side as if lost in thought for a second. "Okay, if I'm being completely honest, that might play a small part in my surprise. But only a small part. I don't really care about that. Mostly I question him being your choice because he's so loud and confrontational. It's as if he's daring us not to like him. Those are not at all the traits I'd expect to see in a man you'd end up romantically involved with."

"Romantically involved?" Syrie echoed. "I have no romantic feelings for Gino. For a fact, I've not met a single man since my arrival here to whom I feel the least bit of physical attraction."

There'd been no one. Not one single man who left her as weak-kneed and wanting as the mystery man in her dream. A mystery man whose face she couldn't even recall.

With the possible exception of the man who she'd just met, Rosella's cousin.

Ellen stopped piling little pastries on the platter and turned toward her, a confused expression wrinkling her brow.

"Then why on Earth would you ask that man to be your date for our party?"

"Because you told me to ask someone I was interested in and, without a doubt, Gino is the most interesting person I've met here. From his manner of speech and the way he dresses, right down to the way he thinks. Though I'm continually at a loss to understand his perspective or reasoning, I never tire of watching and wondering what he'll do next. He is quite interesting. Don't you think so?"

Ellen stared at her for a moment longer, her expression one of a woman examining a never-before-seen insect on her counter. After a moment longer, she began to chuckle, finally turning back to the business of filling the platter.

"What is so funny?" Syrie asked, not at all sure she was comfortable with her friend's reaction.

"Oh, Syrie. I keep forgetting that your understanding of the words I say to you is frequently nowhere close to what I meant when I uttered those words." Ellen sighed and handed the now-filled platter to Syrie. "And I still find it surprising that you'd be interested in a character like Gino simply because he behaves so differently from everyone else."

Syrie accepted the platter and started to leave but stopped. For some odd reason it was important to her that her friend understand.

"It's not just that his behavior is different. He's struggling to find his place in the world, much as I am. There's something about him, Ellen. Something I see deep in his eyes. It's almost as if I've known him before."

Though she knew her reasoning sounded foolish, she wasn't at all prepared for her friend's shocked response.

Ellen gasped, her fingers flying to cover her lips as her eyes rounded. "Are you remembering things? Remembering him? Can he tell you anything about your old life? About who you really are?"

"No, I didn't mean…" Syrie stopped speaking, shaking her head as she realized her mistake. "When I said I feel as though I've known him before, I didn't mean that as if it were a returned memory. It's more like he houses a familiar soul. A soul I've known in another lifetime."

"Oh," Ellen said, confusion coloring her expression. "In another lifetime, you say. Let me make sure I understand. You're not talking about this particular lifetime, the one where you can't remember anything but your name. Not this one here and now, but some *other* lifetime." She shook her head, a little frown wrinkling her face. "Have you thought about how, since you can't remember anything from before Danny found you, you can be so sure about that? I mean, maybe you did actually know this guy and that's why he feels so familiar to you."

"It's not that kind of familiar."

Not at all the kind of familiarity she felt when she'd been introduced to Rosella's cousin. Being in his presence felt like coming home.

"Then what kind of familiar are you talking—"

Ellen's questioning was cut short by a scream and angry shouts from the other room.

"And that's without serving even a single drop of alcohol yet," Ellen muttered as they both headed out toward the noise.

* * *

Patrick didn't like this man, this friend of Syrie's. Not one little bit. From the challenge of his jutting jaw to the possessive manner in which he draped his arm around Syrie's shoulders, nothing about this Gino was endearing.

"Be cool," Clint had whispered when the oaf had pulled Syrie's hand from his. "Fit in."

Fit in. Go with the flow. Do as you're told.

All the advice Clint had given him for the past few hours warred in Patrick's head with his instant and intense dislike for the man in front of him.

"You at one of the houses on campus?" Gino asked.

"I am," Clint answered. "ROTC," he finished, a note of challenge in his tone.

"Figures," Gino said. "You hawks all stick together. But you know what I always say?"

Patrick didn't particularly care what this Gino had to say. He only cared that Syrie had slipped away from the man's grasp and followed another woman out of the room.

"I say make love, not war," Gino said.

As Gino lifted two fingers into the air, Patrick turned his full attention on the man, fighting an unreasonable need to plant his fist in Gino's face. Perhaps not so unreasonable, in truth. The idea of this man with the strange comb stuck in his hair making love to Syrie was beyond unacceptable. Jealousy was a reasonable emotion. Not an attractive emotion, but completely reasonable and distinctly difficult to control.

"Fit in," Clint hissed under his breath, apparently sensing the emotions that flowed through Patrick. "Just go with it."

Patrick clenched his hands into tight fists and pressed them against his thighs to stave off the act that was his first and strongest instinct.

"You got something to say to me, warrior man?" Gino asked, moving closer. "I'm all ears. Sock it to me, man. I can handle it."

Sock it to him? He obviously wasn't talking about footwear, so it must be the other meaning. Although why someone would ask to be hit was beyond Patrick's ability to reason. Also beyond his ability to care. It was what Syrie's friend had asked him to do.

"Go with the flow," Patrick said as his fist shot out to connect with Gino's chin.

The world around them broke into a frenzy of squeals and activity as the young man's eyes rounded before rolling up in his head. By the time his body hit the floor, Clint had pushed Rosella behind him and it seemed as if everyone in the room was shouting at him. And then, as if she'd appeared by Magic, Syrie was there, dropping to her knees at Gino's side.

"Why would you do such a thing to the Dark Elf?" she demanded as she glared up at him, sounding so much like her old self, he was sure for an instant that her memory had returned. "Unarmed as he is, he's obviously of little danger to you. You know they're completely harmless in this realm."

She froze the moment the words were out of her mouth, as if she'd just heard what she said and was momentarily stunned to silence.

Gino, on the other hand, had plenty to say.

"Dark Elf?" he asked, rolling up to sit while rubbing his jaw. "What kind of racist bullshit is that?"

Syrie reached out to help him, but he pushed her hands away and stood up on his own.

"I didn't mean—" she began, but he cut her off.

"I think we all know what you meant. I do, anyway. Dark Elf, my ass. It's been real, baby, but I'm outta here."

Gino pushed through the people who had gathered around him and stormed out the door. From her spot on the floor, Syrie glared up at Patrick.

"This is all your fault," she accused.

"I only did as he asked of me," Patrick said, hoping to allay her obvious anger.

Her memory might be gone, but he sincerely doubted she'd lost her famously quick temper.

"I'm not having any bit of that garbage. You're to blame and you know it." She rose to her feet and strode toward him, stopping only when she was mere inches away. "You overgrown barbarian!" She punctuated each of her words with her index finger, poking it into his chest. "Your solution is always to use brawn first and brains later."

Just like old times.

Only it wasn't old times.

As if she'd caught herself again behaving in a way she simply couldn't explain, Syrie turned and ran from him, disappearing up the staircase at the far end of the room.

"Hardly a normal, everyday little party scene," Ellen said, her gaze traveling from Rosella to Patrick and back again. "I'm open to any and all explanations you'd care to give. The sooner the better, I'd say."

"There might have been a thing or two I neglected to mention when we spoke about Patrick this morning," Rosella said meekly, reaching for the other woman's hand and leading her off in the direction of the kitchen. "Maybe I should fill you in on all of it."

"What the hell was that all about?" Clint asked when people had drifted away from them. "Decking that guy like that. I thought we'd agreed you'd try to fit in."

Patrick shook his head, confused by much that had just transpired. "You said I should follow along with what was asked of me, aye? He asked me to sock him and I did. I canna for the life of me understand why everyone would be so upset when I only did as the man himself asked me to do."

Though he would be the first to admit, it had felt damn satisfying to do it.

Clint rubbed a hand over his face, a deep sigh coming from beneath the hand. "Well, I'll say this much for you, Patrick. Completing your quest is in no way going to be a walk in the park. My Rosie has her work cut out for her."

Indeed, she did. And as for the task that lay ahead of him, Patrick suspected that he'd gotten off to a very bad start.

CHAPTER FOURTEEN

Clearly, she was losing her mind.

Syrie stopped pacing to sit on her bed, her legs weakened at the very thought of how she'd behaved downstairs. *Dark Elf?* How could she have said such a thing about Gino? Where had such an idea even come from, let alone the words themselves that had popped out of her mouth? It was as if another person had taken over her body and spoken for her. Some wild and fearless person, determined to right the wrongs that had just occurred.

If her bizarre behavior alone wasn't enough, what about her reaction to Patrick MacDowylt?

She flopped back on the bed to stare up at the ceiling, her hands rising to cover her heated cheeks.

By all that was holy, just looking at that man downstairs had set her adrift, lost in the sea of his eyes. It had done something to her insides that she couldn't begin to explain. It was as if some invisible force had pulled her to him and stripped her of her will to resist, very like the little black-and-white kissing dog magnets Ellen kept in her kitchen window.

Syrie's hand drifted down her neck and across her breasts to come to a rest on her stomach, as if she almost expected to find a similar magnet affixed to her body.

And when he'd touched her?

As she thought about it, a shiver ran down her spine, leaving a trail of little bumps and raised hairs all along her arms and legs.

Her hand had fit into his palm as if it were meant to be there. The memory of his lips hovering over the back of her hand heightened her physical reaction even now. His skin had barely brushed against hers, his warm breath feathering over her when he'd lifted her hand to his lips, and yet there was no denying that the feel of him had ignited a desire in her, like an old fire, never fully extinguished. Like a memory of an old lover.

What a ridiculous line of thought! Pure indulgence in fantasy. It wasn't as if she had any memory of ever having met Patrick before, let alone any memory of having been his lover.

Not that she had any memories of *anything* before.

With a sigh, she pushed herself up to sit and scrubbed her hands over her face, but it did little good. Even with her eyes tightly closed, she could still see him, gazing down at her, his eyes filled with emotions she couldn't easily identify. Self-confidence? Likely. Arrogance? Absolutely. Desire? Possession? She could almost swear she'd seen those as well.

Or was she simply imagining those last two to cover for her own feelings?

She refused to allow herself to wander too far down that particular path. Her whole reaction to her friend's cousin had been beyond unreasonable, sending her scurrying up to her room to hide for far too long. She should have been downstairs hours ago helping to clean up after their guests left rather than pacing the length of her bedroom, berating herself for her bizarre behavior. She hadn't any reason to be cowering up here for the whole evening. She wasn't the one who'd behaved abominably.

Well, except for the Dark Elf comment.

Even that probably could be explained away. She hadn't been herself. She'd allowed the newcomer to upset her. Perhaps it was the violence that had shaken her so that she'd pulled something out of some book she'd read when she spoke. She certainly hadn't made any sense. And poor Gino. He was so offended, he might never speak to her again.

As for her bizarre reaction to Patrick, there could be a million reasons for it. Perhaps he resembled someone she'd known before. Perhaps his arrival had triggered some bit of latent memory.

"Or perhaps," she said as she rose to stand. "Perhaps he's just an arrogant brute who set off all my warning signals to keep my distance."

That was much more likely than anything else she'd considered. No wonder Ellen and Rosella had been worried about telling her he would be staying here for a while. Rosella must have told Ellen how very uncivilized her cousin was and they'd both had concerns about how she would react to him.

"Well, they needn't worry anymore."

It wasn't like she was some delicate young thing. She'd show them that his presence had absolutely no effect on her. Just a quick washcloth over her still-heated face and she'd go back downstairs to help clean up after the party. And, as far as Patrick MacDowylt was concerned, she'd simply keep her distance and ignore the big Scot, putting him out of her thoughts completely.

"I so swear," she whispered, bolstering her determination.

That determination, along with her vow, lasted for approximately the five seconds it took for her to open the bathroom door and step into a billowing cloud of steam. As the steam cleared, she spotted the man she'd vowed to ignore, standing beside the shower he'd apparently just finished using, gloriously naked and absolutely impossible to ignore.

* * *

"What do you think you're doing in here?" Syrie demanded, her voice cracking just enough to ruin any real display of indignation.

Patrick had heard the door open and the gasp that had followed. He had forced himself to pretend he hadn't noticed as he waited for the long seconds to pass before she spoke.

"I think it's called showering," he said as he cast a single glance in her direction, keeping his body angled slightly away from her. "Though I was led to believe it was an activity conducted in private."

She actually sputtered as she stood in the doorway, forcing him to bite into his inner cheek to keep a smile from reaching his face. There were few pleasures as great as seeing Syrie flustered.

"You arrogant piece of—" She stopped speaking abruptly, obviously gathering her senses, the sound of her breath coming in erratic little puffs. "I know *what* you're doing. What I want to know is why you're doing it in my bathroom."

"Our bathroom," he corrected. "My bedchamber is through that door, so I was told we're to share. You've a problem with that, do you?"

"A very big problem," she muttered, but not quietly enough that he couldn't hear. "In that case, the least you could do is to lock the door when you're using this room."

"I've no need for locks." He turned to face her as he spoke, careful to ensure that the towel he held draped artfully down the center of his body. "I've naught to hide."

Her cheeks bloomed a mottled red as she quickly snapped her eyes up to meet his gaze. But not quickly enough that he failed to see where they had been focused before.

"This is not going to work," she said, backing out of the room and slamming the door shut. "And make sure you lock the damn door from now on!"

Another moment passed and he heard a second door slam. Clearly, she had left her bedchamber. Knowing Syrie, she'd likely be headed out to find someone to demand that he be moved to another room. The Fae might have stripped her memories, but they hadn't been able to take away the fiery spirit that drove the woman.

"Thank the Goddess," he murmured as he moved back into his own bedchamber.

From the beginning a fear had lurked in his heart that Syrie's punishment might have somehow changed who she was. The very idea had gnawed at his innards like some starving animal.

Before Syrie, no woman had ever made him regret his lot in life. In his world, the third son of a powerful man such as his father rarely had the same choices as his older brothers. Patrick had long settled for the solitary path the Fates had woven for him. He was right hand to his older brother, the laird, content to spend his days defending and protecting his people. Though he counted himself lucky that his life was as good as it was, he was a realist. He had no home other than that which his brother provided, and no income or means to support a family. A man in his position could hardly expect any woman to cast her lot with his.

Not that he'd met any worth pining over.

Not until Syrie had entered his life.

From the first moment she'd crossed his path, he'd felt a strange attraction to her. In his experience, women were docile creatures, devoid of personality other than the drive to find a suitable husband.

But not Syrie.

Syrie was like fire raging through a dry forest. She had her own set of priorities and ideas as to how things should be done, and she never hesitated to voice her views. No one could hold her own in a duel of words like Syrie. He might not always agree with her, but he always admired her tenacity and fearlessness.

And her temper.

Memories of her face coloring with the heat of a good argument brought a smile to his lips.

It was that temper that kept her from being perfect. That and her stubborn nature, always so positive that she was right in every argument.

Those were the things he loved most in her. He'd loved them in her even before he'd known how beautiful she was. They were what made her Syrie.

Now, being near her, seeing that all he loved in her was unchanged, for the first time, he felt sure he had more than just a chance at success.

There was nothing his Syrie loved more than putting an arrogant male in his place. Without a doubt, there was no man alive who could be more deserving of being put in his place than he. Especially not if that was what it would take to hold Syrie's attention.

And once he had her attention? The smile on his face broadened. Why, then it was only a matter of time until he could capture her heart.

* * *

"I'm sorry, Syrie, but I can't move him anywhere else. The room next to yours was the only unoccupied room I had left."

Ellen might be saying she was sorry, but she didn't look at all sorry to Syrie. If anything, she looked rather pleased with herself.

"Maybe I could change rooms with one of the new girls on the third floor?"

She had to ask, even though she had a good idea of what the answer would be. The fact that Ellen was shaking her head before Syrie had even finished speaking was clue enough.

"Those girls only moved in here so that they could be next door to each other. They've apparently been best friends since kindergarten, so I don't see that as even a remote possibility. You'll just have to make do with things as they are for the time being."

Make do. Syrie gritted her teeth to keep from snorting. How was she supposed to *make do* with a naked god hanging out in her bathroom?

"Fine," she said grumpily, flouncing down on the sofa next to Ellen. "But will you at least tell him he has to lock the door when he's in there?"

Ellen's smile spread, and Syrie could almost swear her friend was biting her lips together.

"I will," Ellen said after a moment, reaching across to pat Syrie's hand, obviously struggling to maintain her composure. "He's really not all that bad. Maybe you should try to get to know him better. Maybe if you make an effort to see more of him."

See more of him?

"After our little bathroom encounter, I'm pretty sure there isn't much of him I haven't already seen."

And what she had seen was no doubt going to be enough to keep her dreams filled for days. Weeks. Months. His image was burned into the backside of her eyelids even now. Water droplets glistening on his skin, his long, dark hair plastered to shoulders that appeared to have been sculpted by some master artisan. No, that wasn't a scene she was likely to forget anytime soon.

"So, what do you think?" Ellen asked, looking at her expectantly.

Uh-oh. She must have missed something during her little sojourn into Patrick-land.

"Think?" she asked, hoping Ellen would repeat whatever she'd said before.

"Come on," Ellen wheedled. "It will be fun. For both of us. Robert can be so direct sometimes when it's just the two of us. But if you're along, he'll agree to spend some time just hanging out. Say yes. As a special favor for me."

"Of course," Syrie agreed. As if she would ever deny her friend any request. "When is this?"

And please, by all that was holy, repeat what it was she'd just agreed to.

"Wonderful!" Ellen said, clapping her hands together. "Robert will be here tomorrow afternoon and then the four of us can head down to Boulder. We can run my errands and then walk around Pearl Street and see all the strange people Danny told me are gathering there. Oh! And we'll plan on dinner out before coming home, too. We'll have such a good time. I just know it!"

The four of us?

Oh, great. Syrie should have guessed from the look on Ellen's face that she was cooking up something like that. A whole afternoon and evening with Patrick. And a long car ride, too. It took everything she had not to groan aloud.

After that encounter in the bathroom, she had no idea how she'd ever be able to look the man in the eyes again, let alone be trapped in a car with him.

"Fine," Syrie said, standing up to go back to her room. "How long do you think it'll take us to get there?"

She could handle their being with Patrick in a group of four people. Ellen and Robert would be enough of a buffer. It was only the car ride down that really concerned her.

"About an hour and a half," Ellen answered. "Robert's a stickler about obeying the speed limits."

Syrie leaned down to give her friend a quick hug and then headed back upstairs, praying her neighbor was tucked away in his room for the night. Right now, all she wanted was to escape to the privacy of her own room, where there was no possibility of bumping into Patrick again.

Something told her she'd need all the alone time she could get to prepare herself for being trapped in that small metal box with him only a few feet away from her for over an hour.

It would, without question, be one of the longest, most uncomfortable hours of her life.

CHAPTER FIFTEEN

Syrie had expected the drive to Boulder to be emotionally trying. But this? No. She'd never in her wildest worries imagined it would be like this.

She'd come downstairs to find that Clint and Rosella were joining them on their outing and that they had already taken their places in the backseat of Robert's car. Patrick waited patiently by the door, offering a hand of assistance as she climbed inside.

The interior was much larger than any she'd ridden in before, and she'd just begun to count herself lucky when Patrick had folded himself into the seat next to her, his body all but wrapped around hers in the suddenly cramped space.

"Sorry about the crowding," Ellen had said cheerily as she slipped into the front seat. "But once Mrs. Whitman learned we were headed down to Boulder, there was nothing doing but that I should make her honey delivery to save her the trip. One of you can move up here on the way back, if you want."

That would be wonderful. *If* Syrie could manage to survive the current trip.

The backseat that had seemed so luxuriously large only moments earlier now closed around her like a cave-in. A cave-in where the big man next to her was sucking up all the available air.

No matter how she tried to reposition herself, his body fit around hers. From his arm casually resting along the back of the seat cushioning her head, to the length of him that pressed against her side, there simply was no escaping him. Even his legs, longer than hers by far, snugged up next to hers.

She shifted in her seat for the hundredth time, doing her best to shrink into herself, but it did no good.

"Sorry," she mumbled as her elbow bumped against Patrick's chest.

"It's no' a hardship for me, lass," he said, his voice a low rumble in his chest. "Though, if you'd but try to relax, yer journey likely would be more pleasant."

Try to relax. Seriously? As if she could even conceive of relaxing with his breath puffing down over her each time he leaned close to speak. The low hum of his words washed down over her, coating her nerves with a blanket, every bit as smooth as the honey perched in the front seat.

She pushed the blanket away, rejecting any comfort he offered. Trying to reject him.

How dare he? How dare he sit there, possessively curving his body around her as if she needed his protection from the door on his other side? Speaking to her as if she were the only person in the car.

How dare he behave as if he hadn't stood in the middle of her bathroom not twenty-four hours earlier, stark naked, sucking all the air out of that room, too?

Just as he did now.

She'd feared this trip would feel long with him in the car. She'd had no idea that scooted up next to him as she was, it could feel like an eternity.

"Look at that," Patrick whispered, dipping his head closer to hers.

She'd been prepared to rebuff any of his attempts at conversation, but a glance out the window drew an involuntary gasp from her.

The mountains!

Sure, she'd seen the mountains in Ft. Collins, but the view there wasn't at all the same. Here, in Boulder, they rose up around the city in a way that she couldn't ignore as just background scenery. It was beautiful and somehow eerily familiar.

"Reminds me of home," Patrick said. "Does it no'?"

She froze the instant she found herself nodding in agreement. There was obviously something in the man's voice that lulled her into a suspension of reality and bent her will to his way of thinking. How in the world was she supposed to know what his home looked like?

"This looks like a parking spot I can fit this boat into," Robert said from the front seat. "We've made it, gang! I never know for sure with these old cars out of my dad's collection."

"Are you kidding?" Clint shook his head in disbelief and opened the car door to exit, reaching back to help Rosella out of the car. "She's a Nash, right? Forties era. Nobody ever made them any roomier than this."

"Forty-six," Robert said, nodding. "One of my dad's favorites in the collection. Handles pretty darn good, too, if I'm being honest."

Patrick had exited the car and leaned in now, holding a hand out to assist Syrie. She hesitated for a moment, realizing it would look peculiar if she didn't accept his help, since Rosella was sitting on the edge of her side, waiting for Clint and Robert to finish their discussion of the merits of older cars.

When she put her hand in his, that odd feeling returned, the one of familiarity and fit. Once out of the car, she couldn't quite bring herself to withdraw her hand from his grasp. She'd looked up into his eyes and managed to start drifting in those endless blue pools when she heard her name, snapping her out of whatever daydream she'd fallen into.

"No, babe. I want to give Clint a tour through the Nash workings," Robert said as he lifted the hood of the big car. "Syrie can help. And Rosella. The store isn't more than a block or two. Clint and I will meet you there."

Ellen sighed and handed one boxed layer of honey-filled jars to Rosella. She'd just reached in for her second layer when Patrick dropped Syrie's hand and strode forward.

"I'll carry that. Yers as well, Rosella, hand it over. There's no point in any of you lugging these about when I've a perfectly strong back not in use."

"You're sure?" Ellen asked, looking more than a little skeptical of his offer. "You don't want to stay here and pretend you're a car expert, too?"

"Aye," he answered. "I'm sure. Now, if the three of you will lead the way."

He waited, the muscles in his arms straining against the soft blue cotton of the shirt he wore.

Syrie found herself drawn to walk next to him as their little group paraded down the street. Once they'd reached their destination, they were forced to make their way into the store single file, where Syrie's senses were bombarded by what felt like a million different aromas.

"Like opening the door to the home of Orabilis," Patrick muttered, looking much like a giant in a child's room as he threaded his way delicately between stacks of dried flowers and elaborately colored boxes to deposit his burden on the counter at the back of the shop.

"A witch's shop, indeed," Syrie agreed, starting at what she'd just said.

Where had such a thought come from?

"Take yer time as you will," Patrick said, backing away. "I believe I'll bide my time outside the shop. I'm no' so comfortable in such a close place with so many delicates just waiting for me to break them."

Syrie thought a moment about joining him, but the wares in this little shop were far too enticing for her to leave without having a quick look around. Besides, Patrick was the last person in the world she wanted to be stranded on the sidewalk with, forced to make small talk while they waited.

She'd almost convinced herself of that, too, until she glanced out the window to see him talking with a lovely young woman outside. And not just talking. The woman had the nerve to place her fingers on his chest, and he, great brute that he was, didn't even flinch. Not only did he not flinch, he placed his hand over hers, caressing it, as if having some strange woman touching you on the street was perfectly normal!

Unless she wasn't a stranger.

Syrie turned toward the door, remembering at the last minute that she carried a scarf and some dried herbs she'd picked up for purchase. With a deep breath in and an equally great one out, she turned back toward the counter to pay for her treasures.

Giving him, and the lowborn wench who laid hands on him, a piece of her mind could surely wait until she'd made her purchase.

* * *

Patrick drew a deep draft of air into his lungs as he stepped from the shop, grateful to be out of the cramped, dark interior. It was certainly no place for a warrior. He moved clear of the door and stationed himself in front of the window so that he might keep an eye on the women he'd left inside. He doubted witches would be so open in this day and age as to harm them in any way. Nevertheless, one never said never when dealing with a witch or a Fae, and one of those, undoubtedly, owned the shop he'd just escaped.

Another deep breath to clean his nose of the myriad herb smells that had assaulted him inside, and he began his survey of his surroundings. Young men and women in all states of dress, and undress, loitered along the sidewalk. Someone played upon small drums and another accompanied him on a pipe of some sort. Women, barefoot and wearing long, flowing skirts that might well have found a home in his own time, danced to the music, their arms upcast, their long hair flowing around them. This century's incarnation of Tinklers, no doubt.

He watched with only minimal interest until one of the women, made her way toward him, twirling and gyrating until she was mere inches away from him.

"They know you're here," she said, the smile on her lips not reaching her eyes. "They'll not allow you to succeed in your quest."

He wasn't foolish enough to waste precious time in denying any knowledge of what she said.

"Where are they?" he asked, his eyes darting to the crowds behind her. "Are they here now?"

The young woman twirled away and back again, still swaying to the rhythm of the music playing behind her.

"They are here, they are there, they are everywhere. They are relentless in their quest for power and their hearts are void of mercy. They will not hesitate to kill her. Or you. Or anyone else who gets in their way."

At her warning, a verse his mother had often quoted to him flowed through his mind. He could hear her voice in his memory so clearly, it was as if she stood directly next to him. He joined his voice with hers in the words she spoke.

"The Fae can neither commit nor experience violence in the Mortal world."

"Don't be fooled by that old saying, warrior. They can be harmed if they are weakened. If their powers are fully engaged elsewhere, they are vulnerable. If all that makes them who they are has been stripped from them, they wouldn't be strong enough to protect themselves. It would be as if they were Mortal. And though a Fae cannot commit violence in this world, they don't need to. There are a multitude of Mortals, their minds weakened by greed and their own desire for power. These minds the Fae can easily control, as a child might control the movements of his toys. Through them, the Fae can accomplish whatever they wish."

"I will not allow them to harm Elesyria," he said, his voice as unwavering as his determination.

"Orabilis chose her champion well, it would seem. With your bravery, you might have a chance to save her. But know that it will take more than bravery. It will take what you carry in here." She touched her fingertips to his chest, just over his heart. "I can say little more about them, warrior," she said. "Only that you must be constantly alert to the dangers around you, and to remind you that your time is running out."

When it appeared she would leave him, he placed his hand over hers, holding her still.

"I was warned of dangers and challenges aplenty," he said quietly, his eyes locked on hers. "But I'd no reason to believe that time was one of them."

She stilled her dancing and tilted her head to one side as if it had suddenly become important to study him more intently. "In that case, let me share with you what no others have. The longer your Faerie is trapped here away from her memories, the more of herself she will lose. In time, there will be nothing left of herself to reclaim. When that happens, when enough time has passed, she will become the woman she has had to invent for herself and she will be the Fae you sought to rescue no more."

With a delicate twist of her wrist, she was free of his hold and dancing away, once again twirling and gyrating into the crowd gathered along the sidewalk.

Patrick watched her progress until she had disappeared into the flow of people. Danger he had expected. Orabilis had warned him of as much, just as she'd warned him that he'd be stranded in this time if he failed in his quest. That he would be fighting against time as well was not something he'd expected.

He had little enough time to consider the Tinkler's warning before the women came out of the shop, each carrying a bag tied up with colorful ribbons. Ellen and Rosella chatted with one another about the treasures they'd discovered inside, but Syrie had eyes only for him.

The expression she wore was one he'd seen often enough to recognize, putting him instantly on his guard. Something or someone had angered her and, from the intensity of her glare, he suspected it could well be him.

"Who was that woman?" she asked as she drew near. "The one speaking to you out here."

If she'd seen that, she must have been watching him. A good sign, perhaps?

"What woman?" He answered her question with a question, doing his best to portray an innocent memory lapse.

"You know very well what woman. The one with her hands all over you."

If he didn't know better, he'd be tempted to believe Syrie was jealous. A definite good sign.

"The Tinkler, you mean?" He shrugged casually. "You've no call to worry yerself over that one. You ken as well as I do how Tinklers are."

"Worry myself?" she squeaked, her eyes flashing. "It's hardly as if I care in the least what—"

"Hippies," Ellen interrupted, placing a firm hand on Syrie's shoulder as if she hoped to calm her friend. "They've been flooding into Boulder for a while now, camping in doorways, clogging the sidewalks."

"But there are so many more than the last time I was down here," Rosella said, as if to herself. "I wonder why?"

"Because this is the best place to survive Icarus," a young man said from his spot on the ground near where they stood. "When it hits, the Rocky Mountains just outside of town are one of the few places where anyone will be safe."

"I've heard of that," Clint said as he and Robert joined them. "Icarus is a comet. We discussed it in an astronomy class I took last semester. But it's not on anything like an intercept approach. It won't pass close enough to have any kind of effect on us at all."

"You're wrong," the young man said, his eyes closed. "It's coming. It's coming for all of us."

"Not an argument logic is going to carry, Clint," Robert said, putting an arm around Ellen to steer her away from the people in their path. "With all the chemicals these freaks have in their systems, there's no telling what they believe."

"Do you guys want to find a restaurant down here?" Rosella asked. "I'm starving."

"Away from this place," Patrick said.

"I agree," Clint said. "This is the kind of situation that could easily get out of hand. Cops showing up would be all it would take to set off a riot."

Patrick didn't know whether or not Clint was right, but he trusted the man's instincts. Besides, he had his own reasons for getting away from here. It seemed that more and more people were gathering in the area, making it harder to judge who might be watching them. In this place, anyone could emerge from the crowd, strike, and blend in again much too easily. After the warning he'd just received, this was the last place he wanted to be. The last place he wanted Syrie to be.

"Don't think I've forgotten what we were talking about," Syrie said quietly, her words meant only for him. "We'll finish the conversation about your little friend when we get someplace quieter."

More people had arrived, pressing in on them as they started back to the car. The path ahead of them narrowed, forcing them to a single file. Patrick fastened a hand on Syrie's elbow, pulling her close in front of him, her back touching his chest. Though her expression when she'd glanced up at him still reflected her aggravation, she didn't pull away.

Yet another good sign?

Patrick smiled, deciding he'd consider that to be the case until something came along to prove otherwise.

Their progress was slow along the packed walkway, the noise growing as more of the *hippies,* as Ellen called them, began chanting and playing instruments of their own.

They had passed no more than two storefronts before a woman nearby screamed. Instinctively, Patrick wrapped his arms around Syrie and lifted her from her feet, forging his way into the center of the crowd, away from the path they were traveling.

Mere heartbeats passed before a large concrete planter crashed onto the sidewalk where he and Syrie had stood only seconds earlier.

The planter shattered into pieces, some larger than his own head, spewing dirt, flowers and concrete in every direction.

"Did you see that?" Ellen asked breathlessly as she reached the spot where they stood. "It must have fallen from the rooftop. Lucky thing you guys had moved from the sidewalk or an accident like that could have crushed you both."

"Aye," Patrick agreed, his arm tightening around Syrie. "Lucky indeed to escape such an accident."

"Luck wasn't what saved us back there, and you know it. You did. And you don't sound to me like you think it was an accident, do you?" Syrie asked quietly, the fabric of his shirt locked in her grasp the only outward signal of her fear.

Patrick didn't answer, instead tightening his hold on her as he hurried her back to where they'd left the car.

"You don't, do you?" she asked as he helped her into the door and seated himself next to her. "You don't think it was an accident."

"No," he answered once the car was in motion. "No more an accident than it was luck we escaped."

An ordinary man under ordinary circumstances could well chalk it up to luck that the Tinkler had found him to deliver her warning. Or that some woman in the crowd had screamed as she spotted the enormous planter tipping over the edge of the roof.

But he was no ordinary man and these were anything but ordinary circumstances.

"No luck but vigilance."

"There's a place just outside Boulder that Ellen and I like," Robert said as he drove. "We can stop there without even going out of our way."

While others murmured their agreement, Patrick sat quietly. Where, or if, they ate was of no consequence to him. His only concern was the safety of the woman pressed against his side. Her safety and the awareness that, unlike on the ride down to Boulder, she now made no squirming attempts to distance herself from him.

If anything, she had molded herself into his side as if she belonged there.

Which she absolutely did, even if she didn't know it yet.

CHAPTER SIXTEEN

Knife, fork, spoon, flip the corners and roll.

Syrie repeated the litany of her actions over and over in her head as she prepared the flatware rolls to be placed on the tables. Anything to keep her mind off the events of the last couple of weeks. Anything to keep her mind off Patrick.

Too bad none of it was working.

Since he'd saved her life on their trip to Boulder, no matter what she did, there he was, lurking at the edge of her thoughts, watching over her, waiting. Much as he did in real life.

Not that he was actually doing anything of the sort. It was more likely a matter of her being hypersensitive to his presence in the house. She'd come out of her room and he'd be there, in the hallway, as if he were somehow on the same cycle as she. Moving from the kitchen to the living room, he'd be there, sitting on the sofa, his nose buried in a book or his gaze fixed on the television set. But always, the moment she encountered him, it was as if those other things were only to pass time. It was as if he was simply waiting for her.

And at night? She shuddered at the thought, pushing away another basket filled to the brim with silverware rolls all ready to go.

Nights were the worst. Just knowing when she crawled into bed at night that he was next door, with only one thin wall separating them, made it almost impossible to sleep. Instead, she spent her nights listening for any noise that might come from his room and conjuring visions of him as he'd looked when she'd blundered into him in the bathroom. Water glistening on his chest, drops coming together to form little rivulets flowing across his muscles and down toward—

"Damn, girl! What's up with you? We aren't going to run out of silverware rolls for the rest of the week."

Syrie jumped at the sound of Gino's voice next to her.

"Just...just passing time until the end of my shift," she stammered. "You know how it is."

Gino nodded and leaned back against the counter. "I do. And thanks to your overactive efficiency, I got nothing to do until we get some customers. I can't even count on a good visit with you, since your shift ends soon."

A glance up at the clock on the wall in the service station showed that Gino was correct. Another ten minutes and she would be due to leave. Until then, she'd try to simply enjoy her friend's company.

In spite of her fears after the party, she'd come into work and apologized to Gino and he had forgiven her. Things were almost back to the way they had been before. He'd even asked her out on a date tonight, so she felt confident that his forgiveness was real.

Real unless she managed to completely mess everything up again.

"Don't look now," Gino said in a loud, faked whisper, leaning back on his elbows. "But here comes George of the Jungle, right on schedule for quitting time."

"George of the…what are you talking about?"

As was frequently the case, Gino had lost her completely.

"You know." He grinned and broke out in a sing-song litany. "George, George, George of the Jungle."

When she continued to frown, he tried again. "Saturday morning cartoon? Musclebound, handsome, not too smart? Damn, girl, you need to watch more Saturday morning television." Gino laughed and held up a hand in greeting. "Back here, George."

"I rarely watch anything on the television, Gino. You know I work on Saturday mornings." She turned to look in the direction Gino indicated and saw Patrick standing at the front door of the restaurant, a large basket in his hand. "His name is Patrick, not George."

"Right you are, Miss Literal. As for me, there has to be something I need to do in the kitchen. I'm outta here, but I'll see you at eight."

The smile she gave him as he ducked through the door was more out of relief than anything else. Relief that he was leaving before Patrick could engage him in conversation.

Heaven forbid her evening's plans should come up. Though she couldn't explain why, she was more than a little reluctant to have Patrick learn of her upcoming evening out with Gino.

Syrie waited as Patrick set down the basket he carried and walked in her direction. She also made a mental note to look for the program Gino had mentioned the next time she had a Saturday morning free.

"What are you doing in here?" she asked as Patrick reached her side, flinching when he looked hurt.

In the almost two weeks since their strange outing to Boulder, Patrick had made himself an omnipresent part of her life. Every morning that she walked to work rather than having a ride, he was there, following her every step. When her shift was over, once again, there he was, waiting outside the door to walk her home.

At first she had tried to avoid him, even going so far as to slip into a nearby shop to pretend to look for a new dress. She'd spent over an hour trying on everything the shop carried in her size just to waste time. But when she'd come out, there he was, sitting on the hot sidewalk, waiting for her like a devoted puppy.

She had given up at that point, deciding having his company wasn't really so bad after all. But usually, when he came after work, he waited outside. His coming in to meet her was something new.

"You agreed to an outing with me," he answered. "Last night."

"Yes, but—"

She stopped herself when it would have been all too easy to waste time debating the issue. He had just last night asked her if she would let him take her someplace special one day. She'd simply had no idea that by *one* day he had actually meant *this* day.

"Okay. Let me sign out and I'll be right with you."

She slipped into the back room and signed her name and the time to the list her supervisor had begun to use a few weeks ago. When she returned, Patrick was standing by the front door, the big basket once again in his grasp.

"What's in there?" she asked, nodding toward the basket as he held the door open for her.

"It's a meal for us to enjoy together," he said with a grin. "And enjoy we should, since it was no' my efforts, but Rosella and Ellen who spent the morning putting this together for us."

Rosella and Ellen encouraging this? That was something she'd need to look into when they got back home this afternoon.

"And where are we to have this great feast of yours?"

Another grin lit his face, making him twice as handsome as when he scowled. "I've found a place I think you'll like, though it will require a bit of a walk, if that's agreeable to you."

Good thing she was wearing her work shoes.

"Lead the way."

Patrick led her north from the restaurant, past the stores she recognized and beyond. They kept going, even beyond the place where the sidewalks ended, and on through a long stand of trees. Once through those trees, they stood on the bank of a wide, slow-moving river.

"How's this?" Patrick asked, indicating a wide spot of green off to their right.

"It's…it's good," she stammered, overcome for an instant with a wave of familiarity, as if she'd seen this place before.

This place or one very much like it.

Patrick pulled a blanket from the basket and spread it out on the ground. He then reached out a hand to assist her in sitting down before he sat beside her.

"I'm glad you like it here," he said. "I picked this spot because it reminds me of home."

If it reminded him of home, what did it remind her of?

He pulled out sandwiches and set them on the blanket, along with two glasses and a bottle of red wine. She would definitely be having a chat about this conspiracy with her two friends when she got home.

"Isn't it a little early in the day for alcohol?" she asked.

"Nonsense," he responded, pulling the cork from the bottle and pouring a splash of liquid into each glass. "Where I come from, we have wine with every meal."

Maybe that was why he'd traveled across an ocean, to escape from a family of alcoholics? Probably not, but there must be some reason he'd come to stay with his cousin.

With a sip of wine to strengthen her courage, she decided to ask.

"Why are you here, Patrick?" She felt herself blushing as he turned those unfathomable blue eyes fully on her. "I mean, at first I assumed you'd come here to go to school, but you're not attending classes. And you're not hunting for work. So, why have you come here?"

He stared at her through several long moments, his gaze unwavering while it seemed as if he tried to find the words to answer her.

"I lost something that I've come to find." He sipped from his glass and ran a tongue over his lips, as if he wanted to say more, but instead of speaking, he sipped again from his glass.

"Something of some value, I'd guess?" she probed, curious now and hoping for more specific information. "This thing you're seeking."

"Too valuable to ever put a price upon," he responded. "Precious. Priceless."

A nice answer, but really no answer at all. Certainly not enough of an answer to satisfy her growing curiosity. Only a direct answer could do that. To get a direct answer, though, she'd need a direct question.

She drained her glass and held it out to him for a refill. "Maybe I can help. If, that is, you'll tell me what it is, exactly, that you're searching for. And what it is that makes you think you'll find it here."

"My destiny," he said with another of those smiles. "My future. And, as to finding it here, I've no' a single doubt on that count. I've seen it already, so I know it to be here. I've but to capture it now and draw it close."

His answer came as her glass was halfway to her mouth, and it was as if her hand froze there, midair. He looked so serious, so vulnerable, so sincere as he spoke, her heart went out to him.

Or maybe it was simply that deep, rumbling brogue of his coupled with the two glasses of wine she'd already downed.

Then again, it could be that searching for his destiny was something that resonated deeply with her.

"I guess we have something in common, after all," she said, allowing her glass to come to a rest on the blanket beside her. "We're both searching. You're searching for your future while I'm searching for my past."

He watched her so intently, she found herself at a loss as to what to say next, and, rather than say the wrong thing, she lifted her glass to her lips and emptied it for the third time.

"A man." He paused and smiled, filling her glass again. "Or a woman, for that matter, can live well enough without their past, aye? But their future? That's the important thing, Syrie. That's what they must find. No' a past, but a future with the right person so that they can live out their lives happily ever after."

He tucked the empty bottle back into the basket and the movement caused his hair to drape softly over his shoulder, just as it had that first day she'd seen him. There in the front room of Ellen's home, when he'd dipped his head over her hand, his hair had fallen forward in exactly the same manner. His warm breath had flowed over her skin and she'd been captured by his gaze then, just as she was now.

From that thought, it was only a short memory jump to remembering the sight of him as he'd stood in the bathroom. Beautifully naked and…

A shiver ran the length of her body and she shook her head in an attempt to clear her thoughts of him and the effect he had on her. Unfortunately, she didn't find the exercise to be particularly effective. For a fact, none of her thoughts were anything even approaching straight right now. Was an unknown future more important to her than her unknown past? She couldn't begin to say.

But one thing she did know. The man sitting across from her was going to make some lucky woman very, very happy one day. Some woman. Some lucky woman. But not her. Not her.

"Why not me?" she muttered, realizing only as she heard the words that she'd spoken the thought aloud.

"Why not you what?" he asked.

"Nothing," she whispered, surprised that he was sitting so close to her.

When had that happened? She didn't remember him moving, but there he was, only a hand's span away. If she but leaned forward a little, she'd be close enough that she might once again feel that warm breath on her skin. Feel those big hands on her arms. Feel those expressive lips against hers and discover whether they tasted as good as they looked.

She swayed toward him and it was exactly as she'd hoped. His hands fastened on her shoulders and, as her eyes drifted shut, his lips touched upon hers.

So much better! They felt a million times better than they looked, and she could hardly believe she'd waited so long to sample them.

She fastened her arms around his neck, pulling him toward her. As he lowered her to her back, covering her body with his, the world around them seemed to disappear. He deepened the kiss, his tongue playing around the edges of her lips, and she opened her mouth. Another shiver rippled through her body as his tongue swept inside her mouth, the taste of him, the feel of him so right. So familiar.

Her eyes opened on the thought, just as he lifted his head away from her, his eyes glazed with an unmistakable shimmer of desire.

"I've no wish to deny you, *mo siobhrag*, but I've also no wish to start something we canna finish here and now. As it is, if we leave now, the sun will be close to setting before we can make our way back to the house. Exposed and vulnerable out here in the dark is no' the safest place for you to be."

"Sun setting?" she asked, those being the only words that actually penetrated the lovely haze in which she floated. "What?"

"Aye. We've lingered over our meal for more than a few hours," he answered. "Best we were on our way. We can pick up where we left off later."

"Pick up where we left off?" Syrie wasn't sure whether to be offended or grateful they'd stopped when they had. "What time is it?"

Patrick shrugged. "Time is of no matter, is it? I'd only like to have you inside protective walls before night falls."

"Oh, no," she groaned, buttoning the blouse she didn't remember having unbuttoned.

Not only had she made a complete fool of herself over this man, but she feared that, if she was late for Gino's arrival, she'd alienate him forever. She sincerely doubted he'd forgive her inexplicable behavior a second time.

"We have to hurry," she said, wiping her hands over her face, hoping to clear the cobwebs from her brain. "I'm going to be so late."

"Late for what?" Patrick asked, stuffing their trash in the basket.

"Gino's supposed to pick me up for dinner at eight."

Her eyes darted up at the last second, as if her mind had just remembered for her that she hadn't wanted Patrick to know about her date with Gino.

That settled it. She was never touching wine in the middle of the day again.

"Gino?" The name left Patrick's lips on a growl. "Yer planning to see him tonight? Even after what has just passed between us?"

"After what passed…" Her words dried on her tongue. What the hell was he talking about?

"Aye, just now." Patrick's expression was as dark as a storm cloud. "Or, more accurately, what was about to pass between us had I not had the good sense to stop you."

"What?" she squeaked. "*You* had the good sense to stop? You are the most conceited, most annoying, most…*most*. Period. You listen to me, Patrick MacDowylt. Nothing passed between us. No matter what you think was about to happen, it didn't. It wasn't going to happen. And it never will. You understand that? Never."

Syrie pushed up to stand, wavering only a little. She should never have taken even the first sip out of that first glass of wine. What had she been thinking, anyway? Without the alcohol, she never would have allowed her inhibitions to slip like that. Never.

A glance in Patrick's direction found him calmly folding their blanket and packing it into the basket, his expression completely blanked of any emotion, as if he wore a mask of stone.

A mask of stone to match those muscles that rippled in his back as he leaned over his work.

Her fingers twitched at her side and she clenched them into a fist. No, she absolutely did not want to run her hands over those muscles. Not even out of simple curiosity.

She never would have kissed him, never would have allowed her inhibitions to slip without the alcohol. Maybe. Lord, but he was beautiful.

"We'd best put a foot to it if we're to get you home in time for yer dinner engagement," he said, his voice none too friendly.

Beautiful, yes. But without a doubt, he was the most aggravating creature she'd ever encountered and she wanted nothing more to do with him.

Except for those moments, like now, when she wanted so much more.

CHAPTER SEVENTEEN

Patrick slumped on the sofa, his arms crossed in front of him, staring at the box of moving pictures across the room. *The News,* Clint had called it. To him, it was little more than an ongoing litany of war and mayhem. If this news thing was to be believed, not only had relations between the clans not improved, the whole of the world had slipped into madness, posting little stick figures on a board to indicate hundreds of men killed daily in their battles. This was certainly not the future he would have hoped to see.

Not to mention how his new knowledge of this bleak future was adding to his already dark mood.

He was all too aware of the intensely negative atmosphere building around him, but knowing did nothing to aid him in doing anything about it. Certainly, he could go upstairs to his room and hide his dark mood away from everyone, but he was unwilling to hide from the issue that had brought on that same dark mood.

Syrie would be out, after dark, unprotected, save for that pitiful excuse for a man that she insisted on seeing again.

Patrick felt his mood darken at least two shades. First, because she'd chosen to see any man that wasn't him and, second, because he knew he was being monumentally unfair to the man in question. Gino wasn't really a bad sort. For a fact, now that he'd spoken to Gino a few times, he was beginning to actually like the man. If Gino were escorting any other woman to dinner, Patrick would be the first to support him.

But he wasn't escorting any other woman to dinner. He was coming to get Syrie.

Patrick's Syrie.

Patrick huffed out a breath that sounded so much more growl than sigh that Clint, sitting at the other end of the sofa, started.

"What is your problem?" Clint asked, obviously irritated that Patrick's demeanor had rattled him. "So what if she's going out with some other guy? It's just dinner, not some weekend getaway. You need to relax."

"Would you relax if it were me?" Rosella asked as she handed him a glass. "Or would you be pouting just as he is?"

"I doona pout," Patrick muttered, but loud enough that his friends could hear. "And it's no' just a matter of her having dinner with the man. She'll be out there unprotected. I told you of the Tinkler's warning the day we visited Boulder."

Once they had arrived back at Ellen's, Patrick had confided in both Clint and Rosella about the strange encounter. To Clint's credit, he had helped Patrick keep watch whenever his classes would allow. Tonight would be the first time neither he nor Clint would be watching over Syrie, and Patrick didn't like it one damn bit. The whole idea had him so on edge, he felt as if it would take only the smallest nudge to send him tumbling over into an absolute maddening chaos.

At that moment, the *smallest nudge* stepped from the bottom stair and into the room where he sat, bringing him immediately to his feet. Syrie, dressed in such a scant amount of cloth that he had to fight the urge to cover the eyes of every person in the room as she approached.

"And *that*," he choked out, pausing to catch his breath before he continued. "*That* is what you propose to wear out in public this night?"

"It is," she said, her chin lifting in the stubborn manner he recognized all too well. "It's called a miniskirt and it's quite fashionable. Not that I'd expect you to know anything of what women of fashion wear."

A haze filled Patrick's mind, dark and muddy, a nasty mix he didn't at first understand. Much like the battle frenzy he'd experienced on so many occasions. But battle frenzy alone couldn't account for the emotions tumbling through him now. Anger at an enemy could be controlled. Even fear could be overcome by a rational man. But the beast that gripped him now was very nearly beyond his control. A green, howling creature, threatening to swamp all that was sensible in him.

Jealousy.

He'd had a taste of this beast once before, the first night he'd seen Gino's hand caressing Syrie's shoulder. Now, with her arms and legs bared to the world in that tiny bit of plaid cloth she wore snugged around her privates, all the beast could imagine was Gino's hands on all that exposed skin.

The vision, colored by the ugly haze of his emotions, was more than he could take. More than any warrior could take. And with it, he tumbled quickly over the emotional cliff he'd feared he faced all evening.

He'd been on his best behavior for weeks and tried everything he could think of to get into her good graces. Nothing had worked to remind her of what they had meant to one another. Or, more accurately, what he'd thought they had meant to one another. Whether or not it meant losing her and stranding them both in this time, he was done trying. Better she should be stranded here alive than that he should be returning home with her dead body.

It was time for him to take charge of the situation.

* * *

There was no missing how angry Patrick was. His face had mottled a deep red under the dark shadow of whiskers that appeared each evening no matter that he'd shaved earlier in the day. The man was clearly furious.

And Syrie was happy about that.

He was getting what he deserved for trying to take advantage of her. And then, when she'd almost fallen for his romancing, calling a halt to it and jumping to the assumption that, somehow, just because she'd kissed him, she belonged to him or something. Like some kind of property. Well, this overbearing foreigner had a lot to learn about life in America, and she was just the girl to teach him.

She picked up her lecture where she'd left off, ignoring the fact that he had begun to move in her direction.

"As it so happens, I bought this to wear for some special occasion and tonight is—oof!"

The *oof* was a natural response to his picking her up by the waist and tossing her over his shoulder like a bag of sheep's wool.

"What do you think you're doing?" she gasped, her face banging into his back as he took the stairs two at a time. "Put me down this instant!"

"So it's down you want, is it, Elf?"

A door slammed open, hitting against the wall before swinging back and almost smacking into her as he strode into what appeared to be, from her upside-down vantage point, her own room.

"Then it's down you'll get."

The room spun around her as Patrick flipped her back over his shoulder and into his arms like he might carry a baby. Too little time to make anything of that as, before she could even catch her breath to berate him again, she was flying through the air to land with a *thump* in the middle of her bed.

Surprised? An understatement. But Syrie was not one to give up a fight easily. She was on her feet and filling her hands with the back of his shirt before he could make it to the door.

"What the hell do you think you're doing?" she demanded once again, tugging at his shirt to reinforce the seriousness of her question by pulling him toward her.

He turned around quickly, pulling the cloth from her grasp as easily as if she were a child. He stood toe to toe with her, leaning down so that his face, a furrowed road map of emotion, was only inches from hers.

"What am I doing? I'm putting you where you belong wearing naught but a…a scrap of cloth to cover yerself like that. No' even the lowest strumpet would be seen in public as naked as you are."

"How dare you?" she shouted, though, in truth, she was having a hard time working up a great deal of argument for what he said.

She'd debated over the skirt and top for quite some time before deciding to wear it. She'd even changed out of it once, but put it back on again, simply because she'd hoped to make him jealous.

Apparently her plan had worked. Maybe a little too well.

"Fine, then. I'll change before I go out, if you find my outfit so repugnant."

But only because she hadn't really wanted to wear it from the beginning.

"No," he said, turning back toward the door.

"What do you mean, no?" she asked, following after him. "If you think it's so bad, then, like I already said, I'll change before I go out."

"I mean, no, as in yer no' going out tonight. I forbid it."

"You *forbid* it?" Syrie all but strangled on the word. "Who do you think you are, anyway? You don't get to forbid me from doing anything."

Jealousy was one thing. But this? This was completely unacceptable behavior.

"I do," he said, calmly now, an eyebrow arching in a way she found particularly irritating. "I can, and I did. Yer no' to leave this room tonight and that's the end of it. On the morrow, when you've come to yer senses, then we'll talk."

"When I've come to *my* senses?" Syrie yelled. "You can't keep me in here. You haven't any right to even consider such a thing. I'll call for help and Ellen or Rosella will come open my door and there's nothing you can do about it."

There. See how he liked some good, old-fashioned logic.

His smile, the one she'd thought so beautiful earlier today, now struck her as more irritating than the arched eyebrow.

"But I can keep you in here, dearest Syrie. I've but to spend my night outside yer door. No one comes in and no one goes out. Simple enough."

With that, he stepped outside and pushed the door shut behind him.

"No you can't!" she yelled after him, actually stamping her foot in her outrage as she pounded on the closed door.

All protests to the contrary, it would seem he actually could do what he threatened.

Syrie waited at the closed door, certain that he would shortly see the error of his ways and open the door. When that didn't happen, she turned the knob and pushed.

Nothing happened.

The second time she tried, she put the whole of her weight into her effort. Still the door didn't budge.

"You might as well give up yer efforts and take to yer bed for the night. Yer no' passing through," he called, his voice muffled by the wooden door. "I've made myself comfortable here on the floor and yer hardly strong enough to move me."

He was leaning against her door?

She fumbled for words, and when she found none that could break through her fury, she stamped her foot again before pacing the room to calm herself down.

Clearly, she was no match for him in a contest of strength. But wits? She had little doubt that she could best him there.

"What about my dinner, then?" she called out, leaning against the door so that he couldn't pretend not to hear her. "I haven't eaten since lunch."

"You'll survive until daybreak," his answer came. "From what I felt in hefting you up the stairs, there's little enough fear of yer starving any time soon."

"Oh! You…you great slavering man-beast!" she cried out, pounding her fist against the door. "You worthless piece of Mortal man-flesh!"

With her back to the door, she sucked in great gasps of air, consciously slowing her breathing as she fought back her anger. Anger such as this was no solution to her problem. It could only lead to more rash behavior that would end in little more than her own embarrassment.

Almost as soon as that realization settled in her thoughts, a strange little spark of acknowledgment followed, as if she'd just experienced a great breakthrough. Perhaps her temper had always been a problem for her. Perhaps it was even behind her having lost her memory. She pushed at the fuzzy edges of those thoughts, seeking any bit of that missing memory that might be hidden from her, but all she found was a hard wall of darkness beyond which she couldn't tread.

Fine. Temper didn't serve her purpose any more than strength would.

Her back against the door, she scanned her surroundings for any suitable alternative. There was the window, but, in truth, she didn't want to win this conflict badly enough to drop two stories into the bushes below. Her eyes lit on the bathroom door. That was it! She hurried over and opened her door and grabbed the knob to his.

Locked.

Just her luck. The man who never locked a door in his life had suddenly learned how to twist that little key.

She crossed back to the bedroom door and tried once again to nudge it open, unsuccessfully.

"I don't want to stay in here," she said, hoping to appeal to Patrick's better self.

"I know, *mo siobhrag.*" He answered so quietly she had to strain to hear his words. "But it's for yer own good. Go to bed now. We'll discuss the whole of this on the morrow."

Obviously, the man had no better self to appeal to.

Syrie leaned against the door, feeling as if she were a hundred years old. The fight—heck, the whole day—had taken its toll and she simply didn't want to fight any longer. She didn't even care what kind of awful name Patrick had used for her in what was obviously some foreign language.

Crossing to her closet, she slipped out of her boots and the tiny skirt that had so infuriated the man barricading her door. Once in her nightgown, she went back into the bathroom to wash off her makeup and brush her teeth. Everything, every move, seemed to take twice as much energy as usual, so climbing into bed was more relief that capitulation.

Or so she told herself.

Their battle could wait for morning.

That great hairy brute could spend his whole night on the hard floor, cramped and miserable, guarding her door if he wanted. She hoped he had no sleep at all. And if he did manage to doze off, she hoped he awoke with a sore neck and an aching back.

As for her, she wanted only to escape into her dreams and into the arms of the man with eyes of blue meant only for her.

CHAPTER EIGHTEEN

Syrie awoke with the rising sun. Little enough surprise considering how early she'd gone to bed.

Just thinking about the events of the prior evening brought a little ripple of anger dancing through her mind, but, in line with last night's epiphany about the wasted energy of her temper, she refused to let her anger have its reign. She was done with those days.

Besides, unless Patrick was still camped in front of her door, it didn't really matter. She would deal with him and his ridiculous behavior later.

She dressed quickly and held her breath as she tried the door, but she needn't have bothered. The door swung open easily and she stepped into the quiet, empty hallway.

Good. Perhaps he'd realized what an ass he'd been. There was a good chance that his actions had been as clouded by the bottle of wine they'd shared as had hers.

One thing she'd admit though, at least to herself, while the wine had done nothing for her attitude or judgment, she had slept really well. It all boded nicely for a long, lazy, much-anticipated day off.

There was still the whole issue of what had happened when Gino had arrived and she hadn't come down to go with him. But that was something she'd just have to deal with after she was able to find out how that whole scenario had played out. For now, she was determined to enjoy her day off.

With a smile blooming on her face, she headed downstairs, hoping for a lovely cup of tea to start her morning. Instead, she found Ellen, looking much too frazzled for this early hour in the morning, standing in the middle of the kitchen, fully made up, with dress shoes clutched in her arms.

"What's wrong?" Syrie asked, ushering Ellen to take a seat as she spoke.

"It's Robert's mother," Ellen answered. "He called late last night to share the *wonderful* news that she was coming up from Denver and that we're to meet her for breakfast to discuss the wedding. Honestly, Syrie, that woman is so perfect, she absolutely terrifies me."

There was no question from Ellen's tone of voice that she considered this visit anything but wonderful.

"Nonsense," Syrie huffed. "There's no reason at all to let her intimidate you. You're every bit as good as she is."

Ellen's snort of disbelief did little to back up Syrie's claim.

"She's always judging me, Syrie. She totally hates my background and my family. And the fact that I want to keep my home as a boarding house is completely unacceptable to her. I feel like she's always watching, just waiting for me to screw up so she can convince Robert how completely unsuitable I am for him."

"Again, utter nonsense," Syrie consoled, sitting down across the table from her friend. "Robert adores you. You know that, right?"

"I suppose he does," Ellen said quietly. "I mean, he's not an expressively romantic man by any means. But he says he loves me and he puts up with everything I ask of him, even when he doesn't agree with what I do. So, yes, I am confident in his feelings for me."

Not exactly the ringing endorsement Syrie had hoped to hear from her friend.

"We both know that you're the best thing that has ever happened to Robert. You're in love with him, and that alone matters more than anything his mother says or does." Syrie waited for a response, and when none came, she prodded further. "You are in love with him, aren't you?"

"Well, yeah." Ellen chewed at her bottom lip, the worried frown still in place. "I mean, yes, I'm good with Robert. I'm looking forward to my life with him. Sometimes, I just wish..."

When Ellen didn't finish voicing her thought, Syrie reached for her hand. "You just wish what? Either you love him or you don't. It's really pretty simple."

Ellen shook her head. "No, it's really not simple at all. At least not for me. Yes, I think what I feel for Robert is love. But what do I know about love? My parents barely tolerated each other. How I was ever conceived is beyond me. That's why Danny and I spent so much time here with my grandmother. And what Robert and I have, though completely comfortable and satisfactory, certainly isn't what I see passing between Rosella and Clint. It's not that no-questions, no-doubts kind of love. I just wish I knew for a fact that I'm making the right decision for both of us in marrying him."

Silence settled over the two of them, with Syrie not knowing what to say to console her friend. Of all the things beyond her own realm of experience, knowing what real love felt like was pretty high on the list.

"You know that if there's anything I can ever do to help," Syrie began, but Ellen shook her head and got to her feet, her usual smile back in place.

"I'm just being stupid because Helena Shaw gives me the hives," Ellen said, as if she could easily dismiss everything that had come before. "But if you really want to help, it would be lovely if you could get a head start on tonight's dinner. Rosella and Clint will be joining us, but she left with him before sunrise. They went up the canyon to get some of that fruit jam he loves that they only sell in a little shop up there, so I can't ask her. I have everything pretty much ready to go, except that I'd planned to bake Robert's favorite cake. The recipe is out on the counter. If you could do that for me, I'd be grateful."

Bake a cake? Her? Syrie swallowed hard at the idea. Everything in the kitchen other than boiling water for tea baffled her. She didn't even think it was a part of her memory loss, but something else entirely. Something like her never having cooked in a kitchen in her entire life. But for Ellen? For Ellen, she'd give it a try.

"Don't you worry about it," Syrie said, forcing a smile to her lips.

She would do the worrying for both of them.

"Okay. In that case, I think that's everything." Ellen paused, looking around the kitchen as if the surroundings might remind her of something else. "Don't forget the tricky faucet and—"

Anything else she might have thought to say was halted by the sound of a car's horn honking outside.

"There he is now." Ellen started for the door, stopped and laughed, turning back to the table to retrieve her shoes. "Guess I'd better put these on. That's all I'd need, to show up barefoot at some fancy breakfast with Mrs. Shaw. She'd never forget that!"

Syrie sat at the table until she heard the front door slam shut and then headed for the stove and the kettle. Thank goodness the water was still hot. After agreeing to do something so far out of her comfort area, she needed that morning tea more than ever.

While her tea steeped, she read through the recipe Ellen had left out. Seemed straightforward enough. After all, every woman she knew cooked, so how hard could it really be? She was intelligent and hardworking. If they could do it, so could she.

A spoonful of Mrs. Whitman's honey into the cup and Syrie took her first sip. Perfection! Now she was ready to face anything.

First things first. It was all really just a matter of being organized and following directions, right?

Syrie began gathering all the items called for in the recipe, feeling more confident with each item she set on the counter. By the time she'd measured all dry ingredients into one bowl, she was feeling like an old pro. Then came the wet ingredients.

"Separate eggs," she read aloud. "Add milk and using electric mixer, whip…"

Electric mixer? One large cabinet in Ellen's kitchen was filled with any number of electrical appliances, any one of which could be the one Ellen had meant. How was she ever supposed to—

No. She was too far into this process to allow herself to panic. If everyone else could do this, so could she. She'd simply go through the pieces of equipment and figure out which one it might be. As she began pulling appliances out of the cupboard, she came across one she remembered seeing Ellen use to mix a frozen lemonade drink she'd made one afternoon when Danny had stopped by. This had to be the one she'd meant. Even though Danny, as she recalled, had referred to it as a *blender*, Ellen had said she was whipping up some drinks. The recipe clearly said the next step was to *whip the mixture*. This had to be the right thing. Besides, what could it matter? Blend, mix, whip...if Ellen had used this machine to whip up their drinks, surely it could whip the eggs and milk.

Carefully, she broke the eggs and dumped them into the glass pitcher, followed by the milk. This baking thing was so much easier than she had imagined it would be. The recipe indicated that after she'd whipped these together, she should add half the dry ingredients. That made little sense. Why not add half of the dry ingredients now? They could all mix together while she figured out what to do with the other half.

Confidently, she dumped half the dry ingredients into the mixture, plugged the machine into the outlet and leaned over the opening to watch what happened as she flipped the little *ON* switch.

When the first blast of milk, egg and flour flung itself into her face, she screamed, but only once as the continuing bombardment splattered strings of the thick, wet goo into her open mouth. As she staggered backward from the unrelenting attack, her bare foot slipped in a patch of the gooey mess and she grabbed for the counter in an attempt to prevent her fall. Instead, her fingers latched around the bowl of remaining dry ingredients sending them up into the air as she fell, leaving them to shower down on her as she lay sprawled on the floor, like a helpless bug claimed victim by a kitchen snow storm.

Just when she'd thought the whole scenario couldn't possibly get any worse, Patrick appeared, racing through the door wearing nothing but his jeans and an expression that said he was ready to murder someone. An expression that quickly changed to one of shocked surprise as he, too, encountered one of those little goo patches and lost his balance, landing almost on top of her. His face was only inches from hers when another flying glop of the mixture slammed into his forehead and oozed down over one eye.

She revised her earlier opinion. The kitchen snowstorm had claimed two victims: one helpless bug and one very big, very angry bug-squasher.

* * *

Patrick lay in the big, soft bed, a smile lifting the corners of his mouth as he remembered how furious Syrie had been last night. She was the one woman he'd ever met who could do furious with style and beauty. Fury suited his red-haired Elf well. As did every other expression he'd ever seen her wear.

Wear. The word brought to mind the skimpy bits of cloth the woman had thought to wear outside the house last night. And those skimpy bits of cloth brought to mind how she'd looked in them.

If he'd thought her beautiful in the midst of a temper, he'd not counted on just how beautiful she could be. All that lovely, creamy skin exposed.

He felt himself harden uncomfortably against the metal closure of the pants he'd not taken off before falling into bed sometime before sunrise this morning.

He wanted Syrie, in every way it was possible for a man to want a woman. He wanted her as his own for all time. And, likely as not, in his effort to keep her safe last night, he'd ruined any chance he'd ever had of having her.

With a sigh, he scrubbed his hands over his face and sat up, swinging his feet to rest on the polished wooden floor. He'd just risen to look for a shirt when he heard the scream.

Syrie!

Without thought, he was out the door and through the hall. He took the stairs in one leap, landing in a crouch ready for battle. When he saw nothing, he followed an ungodly buzzing noise straight to the kitchen, ready to rip out the throat of whoever threatened his woman.

In one glance, he took in everything in the room. Everything except the slippery patch in front of him that robbed him of his footing and sent him pitching through the air toward the spot where Syrie lay, covered in blotches of some monstrous concoction of white and yellow. Twisting, to avoid his full weight landing on her, he managed to slide to a stop just over her, his face only inches from hers.

"At least now I understand why so many cooks wear aprons," she muttered, her eyes squeezed tightly shut.

He quickly ran his hands over her face, wiping away the thick goo before continuing down her arms, searching for any injury.

"Are you unharmed?" he asked, fearing what she might answer after that awful scream.

"My body isn't hurt, if that's what you're asking." She opened her eyes and grinned ruefully. "But my ego? That's bruised all to hell and back."

His heart rate slowed to normal as he studied first her and then the disheveled state of the kitchen. Clearly there was no one around responsible for Syrie's dilemma. No assassin sent by the Fae. No all-powerful being set on keeping her in this time by any means necessary.

"What happened in here?" he asked, turning his attention back to her.

"I was trying to bake a cake as Ellen had asked me to do." She wiped a hand over her face, leaving a trail of batter in the wake of her action. "I was so sure I could do it. She left me a recipe and everything."

"Bake?" Patrick snorted his disbelief. "Yer barely able to boil oats without burning them beyond recognition. How'd you ever expect to master baking? And on yer own, at that."

Other than one quick glare, Syrie ignored him, seemingly more intent on assessing the damage around her.

"Ellen's going to kill me. She's so picky about the state of her kitchen and I've turned it into a complete disaster area."

"Then we'll clean it," he said.

She turned her gaze back on him and, as if realizing their position for the first time, she placed her hands on his chest and pushed, though not with any real effort. Her hands dropped away almost as soon as she touched his bare skin, and she began to wiggle beneath him in an attempt to move away. "Get off me! How am I supposed to clean up anything if you're lying on top of me?"

Though her wiggling beneath him did nothing to encourage him to move away, he pushed up to his knees, one straddling either side of her. From this angle, the view of Syrie was priceless.

She lay on her back still, batter muck clinging in clumps to her hair and clothing and more of it smeared across her face. The urge to kiss her senseless had never gripped him more strongly.

"What?" she demanded, her eyes flashing a warning. "What are you grinning about?"

"Nothing," he said, forcing himself to stand and reach down to help her up.

He doubted she'd understand that his grin was a mixture of so many emotions he couldn't begin to explain. Relief in finding her safe, humor in the way she looked, happiness at being so close to her. If the world were bent to his own desires, he'd have taken her here and now on the messy kitchen floor.

But the world, as it frequently reminded him, did not bend to his will any more than Syrie herself did. At least she was speaking to him this morning.

"What a mess," she muttered, hands on her hips. "I'm not even sure where to start."

Clearly it was time for a man to take over and get things organized. Make some soapy water and add in a little elbow grease. Simple as that. A woman's work in the kitchen was highly overrated.

"You start here," he answered, striding to the sink and flipping the handle to full blast as he pushed the faucet toward one side of the double sink.

"No!" Syrie shouted.

But it was too late.

The faucet fell forward, clattering to rest in the sink as a stream of water shot straight up into the air. Patrick had never seen its like and, in the moments it took him to recover from his surprise, he stumbled backward in an attempt to avoid the torrent raining down on him.

As he moved away, Syrie rushed forward, cupping her hands over the gushing water in a vain attempt to stop it. The sight of her there, struggling against the water, spurred him forward. He pushed her away and, after a second or two, thought to turn the handle to stop the flow. He then replaced the faucet in the hole the water had surged from before turning to survey the latest round of onslaught in the kitchen.

Syrie stood a few feet away, her expression of shock giving way to distress. Little wonder. Her hair, still matted with batter, now hung around her in thick, wet clumps. Crisscross trails covered her face where the spray of water had formed little rivulets in the flour mixture that had clung to her.

With no hope of controlling himself, Patrick began to laugh. Only a chuckle at first, to be sure, but swiftly evolving into a heartfelt, gut-twisting laugh brought on by the ridiculousness of their situation.

Anger darkened Syrie's eyes, but only for an instant before she, too, began to laugh.

He moved toward her, supporting her as she sank to sit on the floor, surrounded by water and floating chunks of the mysterious flour mixture. A moment later, he sat next to her, while she leaned against him, her laughter gradually dwindling until it was little more than a series of hiccups and gasps.

"My only...only consolation is that when Ellen kills me, she's...she's going to kill you too," she said between hiccups.

It was then he realized that somewhere in the time they'd sat there on the floor next to one another, while his laughter had simply died off, her laughter had turned to tears.

"Doona fash yerself so, *mo siobhrag,*" he said, laying an arm around her shoulders and pulling her close.

"I've made such a mess of everything," she whimpered, snuggling her face into his chest.

While he would give anything asked of him simply to keep her like this, cuddled in his arms, he couldn't. Not even this pleasure beyond pleasure was worth seeing her so upset.

"Come now, Syrie. Yer made of sterner stuff than this." He pulled her arms from around him and stood. "On yer feet, lass. With but a bit of applied effort, we'll have this room back to rights in no time."

With a sigh, she stood up, wiping her face with her hands, but to little good effect. "You're right. Sitting there sniveling like a child isn't going to get anything done. I'll go get towels."

By the time she returned, Patrick had found a bucket under the sink and carefully filled it with soap and warm water. The dratted faucet wasn't going to catch him unawares a second time.

They worked quietly and efficiently until, at last, all that was left to do was the dishes she'd dirtied in her original baking attempt.

"Not bad, huh?" she asked, the hint of a smile in her eyes. "Guess we make a halfway decent team when we aren't fighting."

"Indeed we do," he replied, reaching over to take a cleaning cloth from her hands. "I'll finish up here. You head upstairs and slip yerself into a well-earned bath, aye? Will do wonders for yer spirit."

"You're sure? You don't mind?" she asked, her eyes darting longingly toward the door.

"I'm sure. Go on, then. Away with you now."

He watched her leave, licking his lips. In her wet shirt and trousers, she looked good enough to eat.

And thinking of *eating*…

He wiped his hands on the last sort of clean towel and picked up the recipe Syrie had shown him earlier. If he remembered correctly, Mrs. Whitman next door was quite the baker. And, considering all the work he'd done for her in moving around her damned bees and honey jars, he suspected he just might be able to convince her to help him out with the one remaining item on Syrie's to-do list.

CHAPTER NINETEEN

That just might have been the worst mess she could ever remember having to clean up. Not that she could remember any instances of cleaning in her past.

Syrie smiled ruefully at her reflection in the mirror and continued to try to drag the brush through her wet hair. She paused to secure the towel she wore as it began to slip and then tried again.

At least the globs of sticky goo were out of her curls at last, even if her tangles were worse than ever thanks to all her scrubbing.

A little rattle followed by a quiet gasp were her only warning that she'd forgotten to lock the door leading to Patrick's room.

"I beg yer pardon. I assumed you were finished, since the door was unlocked."

Her first instinct was to complain about his not knocking, but that annoyingly arrogant raised eyebrow told her without a doubt he hadn't forgotten her tirade at his not having locked the door. Clearly she had no solid ground on which to make a stand.

"Sorry," she said instead, dropping her brush to clutch her towel around her.

He might have given her quite an eyeful the night she'd walked in on him, but she had no intention of returning the favor. Besides, still covered in the evidence of their horrific kitchen adventure, he managed to look rather pathetic in spite of the eyebrow.

"I'm done in here, anyway. I can finish up in my room."

"If yer sure." He grinned. "Ellen and Robert have returned. I barely made it to the stairs before the door opened. Didn't want to have to explain all this."

He swept a hand from his head to his waist, and she had to force her eyes away. He might still be wearing globs of dried batter, but even those had no hope of disguising a bare chest that looked as inviting as his. Or as intriguing. When they had more time, she'd have to remember to ask about the unusual tattoo over his heart.

Have to remember? She almost laughed out loud. Like she could ever forget that bare chest of his.

"All yours," she managed, her voice little more than a squeak.

Syrie started to bend down to pick up her clothing, but, considering the towel was all she wore, she decided better of it. Instead, she shoved at the pile with her foot, flashing him an apologetic smile as she guided her bundle out the door and quickly followed behind it.

Safely on her side, she turned the little key and let out a long breath. How any man could manage to look as good as he did in an equally disheveled state, she simply couldn't imagine.

"Good looking or not, he's still an ass," she reminded herself, feeling a little flutter of guilt even as she voiced the familiar sentiment.

Would an ass have helped her clean up that gigantic mess she'd made? Even though he did help make it worse...

With a sigh, she shook her head, hoping to clear Patrick and any thought of him out of it. Almost an impossible task when she heard the water of the shower switch on.

She remembered all too well what he was doing at this very moment. And how he looked doing it.

Quickly, she slipped into clean clothing, realizing only then that she'd left her brush in the other room. No retrieving that now. Grabbing a rubber band from the top of her dresser, she gathered the unruly curls together and fastened them into a bundle. She could worry about her hair later. Right now she needed to be downstairs, trying to give some sort of explanation for her complete and total failure to do the one thing her friend had asked of her. Not to mention explaining away any of the mess Patrick might have missed after she'd left.

At the foot of the stairs she stopped, deciding that complete honesty was the only defense she had. Ellen's voice drifted to her from the kitchen, followed by the low rumble of Robert's reply. Syrie wished she didn't have to admit her failures in front of him, but it was unavoidable.

Squaring her shoulders, she walked to the kitchen, stopping in the doorway as Ellen met her with a hug.

"The cake looks wonderful, Syrie," she said. "I have to admit, you've always been so uncomfortable in the kitchen, I had my doubts. But you really came through for me."

"Smells great, too," Robert added as he helped himself to a soft drink from the refrigerator.

There, sitting in the middle of the table, was a beautiful cake, exactly like Syrie would have given her left arm to have baked. But of course, she hadn't. Having no possible understanding of what was going on, she simply smiled and offered to help in preparing dinner, tucking away all thought of the complete honesty policy she'd adopted only minutes earlier.

"No need for help," Ellen said with a smile. "Robert and I decided to stop at that little restaurant we like so much and bring home dinner. It was a long day, if you get my meaning, and cooking didn't sound at all like something I wanted to do."

Syrie bit back the temptation to agree with the "long day" comment.

"Come on, El," Robert said, the warning in his tone clear. "Even you have to admit, my mother was on her best behavior today. For her, at least."

"For her," Ellen echoed, rolling her eyes as she turned toward Syrie. "You can help me set the table in the dining room, though. And then, if you don't mind, you can go let Patrick know we're home and we're ready for dinner."

"No, I don't mind."

Much easier to agree than to say that he was in the shower. If she did that, she might be forced to admit why he was in the shower this time of day. Or how she knew where he was.

By the time the table was set, Patrick had come downstairs. He'd obviously hurried through his shower, since he looked as though he could use a shave. But, other than that, he appeared fresh and clean and much too innocent for Syrie to believe anyone in the room wouldn't be suspicious that something had happened in their absence.

But, apparently, they weren't.

"A lovely dinner," Patrick said, rising from his seat after the meal to collect empty plates.

"Leave that where it is," Ellen ordered, standing up to take his plate from him. "I'll clean up. It's the least I can do after Syrie baked this wonderful cake and left the kitchen absolutely spotless to boot."

"Patrick helped," Syrie blurted out, unable to stay silent any longer. "I couldn't have done it without him."

"Really?" Ellen said, her piercing gaze traveling from one to the other of them as though she could see right into their thoughts.

"Kept her a bit of company is all I did," Patrick said with a shrug. "It's no' as though I've any skill at baking. I doona even ken where to light ovens such as yers."

Ellen chuckled, picking up the last plate. "Well, since we don't have to light our ovens, it's apparent that you're telling the truth about your lack of skill in the kitchen. Syrie, on the other hand, has kept her talents hidden all this time. I think that cake was even better than mine. You'll have to share your secrets. What did you do differently to get that lovely flavor and texture?"

Syrie blinked, her mouth firmly shut. How could she share the secret of how she'd made a better cake when she didn't even know the secret of where the cake had come from?

"She's a sly one, our Syrie," Patrick said with a grin. "If I were a betting man, I'd put my money on the extra butter she used. That and a touch of Mrs. Whitman's honey."

"Very clever," Ellen said, nodding as she carried dishes to the kitchen. "I wouldn't have thought to do that. Of course, I rarely alter a recipe once I've found a good one. Perhaps I need to take a page from Syrie's book and be more adventurous."

"Adventure is highly overrated," Syrie murmured.

"On that, I agree," Robert said, pushing back his chair and heading toward the sofa. "Join me for some television, Patrick?"

"I'll pass on yer kind offer. It's been a long day, so I think I'll retire to my chamber." Patrick rubbed a hand over his cheek and grinned. "Perhaps even clean up a bit before I retire. Thank you again for a lovely meal, Ellen."

With a little bow, he left the room and disappeared up the stairs.

Syrie found it almost impossible to drag her eyes from the direction he'd just gone.

"He does cut quite a striking figure, doesn't he?" Ellen asked as Syrie joined her in the kitchen. "With that long hair and those big shoulders. Not to mention that dark five o'clock shadow on his face."

"Quit your matchmaking, El," Robert yelled in from the other room. "And don't you even try to deny it. I know what you're up to when you start that whisper-buzzing of yours."

"Men," Ellen said, but a guilty grin played around her lips. "Still, you could do a lot worse than Patrick. He's handsome and quite obviously helpful. I even suspect he rather likes you."

"Robert's right, you know," Syrie said as she scraped the plates to get them ready to wash. "You should quit your matchmaking."

The last thing she needed right now was to be fixed up with anyone, let alone the most confusing, aggravating man she'd ever met.

CHAPTER TWENTY

Had guilt always been such a powerful force in her life? It was one of those questions that kept Syrie awake at night.

She lay in bed, staring up at the ceiling, wishing she could turn off her overactive mind. She had an early shift tomorrow at the restaurant, and if she didn't get to sleep soon, she was going to be one very tired woman before she left work.

Logic did nothing to help. Her mind still wandered back to Patrick, forcing her to confront the day all over again, playing everything through her mind for at least the hundredth time.

All through dinner, through all the accolades for the wonderful job she did on the cake, she had waited for Patrick to speak up. Waited for him to claim the credit he deserved. Even when she'd made her one, admittedly feeble attempt to direct some of the praise toward him, he'd placed it all back in her lap. Hardly the actions of the arrogant, egotistical man she'd always pegged him to be.

The evening, the whole day, left her with no choice but to re-evaluate her original opinion of the man.

More than anything, she hated being wrong. Almost more than anything. She hated being wrong and being the bad guy most of all. And when she considered the way she had acted toward Patrick on more than one occasion, it left her feeling like the bad guy. True, he'd been way out of line on the night he'd kept her from going out with Gino. But, in retrospect, he had been right about what she had intended to wear.

What he hadn't known, what she never would have admitted to him, was that a big reason for her choice of clothing that night had been to see if she could make him jealous.

"Stupid," she muttered, feeling her cheeks heat at the memory.

She was much too old to behave in such an immature manner. That was behavior she'd expect from some tender young thing suffering through the throes of her first crush.

"Stupid," she said again, sitting up in bed and staring out the window into the night.

Stupid was right. It wasn't like she had feelings of any sort for Patrick.

Or did she?

She closed her eyes tight, struggling to replace the image of him with the one of the shrouded figure from her dreams, but her effort was useless. No matter how hard she tried, it was always Patrick's face, Patrick's eyes, that looked back at her from the depths of that hooded cloak.

Maybe that was because she could hear him banging around in the bathroom right now.

With an annoyed huff of breath, she swung her legs out of bed and stood, hesitating for only a moment to reconsider what she was about to do. No, she might as well get it over with. It wasn't like she was going to get any sleep anyway. Maybe if she thanked him for what he'd done for her today, she could get him off her conscience and get some rest.

At the bathroom door, she paused again, fitting her ear up to the wood to try to determine whether or not he was still inside the little room. The muffled sound of water turning on and off filtered through the door. No question, he was still in there.

Last chance to change her mind and scurry back to her bed like some frightened mouse.

"I am no mouse, frightened or otherwise," she muttered, and knocked.

"Aye?" Patrick called out. "Come in if you like. The door's no' locked."

Of course it wasn't. Not that she could really complain to him on that account, since she'd done the same thing herself this very day.

A cloud of warm, moist air greeted her as she opened the door, and only then did she regret not having asked him whether or not he was decent before she entered. As it turned out, he was, though only by the loosest of definitions.

"Did you want something of me?" he asked, wiping a small towel over his face to remove the remains of shaving cream.

Was he kidding? He stood there, towel in hand, bare feet and bare chest. Her gaze fixated on one single drop of water rolling down the center of that bare chest, like rain down a carved ravine. Did she want something of him? What she was wanting at the moment couldn't be discussed in proper company. At least he had jeans on, though the top button was undone and they seemed to simply rest on his hips, in danger of falling at any moment. Thank the Goddess he wore something.

She barely had time to register the words that had just run through her mind, let alone question them, before he spoke again, sending all her thoughts tumbling around until she could barely form a response.

"I do enjoy the razors they have now. It's a fair, smooth feel they leave on yer skin, is it no'? Here," he said, catching up her hand and lifting it to his cheek. "Feel for yerself. It's nice, aye?"

"Nice," she managed to answer, though the words did their best to stick on her thickened tongue.

More than nice. Once he released her hand, her fingers clenched into a fist at her side so she wouldn't test the feel of his bare chest, too.

"You've yet to tell me what it was that brought you in here," Patrick said, his attention seemingly focused on tidying up the sink. "There was something, was there no'? I doubt you came in for no reason but to admire me shaving."

"There was," she agreed, though she was doubting it herself at the moment. "I wanted to thank you for all your help today. The cleaning, the company, everything. And though I've no idea how you made that wonderful cake appear, I'm grateful to you for it."

Maybe that nasty streak of guilt would be put to rest now and she could get some sleep.

"It's no' me you have to thank for the baking of that cake. It's Mrs. Whitman."

Mrs. Whitman? Syrie couldn't remember having spoken more than ten words to the old woman next door, and almost all of those were Mrs. Whitman complaining about something or asking for a favor of some sort.

"But how? Why would she do that?"

"It was easy enough," he said with a shrug. "After the two days I spent helping with those damned bees of hers, she owed me. And, with no more than the promise of another day's labor, she agreed to help. She's quite the baker, actually. And quite the shrewd negotiator, too."

Manual labor? He'd basically hired out his services for nothing more than a cake. A cake that benefited Syrie, not him.

"Why would you do something like that for me?"

He chuckled, a deep, soothing sound that rumbled up from his chest. "You have yer answer right there. Because it was for you. To make you happy. Do you no' ken by now, *mo siobhrag*, I'd do anything for you." Reaching out, he placed his knuckles against her cheek, his thumb strumming against her temple.

A simple contact, nothing more than his hand lightly stroking the side of her face. And yet it felt as if he held her fast, shackled to him by rope and wire.

Or maybe she only wanted to be shackled to him.

"It would be so easy to believe your words," she said, her eyes captured by his as surely as his touch held her body captive.

"I speak only the truth to you," he said, his eyes darkening as he spoke. "I could do nothing else. You may believe me."

Believe him she did. With nothing more than his words for proof, she found herself falling into a deep chasm where nothing existed except her, him and the reassuring sound of his voice.

The same voice that whispered a string of nonsense words into her ear, soft and low, once she found herself in his arms. And then, somehow, his lips covered hers. A moment later, her hands roamed freely over the chest she'd imagined caressing since the first moment she'd seen him.

If she were ever to find herself in heaven, surely it would be exactly like this.

His hands slid down her shoulders, taking the straps of her nightgown with them. His mouth was on her neck by the time she felt the silky scrap of material pool on the floor at her feet.

"By Freya," he moaned, his forehead against hers. "Yer the most beautiful thing that's ever graced my life."

She would thank him, if she could. Thank him and tell him how beautiful he was, too. If only she could manage to form the words.

But somehow all she could think of was getting his mouth back down to hers. Feeling his tongue as it traced a path over the outline of her lips.

His arm slid down her back, down, to rest behind her legs, enabling him to scoop her off her feet. Talented man that he was, he did it all without breaking the kiss she currently enjoyed.

"Yer room or mine?" he asked, his voice husky, breathless.

"We can't," she said. "If anyone were to come up and find either of us not in our room, it would look…"

She left it hanging, more annoyed with herself than anything else. Why did she care what anyone thought about what she did? Why couldn't she just this once do whatever she wanted?

"No' if they hear the water." He stepped into the tub and, without shifting his hold on her, turned the water on. "Whichever room they come to, they'll think we're in the shower, aye?"

"And we are," she murmured as he slowly lowered her to her feet.

The water, warm and comforting, poured down on their heads, running in happy little torrents down Patrick's chest. Happy little inviting torrents.

She leaned into him, slowly lowering herself as she traced her tongue along one of those torrents. At his waistband, she stopped, her fingers fumbling with the button that blocked her path. His hands fastened around her upper arms, pulling her back up to stand, just before he returned the favor of torrent-tracing.

The pleasure of it all was surely going to drive her completely insane. When she thought she could stand no more, he rose to tower over her, smoothing her wet hair from her face as he pressed his now naked body against hers, her back easing up against the wet tile of the shower wall.

"I've waited for you my whole life," he murmured as he entered her. "I've waited for this."

Their gasps were identical echoes of one another. A moment to regain themselves and he lifted her legs to clasp around his back. She gave herself over to the sheer intensity of feeling as he withdrew and entered her again, repeatedly, going deeper with each thrust.

She missed the beginning of his release, already lost in the throes of her own. It was like standing on a precipice, peering out into the most beautiful valley she'd ever seen. And when she tipped over the edge, she was flying, destined for a perfect landing.

Patrick had said he was searching for his future, his destiny. In this moment, their bodies locked together, she knew she'd found her own.

In that moment of realization, her mind exploded into a miasma of colors and shapes, pulsing around her, demanding her attention. Sounds, feelings, vague but insistent, they pummeled against the inside of her head as if in a mass hysteria of exodus. Colors, shapes, sounds and feelings, building in intensity. Colors, shapes, sounds, feelings and, all at once, memories, tumbling over one another in their haste to return to the place they belonged.

Memories of everything. Who she was, how she'd gotten here, all of it. She could clearly see her life before she'd come to this place. Wyddecol and the Temple of Danu, Castle MacGahan and all the people she'd left behind. All the people she cared for. And towering over it all, with eyes of piercing blue, stood Patrick.

She looked up into the concerned eyes of the man who held her in his arms.

She remembered everything.

She remembered Patrick.

* * *

"I know you," Syrie murmured, tears pooling in her eyes to mix with the spray of the shower running down her beautiful body.

Patrick thought his heart might well burst from the love he felt.

"I should hope you know me," he said, forcing a grin to break the tension of the moment. "After what we just did, I'd no' like you to think of me as a stranger."

"No," she said as she shook her head and brought her hands to rest on either side of his face. "I know *you*. I remember you. I remember me. I remember everything."

His vision misted over as he realized what she was telling him, and he drew her close, crushing her to his chest.

His Syrie was returned to him.

He held her until the temperature of the water changed so that it was as if they stood in a mountain stream rather than a hot spring, and Syrie began to shiver in his arms.

Reluctant to let her go, Patrick reached down and turned off the water. With one hand still clutching her arm, he pulled one of the big towels from its rack to wrap around her before lifting her out of the tub and carrying her to his room. He left her sitting on the stool in front of the big mirrored dresser to go back for her robe. When he returned, he found her using the towel in an attempt to dry her hair. He held the robe for her to slip her arms into and then wrapped his plaid around his own waist before he reached into the top drawer to pull out the comb he'd carried with him to this time. Syrie's comb.

"Where did you get that?" she asked, her eyes meeting his in the reflection of the mirror.

"Yer room at Castle MacGahan."

He didn't add that he'd been wild with grief and fear, searching desperately for any clue as to where she'd gone.

"How did you find me?"

"Orabilis." That name should explain well enough, though perhaps he wasn't giving all the credit due. "And Editha Faas."

Syrie nodded thoughtfully, her eyes once again capturing his in the mirror. "You were aware of where you would have to come to find me? *When* you would have to follow to?"

It was his turn to nod. "I was."

"And you followed me anyway."

It wasn't a question any more than he had questioned whether or not to come after her.

"I would follow you anywhere, *mo siobhrag.* Anywhere in the world. Anywhere in time."

"You'd do all that," she said with a smile lighting her eyes. "But you won't cease from calling me an Elf."

Apparently her memories of the old language had returned with all the others. Interesting she didn't comment on his having referred to her as *my Elf.* He should pursue that. Should question her.

If he didn't fear her answer.

But he had no reason to fear, did he? Hadn't Orabilis told him she would regain her memories only when she fell in love with him again? Her memories had returned, so it stood to reason...

Still, he doubted. Doubted that he, the unworthy third son, should find the good fortune to have a woman such as Syrie return his love.

"Are you ready to return home with me?" he asked, hesitant to face his real question.

Syrie reached up to place a hand over his, stopping him as he drew the comb through her hair. "I'm not sure I want to go back, Patrick. I have a place here. Friends. A new family. A home where I'm wanted."

"Yer wanted in yer own time, as well," Patrick said quietly, the fear growing in his heart.

"Where would that be that you think I'm wanted? I'm but another mouth for your brother to worry over feeding at Castle MacGahan. Certainly not even you could think that I'm wanted in Wyddecol. My people have made it abundantly clear they don't want me there." Syrie shook her head as if to deny any protest he might make and slipped the comb from his fingers to run it through her hair. "No. I think maybe it's best if I go on being Syrie Alburn, the girl with no memory."

"You'll no' be safe here, Syrie. The Fae willna leave you in peace. No' with yer memory returned. Yer too great a danger to them, no matter what time yer in."

"Ridiculous," she huffed. "They threw me away. They wouldn't have done that if they considered me a threat. They could not care less about me. And I'm not needed at Castle MacGahan any longer, so I'll stay here where there are people who care about me. People I might be able to help in some way."

"You were no' a threat without your memory. No' a threat before I came after you. But you remember now. Now you are a threat to them."

His explanation wasn't at all what he wanted to say. *What about me?* he wanted to ask. *What about us?*

Asking those questions would mean giving up any pretense of pride. Asking would mean opening himself up to the possibility of the greatest rejection, the greatest pain he'd ever encountered. And yet asking was the only way he would know for sure.

"Syrie," he began, getting no further, thanks to a bloodcurdling scream from downstairs.

"Ellen," Syrie breathed, her eyes wide with fear as she surged to her feet.

He was already headed out the door and down the stairs with Syrie following closely on his heels.

It took only a second to absorb the meaning of the scene awaiting them in the living room. Ellen held a lamp in front of her, brandishing it like a weapon to keep the stranger with a long knife at bay. Blood dripped from her arm but she seemed unaware of the wound, her eyes flashing with each swing she took at the wild-eyed man.

"Call Danny," she yelled, not taking her eyes off the man. "Come into my home, will you? Threaten my friends? I don't think so."

As if Patrick had any intention of waiting for Ellen's brother in a situation like this! He was vaguely aware of Syrie grabbing the telephone as the bright haze of battle settled around him and he charged the intruder. His body hit the man like a battering ram as he grabbed the wrist of the hand holding the knife. The two of them crashed against the wall and slid to the floor, Patrick on top of the smaller man. Patrick forced the hand holding the knife into the air and then slammed it to the floor, sending the knife skittering across the wood as the attacker's fingers splayed wide.

Beneath him, the intruder kept up a litany of words, repeating them over and over, as if he were unaware that whatever he'd planned to do, it certainly wasn't going to happen now.

"Find Elesyria. Destroy. Find Elesyria. Destroy."

Patrick lifted himself off the man's body long enough to flip him over onto his stomach and pull his arms up behind him. There, he waited, his knee in the man's back to make sure the bastard didn't try to follow through on the threat he continued to repeat.

"Danny's on his way," Syrie said, hurrying to Ellen's side. "It's all going to be okay now. Let me have a look at that arm."

"Sonofabitch," Ellen spat out, her breath coming in great heaves. "Thought you could come in here and attack my family, did you? Not in this lifetime, fella."

As if the statement took the last of her strength, Ellen let the heavy lamp drop, shattering at her feet, before Syrie led her over to sit on the sofa.

With the man still squirming under his hold, Patrick looked toward Syrie, catching her frightened gaze.

"Everything is going to be okay now," she said again, as if to force the statement to be truth.

"You ken as well as I do, yer wrong on that count," he said. "He's no' the first and he willna be the last. They'll continue to come. There will be even more of them now that you remember."

Syrie's expression blanked as she nodded her acknowledgment of his words. Her hands busily worked at wrapping a towel around the wound on Ellen's arm. When she'd done all that she could, she rose to her feet and disappeared upstairs.

Outside, the whine of a police siren shattered the quiet night, while red and blue lights flashed through the window, creating a colorful show on the walls.

Danny had arrived with reinforcements. They swarmed into the small room, relieving Patrick of his perch, freeing him to go after Syrie.

He found her in her room, dressed in a gown he remembered all too well from the few times he'd seen her wear it. A gown of green flowing material he had not one single doubt had its origins in Wyddecol.

"What are you doing?" he asked, already knowing the answer.

"You were right," she said, tears glazing her eyes. "I can't stay here. Not now. Not if it means putting my family here in danger."

"What do you want to do?" he asked. "It's yer call. You've only to tell me your wish."

"I want to go after them," she said, her chin lifted. "I want to make them pay for what they did to Ellen. Make them pay for what they did to the Goddess. Make them pay for what they did to me. But how can I? I'm only one woman."

This was not the Syrie he knew. Not this broken, unsure woman. His Syrie would never admit defeat. Never allow anyone to shake her confidence in herself. She was still in there. He knew she had to be. He had but to drag her out and expose her to the light of day.

"One woman." Patrick snorted, pleased to see surprise replace the defeat in her expression. "You ken as well as I do, yer so much more than that. Yer a powerful Fae who takes a backseat to none. That's why they've come after you. It's the power you wield they fear."

"I don't know," she whispered, sounding for all the world like a lost child.

"You do know. And as to being alone, yer no' that." He crossed the room to fold her in his embrace. "You'll never be that. No' for as long as I draw breath."

"Oh, Patrick," she said, searching his eyes as if she thought to find herself in there. "I think you just might be the best thing that ever happened to me."

That was only fair. Because Syrie was definitely the best thing that had ever happened to him.

CHAPTER TWENTY-ONE

"I still don't understand why you think you have to leave." Ellen held on to Syrie's hand, her eyes pleading as much as her words ever had. "They've taken that lunatic into custody so you won't have to worry about him coming back. Danny assured me of that."

"I have to go because, if I stay, he won't be the last." Syrie hugged her friend before stepping away from her. "I have things I need to take care of. And once I do, I'll be back for a visit. I promise."

"You promise," Ellen repeated, almost as if she doubted Syrie's words.

"I promise," Syrie confirmed, hugging Ellen once more. "I owe you a debt, my friend. Maybe one too large to ever repay, but I will be back to give it a try."

"Pfft," Ellen said. "You owe me nothing. You were meant to be here. Meant to become my heart-sister, every bit as much as Rosella."

Syrie smiled, her heart heavy that she'd miss saying goodbye to her other friend. "You'll give my love to Rosie, right? Tell her I'll see her again, too."

Ellen nodded her agreement as Syrie turned away.

Enough of this emotional farewell. She had business that needed attending to. Fae who needed attending to.

She passed through the kitchen and let herself out the back door, where she found Patrick waiting, just as he'd promised. He had also changed back into his own clothing, for the most part. He still wore the high-top sneakers Clint had bought for him the week before.

Syrie cast a quizzical glance at the shoes and then up to him. "Do you think that's a wise idea? Taking something like that back with you?"

He shrugged, his face breaking into one of those lovely smiles that stole her heart. "It's no' as if I plan to give them to anyone. And should I die, you'll make sure to burn them for me, aye?"

Of course he was teasing. At least, she hoped he was teasing.

"The shoes and you in them, if you allow yourself to be killed. So, best you remember that and stay on your guard."

And whoever dared to try to kill Patrick would burn, too. The difference was, she just might not take the time to kill them first.

"I will keep that in mind, Elf."

His grin kept her from correcting him again. Seriously, she was obviously wasting her time with the corrections anyway.

"What do we do now?" he asked, reaching out to take her hand. "Must we go somewhere special? Orabilis sent me from some glen she said contained special powers, and I know that she awaits our return there."

"Then that is where we'll join her," Syrie told him, tightening her grip on his hand. "I've but to call down the starlight for us to travel upon."

"Starlight, eh?" Patrick shrugged and pulled her a little closer. "To think I never realized you knew how to do such a thing."

Syrie only smiled, not wanting to make her companion nervous. No point in telling him she hadn't ever known how to do such a thing. How she knew now was a complete mystery to her. But she did know, as if it were knowledge that had always been tucked away in some dark corner of her mind. A mind that now had no dark corners at all.

"Perhaps that's what they fear most of all," she murmured. "The light."

"What?"

Syrie shook her head, and smiled at Patrick as she rose up on her toes. "You'll need to kiss me now," she said. "It's part of the process of returning."

"Kiss you? That's not how it worked with Orabilis."

Good thing, too. She'd not want to have to take on a feud with someone as powerful as Orabilis, but she would. If she thought the old Faerie had one single romantic thought about her man…Of course, considering the family connection Orabilis had to Patrick, that would be ridiculous.

Though, it was just possible that Patrick wasn't aware of that relationship. After all, she hadn't known of it until now. That knowledge had lived in one of those formerly dark corners.

"I'm not Orabilis. This is how I do it," she said, threading her fingers into the thick hair at Patrick's neck to pull his head closer. "Hold on tightly."

"I think I rather prefer the way you do it," he murmured, just before his lips met hers and his arms fastened around her.

All around them, the light brightened, turning an intense emerald shade of green.

Patrick might prefer her method of sending them through time, but Syrie quickly found its disadvantage as his touch distracted her from the Magic and the rainbow shards of light that had begun to dance around them disappeared.

"Let's try that one more time," she said, more for her benefit than his.

A life filled with Magic and Patrick was definitely going to take some getting used to.

* * *

One moment they had stood alone, wrapped in one another's arms, isolated in a shimmering emerald cocoon. In the next instant, Patrick's time of isolated perfection was shattered by a raspy voice he found irritatingly familiar.

"About time the two of you showed up."

Patrick forced open his eyes to find Orabilis sitting only yards away as Syrie slipped from his grasp to join the old witch. It took all the strength he had to remain on his feet, fighting an overwhelming grogginess such as he'd experienced only once before.

"Thank you for convincing him to come for me," Syrie said, dropping to her knees next to the rocking chair where Orabilis sat.

They were in the glen, in the exact same spot from which Orabilis had sent him to find Syrie. Everything was the same as when he'd left except for the rocking chair, a strangely out-of-place object that his sluggish brain couldn't quite fit into his memories.

"Convince him?" The old woman snorted, patting Syrie on the shoulder. "Hardly. I doona think I could have kept him from it, even if I had wanted to."

Syrie's laughter tinkled through the glen, reflecting off the water and dancing around his head, much as the strange lights had done only moments before.

"What is our situation, Orabilis? Have we a chance against them?" Syrie asked, all signs of her joy wiped away.

"A state of near martial law exists in the capital of Wyddecol. The Goddess is held captive and the Council searches for any they deem to be in opposition to their rule."

Syrie sat back on her heels, a stricken expression filling her eyes. "How do you know of these things? Who told you?"

We did, echoed through the glen, a chant carried by a multitude of voices, though Patrick could see none present other than the three of them.

"I ken yer too fearful to return to Wyddecol," Orabilis barked over her shoulder in the direction of the deep pool. "But if yer to stay here, you've need to stay quiet, aye? I've business to attend to and need none of yer interruptions."

A whisper of sound greeted her question, barely more than the *whoosh* of a breeze through the trees.

"Attendants to my son," Orabilis muttered, shaking her head. "Almost as useless as he has allowed himself to become over the years."

"They sent assassins after me," Syrie said. "As if stealing my memories and casting me adrift in time wasn't punishment enough. In all my days, I've never heard of such a thing."

"I'd hazard a guess that there are any number of things you've no' heard about, child," Orabilis said, a tired sigh following before she spoke again. "Power is a seductive mistress. You'd do well to remember that now. There are many, Fae and Mortal alike, who canna resist her siren call. Reynalia Al' Servan is one of those, though by no means the first, nor will she be the last. She cultivated her natural gifts and her family's contacts as she rose through the political ranks. But Supreme Leader of the High Council is no' enough for a woman like her. We should have known as much based on her bloodline. In spite of that, no one questioned her intent or her loyalty. No' until it was too late. The lure of the Earth Mother's power was too strong. Reynalia has surrounded herself with those possessed of weak minds and even weaker morals, who support her thirst for control of all Wyddecol. And once they've taken over there, they'll make their move for complete domination."

"But why come after me?" Syrie asked. "I'm a nobody. I was never more than a handmaiden at the Earth Mother's Temple."

"You were never a nobody, my dear," Orabilis said, smoothing a hand down Syrie's wild curls. "But even if you were, thanks to what the High Council did to you, yer anything but a nobody now."

"It's because she traveled with her Magic, isn't it?" Patrick said, as two surprised faces turned in his direction. "Not stripped from her, but merely sealed away along with her memories."

He remembered the conversations between Orabilis and Editha. The conversations that had felt such a great waste of time when all he'd wanted to do was to go after the woman he loved.

"It is," Orabilis agreed before turning her attention back to Syrie. "They sent you, fully equipped with yer Magic, through the Time Flow of the All Conscious. The River of Time, some call it. A place of unbelievable power. And now yer Magic, and you, have gained the power that comes from the river. They sent someone after you because they have begun to realize their mistake and, in their mistake, the danger you present to them."

"So you say, but I feel no different than I ever did," Syrie said. "I cannot see how I am a danger to people as powerful as they are."

"Regardless of how you claim you feel, you are different." Orabilis tilted her head to one side, examining Syrie as she might some new type of flower or insect. "The walls you've built to protect yer heart are strong, child. But they hold as much in as they keep out. One day they will open and then you'll ken the power that you possess. The High Council would prefer to stop you before you realize the extent of what you've become."

Patrick didn't care about any of that. Syrie was Syrie, as she'd always been. Her powers or lack of them meant nothing to him. Only having her home and safe were of any consequence.

"I will take her to Castle MacGahan," he said. "Within those walls, she'll be protected. No one can get to her there, not even yer mighty High Council."

"Even if you could get there, she'd still no' be safe. Mortal walls canna withstand the will of the Fae," Orabilis said, shaking her head. "No' when they've set their minds on destruction."

"What do you mean, *if* he could get me there?" Syrie asked, picking up on the words Patrick had missed.

Orabilis shrugged, returning to the needlework in her lap that Patrick would have sworn wasn't there minutes before.

"A number of men surround the glen, waiting for us to emerge," Orabilis said, her head bent over her work. "I've no doubt as to who sent them or why they've come. We willna be allowed to leave this place unmolested. No' through any Mortal passage."

Patrick bristled at the idea that anyone could think to keep them prisoner in this place. If only he could get word to his brother, those who kept them here would stand no chance.

"And innocent lives would be needlessly lost," Orabilis said, casting an exasperated glance in his direction. "Yer true enemies canna be defeated in this world."

"Then we must go to Wyddecol," Syrie said, rising to her feet. "We must defeat them there."

"Exactly," Orabilis agreed.

No, no, no, the unseen voices protested, the leaves on the trees rustling with their intensity as if a storm approached. *Unsafe, unsafe, unsafe!*

"What did I tell you?" Orabilis barked over her shoulder before turning back to them, an apologetic smile on her lips. "They are correct, unfortunately. I canna go with you into Wyddecol. My presence would almost assure yer being found out the minute you entered. This is something you will have to do without my help."

"You told us this High Council is searching for those who oppose them," Patrick said. "If opposition exists, we have only to gather those who would see the Goddess returned to power."

Fae or Mortal, battle was battle, and wars were often won in the planning and choice of allies.

"Where would I be without your counsel?" Syrie asked, smiling as she came to stand next to him. "Patrick is right. I'll speak to my friend, Nally. She served at the Temple with me and would surely know of many who would help us."

Orabilis stopped her rocking, fixing a look on both of them. "That would be a most unwise action, Elesyria. Someone inside the Temple helped to set up the Goddess in the first place. You need to stay as far away from there as possible."

Shock registered on Syrie's face and she moved closer to Patrick, as if to seek the physical comfort he was more than willing to provide.

"Where would you recommend we start?" he asked, looping an arm over Syrie's shoulders.

"There's a young officer in the Palace Guard. A captain. His mother has remained close to me in spite of my…" She paused, as if searching for the word she wanted to use. "In spite of my absence from Wyddecol. I would recommend you begin with him. His name is Dallyn Al' Lyre, and if what my sources tell me is accurate, he will be an inroad to many more who would readily join yer cause."

"How will we locate this man?" Patrick asked.

"It should be easy enough," Orabilis answered with a chuckle. "When you enter Wyddecol from here, you'll be arriving in his mother's barn. I'm sure she can arrange a meeting for you when you tell her who sent you."

Trust wasn't something that any good warrior gave easily. Not if he wanted to live to be a good *old* warrior. But Orabilis had been a large part of Patrick's childhood. If there was anyone he felt he could trust, it was surely her.

While Syrie and Orabilis busied themselves with a discussion of all that had passed in Wyddecol in Syrie's absence, Patrick slipped away into the woods, intent on seeing for himself the size of the force Orabilis claimed surrounded the glen. Trust was one thing. Knowledge was quite another.

As it turned out, she hadn't been exaggerating. If anything, she'd played down the threat in her disclosure.

"There you are," Syrie said as he returned to the clearing in the glen. "I was beginning to worry about you."

"No need," he said. "Merely scouting our conditions here."

The last he added quietly as she reached his side.

"And?"

"And it is worse than Orabilis suggested. A full company of men at the very least. Strange men."

Before any battle, and certainly when an army felt itself in the superior position, men joked and visited. They prepared their weapons amid a constant din of chatter. Not so with these men.

"Strange how?" Syrie asked.

"Quiet. Not like any warriors I've known. Almost as if they weren't even Mortal men."

"They're Mortal, true enough," Orabilis called across the clearing.

The woman had the sensitive hearing of a wildcat.

"All held under a massive compulsion, is my guess. It's what makes them strange, robbing them of any independent thoughts or feelings. All they know, all that is in their minds, is what they've been told to do."

Patrick had heard stories of compulsions his whole life. He had assumed that was what afflicted the man who had attacked Ellen. But this? He'd never heard of a compulsion on such a grand scale.

"Then it's settled," Syrie said, giving his arm a squeeze before she left him to hurry back to Orabilis. "Straight to Wyddecol from here is our only option."

Large bubbles had formed at the water's edge by the time Patrick approached, appearing to lower the level in the pond. As he watched, the bubbles continued to grow, sucking up more and more of the water, forming a barrier that created a dry path leading to the waterfall at the far edge of the pool.

"You enter there," Orabilis said, pointing a finger toward a dark opening that appeared just below where the water had been.

"We go now?" Patrick asked.

For some reason he hadn't expected they would leave so soon.

"You don't have to come along," Syrie said, keeping her gaze turned away from him. "Wyddecol is a dangerous place for Mortals."

"This one can hardly be called only a Mortal." Orabilis cackled. "Though it's dangerous enough for his kind, too."

As if they thought danger would prevent him from going along. Danger was the reason he would insist on going along.

"Someone has to look after Syrie. As much as I risked to get her back here, I've no intent to see my hard work all gone to waste now."

Syrie's smile was all the reward he could ever ask.

"You might want to hurry yerselves a bit, dearies," Orabilis said. "I canna hold this back forever, you know. I'm no' as young as I used to be."

Syrie grabbed his hand and pulled him forward, across the path between the large bubbles and into the dark opening.

Whatever happened next, he didn't care. As long as he was with her, keeping her safe, nothing else mattered.

CHAPTER TWENTY-TWO

"You've hardly touched your food, either of you. Is there something wrong with it? I pride myself in my ability to serve a Mortal dish at every meal."

Leala Al' Lyre dipped her spoon into the big pot hanging over the fire and lifted it to her lips, her brow drawn tight in concern.

"There is nothing wrong with the bounty you've served us, madam," Patrick said, and downed two bites in quick succession.

"I think it's exhaustion more than anything else," Syrie said. "From our journey here."

No point in explaining that Leala's version of Mortal food in no way resembled anything Syrie would consider edible. No doubt Patrick suffered from the same complaint.

"Or nerves," Leala said, her face breaking into a relieved smile as she laid her spoon on the table. "There's so much distress in our world at the moment. So much uncertainty. My poor Dallyn only picks at his food when he comes home for a visit. Too much on his mind to simply relax and enjoy a meal." She sat down in her chair and took a bite from her own bowl before her brow furrowed and she looked up again. "You're not here to add to my boy's distress, are you?"

A perfect opportunity to change the subject if ever Syrie had heard one.

"That is not our intent. Do you have any idea when your son might arrive?"

Leala shook her head, and rose to ladle seconds into Patrick's bowl. Fortunately, their hostess was too preoccupied with serving to notice the look of resignation on Patrick's face as he set about the task of being a good guest by eating more of the bitter mush they'd been served.

"He should be here anytime now, my dear, any time. It depends, of course, on his ability to slip away from the palace unseen. Such troubled times we live in."

Syrie refrained from pointing out to her hostess that most times in Wyddecol had been troubled in one way or another. The Fae had gone from one internal power struggle to another with only short periods of relative peace in between.

"Eat up," their hostess said cheerfully, apparently satisfied with Syrie's disclaimer. "There's plenty more. Are you ready for seconds, my dear? I've made a huge pot."

Syrie was saved from having to find an appropriate refusal by the door opening and a young man slipping inside.

"Dallyn, my sweet boy, you've arrived just in time to eat with us," his mother exclaimed, jumping up from her seat to scurry over to him. Rising up onto her tiptoes, she pulled his head down so that she could kiss his cheek before turning a happy face to her guests. "This is my son, Dallyn Al' Lyre, Captain in the Guard of the Realm of Faerie."

"I doubt your guests are in need of a recitation of my rank and honors, Mother," the young man said, a fond expression lighting his eyes as he placed a hand on the shoulder of their small, rotund hostess. "Especially not in light of your message as to who has sent them here."

"Oh, you're right, of course, my dear," his mother said, patting his hand before hurrying over to her still-bubbling pot. "Shall I fill a bowl for you? You can eat while you all get to know one another."

"I think not, Mother," Dallyn said. "As a matter of fact, I think I'd prefer my new friends and I adjourn to the stables for our visit. Won't you join me?"

"But surely you'd all be more comfortable in—" Leala began.

"I'd enjoy a tour of yer fine stables," Patrick interrupted, rising from his chair to join Dallyn at the door. "I've heard much about the quality of yer horseflesh here in Wyddecol."

"Men," Syrie said with an apologetic smile aimed toward Leala before she followed after the two, who had walked out into the night.

Inside the stable, Dallyn stopped and lit a lantern hanging by the door. With a flourish, he removed his cloak to spread it over a bale of hay before offering Syrie a seat.

"Let us be clear on this from the beginning," he said, looking from one of them to the other. "My mother is not to be involved in any of this in any way. I know from her message who you both are, and, under the circumstances, I have a very good idea of what you have come to ask of me. But, should anything go wrong, I will not have her endangered. Is this clear?"

"Completely," Patrick said. "We would have it no other way."

"Good," Dallyn said. "My assumption is that you have come to rescue the Goddess. Have you a plan of any sort?"

Patrick took a step back, positioning himself behind the bale on which Syrie sat, making it clear which of them would be answering. With no more than a raised eyebrow, Dallyn shifted his penetrating gaze to her.

"A plan," she said. "Of a sort, yes."

"Perhaps you would care to enlighten me with a few details of what specific sort you have in mind, milady. Before I offer up lives for your disposal."

Likely the young captain wouldn't be impressed with her should she actually tell him she had only the vaguest idea of what they needed to do. Once again a regret pierced through her heart that she hadn't gone to her friend Nalindria first. Nally would have understood Syrie's need to act and would have helped her talk through her ideas until they came up with a plan of action together, as they had so many times in the past.

But she hadn't. She'd done exactly as Orabilis had recommended and now here she sat, facing this stranger. This close she could see he wasn't quite as young as she might have originally determined. His bearing, however, was the epitome of the typical overbearing male Fae. Tall, muscular, with long blond hair pulled back into a strap, he was what any female would consider more than a little handsome. Nothing compared to her Patrick, of course.

Dallyn's eyes were fixed upon her, his face blanked of any emotion so that she had no idea whether he planned to help or to turn her over to the High Council. Studying the Fae before her, she determined that playing her cards close to the chest would be her best move until she trusted him more.

"Perhaps a few details," she agreed, adopting a superior air to match his. "We need men and information before we can proceed."

Dallyn nodded. "What information is it that you seek?"

Syrie faced a moment of truth. To move forward, she would have to trust Dallyn. At least a little. Without that step she would not be able to access what she needed to continue. Trust meant risking her life and Patrick's, but she could see no other way.

As if he'd read her mind, Patrick placed a hand on her shoulder and squeezed, a gentle, reassuring move that helped her decide.

"We must gather a force to oppose the High Council. The three of us could hardly hope to accomplish much on our own. And before I finalize any plan, I need information. I need to know where and how the Goddess is being kept. I need details on the movements of the High Council. Details on their loyal forces and what sorts of opposition we might face. Most important of all, I need details on what sorts of support we might find."

Dallyn continued to nod. "Support is strong for the Goddess. She has been good to the people of Wyddecol and they see little enough need for change. Especially not in this fashion. It is all too reminiscent of the troubles with the Nuadians."

"Are they behind this takeover?"

"I have no proof of that. Yet," Dallyn answered. "But the possibility exists. Reynalia's own brother was exiled in the last round of troubles and rumor has it that he has made himself a prominent figure within the group of Nuadians."

"Perhaps it's no more than ambition run rampant in the family," Patrick said.

"Perhaps," Dallyn agreed. "Or not. Still, it is for that reason that I am unwilling to put my mother's safety at risk. You'll forgive me if I tell you that you are unwelcome here. You are free to stay the night. But on the morrow I will send a friend of mine, a fellow officer, who will take you to a small cabin where you can stay comfortably while we prepare for what is to come."

"I understand completely," Syrie said, rising to stand. "And we will say nothing of this to your mother. Only that we have enjoyed her hospitality and must return home."

"Excellent," Dallyn said, reclaiming his cloak. "Darnee Al' Oryn will wait for you just inside the trees to the north at noon. She will accompany you to the new location."

"Thank you for your help," Patrick said, extending a hand to Dallyn.

The Fae accepted the gesture with a slight bow. "I will come to you there tomorrow after dark with news of anything I can find."

With another bow and a kiss to Syrie's hand, the captain disappeared out the door and into the night.

"So that's it, then," Patrick said, holding the door open for Syrie. "It has begun."

Syrie slipped her hand into Patrick's grasp, stopping just before they entered the house. There was so much left unsaid between them but, for some reason, now didn't feel like the right time to delve into any of it. Any of it save Patrick's safety.

"There's still time for you to go back to the glen. You can wait there with Orabilis. Make sure she's safe until I return for you."

If she was able to return.

Patrick snorted, tightening his grip on her hand and pulling her into his embrace. "Like that old witch needs my protection. More likely those men ringing the perimeter of the glen need protection from her."

He had a point. A Fae of her age and power had very little to fear anywhere.

"You'll stay with me, then," she said, knowing it was not a question. "Even though this may well be your last chance to leave safely."

Again he snorted, though more quietly this time. "My place is with you, Syrie. If it's safe enough for you, it's safe enough for me."

The kisses he showered on her cheek and down her neck could easily have led to something more if not for the scraping sound that warned someone was opening the door. By the time Leala's face appeared in the opening, Patrick had resumed his spot next to the door to hold it open for Syrie to enter as if nothing at all had happened.

Regrettably, this was yet one more thing between them that would have to wait.

CHAPTER TWENTY-THREE

Syrie awoke long before sunrise, an odd, buzzy feeling of constriction gripping her chest and spreading up into her throat. Nightmare, no doubt. Anxiety over the task she'd set for herself. Anxiety over the allies she'd chosen.

What she needed was to see for herself what was going on. What she needed was to speak to someone who had experienced it all firsthand. Someone she trusted.

She rose from the bed and lit the small lamp next to the fireplace before she dressed, wishing she could speak to Patrick before she did what she'd already decided she was going to do. But Leala had made sure to place them in bedchambers on the opposite sides of her own. For propriety's sake, she had claimed, delivering the clear message that there would be no...*togetherness*...in her home.

Syrie smiled at the memory of the little woman's pink cheeks as she'd addressed their sleeping arrangements.

Just as well. If they had shared a room, Patrick would have insisted upon coming with her, and his presence would have stifled any attempt at her connecting with her old friend.

She carried the lamp with her from her bedchamber to the front door. There, she blew out the flame and slipped out into the still morning air leaving the lamp on the bench beside the door. A less impetuous woman would have remembered to bring a cloak along, but that would have required her asking her hostess for the loan of one.

And *that* would have defeated the whole purpose of her slipping out into the dark.

With a shiver, she hurried across the open space of the Al' Lyre homestead and slipped into the woods. A look back showed her the house was still darkened and quiet. Good. She'd made it this far successfully.

The woods of Wyddecol were like no other place Syrie had ever been. The foliage here was perpetually green, and the smell was one that lived in her memory no matter how long she'd been away. She knew these woods as well as she knew the lines on her own hand, so traveling to her destination, even in darkness, was no hardship.

When she arrived, she hunkered down, making herself as small as possible as she watched for any movement. It didn't take long to spot the guards she had suspected she'd find. After all, having taken the Goddess prisoner, it was unlikely the High Council would leave her Temple untouched.

Precisely as the sun began to rise, Nalindria appeared on the steps of the Temple, buckets in hand. Syrie had counted on this. After so many years of repetition, she had hoped that, in spite of the guards, her friend would still be following her usual routine.

The dark-haired woman crossed the open area, headed for the nearby stream. As she passed each guard, the man would nod a silent greeting, allowing her to pass unmolested.

Thank the Goddess that the respect shown to the attendants of the Earth Mother's Temple hadn't waned.

After making sure that none followed Nalindria, Syrie quietly made her way through the forest to the stream where her friend headed so that she could be there waiting when Nally arrived.

Her friend had moved more quickly than Syrie expected, and was already bent over the water, scooping it into her buckets, when Syrie stepped from the cover of the trees.

"Nally?"

Nalindria Re' Alyn dropped her bucket as she turned, a gasp on her lips.

"I'm so sorry," Syrie exclaimed, rushing to her friend's side to catch her up in an embrace. "I didn't mean to frighten you."

"Not frightened," Nally said, her voice hushed as always. "It's only that I thought never to see you again. Not after what we heard had happened."

Syrie pulled back from the embrace, her hands still on her friend's shoulders. This was exactly the sort of information she'd hoped to learn when she'd sought out her friend.

"What did they tell you? I want to hear everything about what's going on at the Temple."

Nally's teeth worked at the corner of her bottom lip before she bent to retrieve her bucket. "I haven't the time to recount all that has passed since I saw you last. The guards watch over every move of the Temple Maidens. If I don't return very soon, they'll come looking for me. Can we meet later on? Tonight, perhaps? I'm sure I can slip away unseen and come to wherever you're staying."

Except that Syrie had no idea where she'd be tonight.

"That won't work," she said, stepping back as her friend refilled the buckets she carried. "If you can get out of the Temple unseen, perhaps I can get in?"

"Perhaps," Nally agreed, turning her head to cast a glance back in the direction of the Temple. "Yes, that should work. I'll meet you inside the entrance leading to the old baths. When the moon rises to its peak?"

"Agreed," Syrie said, watching as her friend disappeared into the trees.

She should have guessed where Nally would choose to meet. They had used that ancient doorway more times than she could count on full-moon nights when they'd wanted to slip out of the Temple unseen.

Retracing her path, Syrie stopped for several minutes to observe the location of as many guards as she could find. Knowing which areas to avoid would be helpful tonight. After she was satisfied that Nally had re-entered the building safely, Syrie quickly made her way back to the Al' Lyre homestead.

Sunlight sparkled off crystal decorations that dangled from every window, sending jeweled rays dancing into the air to welcome her back. An unfamiliar wave of happiness flowed around her like a beautiful new cape as she neared the front door. She'd made it safely to see Nally and back again, all undetected. All she needed to do was slip back into her room before anyone noticed her gone and she could chalk up a perfect adventure. Everything was as it should be in the world, if only for a moment or two.

And then she opened the door to find Patrick staring down at her, accusation burning in his gaze.

Perhaps she'd been a bit hasty with the *as-it-should-be* declaration.

* * *

Patrick had searched everywhere. Every possible chamber, every outbuilding and stand of trees. Syrie was nowhere to be found. An unwelcome emotion began to bubble in his gut, the dreaded fear he had rarely known before discovering himself in love.

"If she's allowed herself to be harmed," he muttered, not finishing the dire threat as he entered the main chamber of the little house to find their hostess humming to herself as she stirred a large stick in the pot bubbling in the fireplace.

"Good morning, Patrick," she chirped, her face crinkling in a smile as she spotted him. "First up and in here this lovely day?"

"First in here," he confirmed, not wanting to alarm Leala. Not yet.

"I'll have our wonderful porridge prepared for you in short order," she said, stirring furiously. "And then, once I've carried the feed out to the chickens and the goats, we can wake your little friend and have ourselves our morning meal."

"Allow me," Patrick offered, none too keen on the smells wafting from the pot. "I'll see to yer animals this morning. It's the least I can do to repay yer kindness in allowing us to stay the night."

"Oh, my," Leala said, her free hand fluttering around her in the general direction of the door. "So good of you, lad. You'll find the feed sacks just inside the stable."

Outside, Patrick sucked in a deep breath, shoving the fear into a little box and putting it to the side. He'd concentrate on the task at hand. If by the time he returned to the house Syrie was still missing, he'd have no choice but to alert his hostess and plead for her son's help.

Chores finished, he'd been inside only long enough to check Syrie's chamber one last time before he returned to the main room, his mind made up. It was time to ask for help.

"Leala," he began, just as the front door opened.

Syrie had returned and the growing ball of fear rumbling around in his guts began to change to anger.

"Where have you been?" he demanded as she entered, surprise coloring her expression.

"I was…just out in the stable. Visiting the horses."

Lying! To him, of all people!

"I didn't see you get past me, my dear," Leala said, still bent over her pot. "But I do tend to put all my attentions into cooking."

"I didn't want to disturb you when I went out," Syrie said. "It smells very…fresh."

Patrick tried to unclench the muscles that held his jaw tight, but it felt beyond his control. Not only had he feared the worst but then, when she returned, Syrie lied to him. This wasn't something he could simply let go.

He scooped up a couple of buckets from the stack by the doorway and tossed one to her.

"Come with me. We'll replenish Leala's water for her so she doesn't have to do it later."

"So helpful," their hostess said, to no one in particular. "Such lovely young people."

Syrie hesitated, but only for a moment, resignation coloring her expression as she stepped out the door he held open for her.

"Where were you?" he asked as soon as he pulled the door closed. "And why did you lie to me?"

"Lie to you?" she said with mock innocence. "Whatever—"

"I was just in the stables. Feeding the goats and the chickens and the horse you claimed to be visiting." He worked the handle on the pump, filling her bucket as he attempted to compose himself. "In the stables for the second time this morning. The first time was when I was frantically searching for what had happened to you."

"I didn't want to tell you because I knew you'd just get upset with me," she said. "And sure enough. Look at you. You've gone all indignant warrior mode, just like I knew you would."

No matter the anger, no matter the fear, he wouldn't allow her to distract him so easily, though he knew well enough it was her intent to do exactly that.

"Where were you?" he demanded again, blanking the emotion from his voice.

"Oh, very well." She huffed and leaned over to set the bucket at her feet, no doubt stalling for time. "I've nothing to gain by hiding it from you now. I went to the Temple. I waited in the woods until my friend Nally made her daily visit to the stream to collect water. We talked and then I came back here."

A bright red haze filled his mind, forcing him to fight his way through it to even think upon the foolish actions she'd taken.

"Have you no idea what a risk you took?"

It was all he could voice at the moment.

"Not so much of a risk," she said. "It was something I needed to do and I was very careful. It wasn't as if I were going to walk into a trap, Patrick. No one knew I was coming. And even if they had, I'm quite sure I could have dealt with whatever came up."

This was the old Syrie. The one he'd verbally sparred with so many times. The impetuous, overly confident Faerie he'd fallen in love with. He just didn't love that she thought nothing of the danger to herself in what she'd done. Or to... That was it! That was the one thing she wouldn't have considered.

"Were you followed when you returned here?" he asked.

"Of course not," she answered, but she sneaked a quick look over her shoulder nonetheless.

Just as he'd thought.

"Even if you care naught for the danger to yerself, we gave our word that we would do nothing to jeopardize our innocent hostess. Do you think Dallyn would look upon your morning escapade as harmless? Especially if yer carelessness brought the Council's guards to his mother's door?"

He could see almost immediately he'd hit his mark as her expression changed.

"I never considered..." She paused, looking first to the woods and then back to him before taking a step closer. "I'm sure I wasn't followed. Had I been, I'd think they would have stormed the house by now."

He shrugged, his anger fading in the face of her worry. He pulled her into an embrace and ran his hand over her unruly curls.

"Doona be so foolish in the future, wee Elf. I'd have yer word upon it."

He needed to hear her swear to it. Swear that she wouldn't slip away again. Swear that she wouldn't take such foolish risks again.

"You've my word," she said, her voice muffled as she pressed her forehead against his chest. "I'll never again slip out in the early morn without letting you know first."

Good. Perhaps she'd learned a lesson. Although, now that he thought upon it, her vow had been a little more specific than he would have liked to have heard. He would have questioned her on that, but the sound of a throat clearing just inside the trees brought them both to attention. A moment later, a tall woman wearing the uniform of the Palace Guard stepped into the clearing.

"I hope I haven't interrupted at a bad time," she said, though her expression indicated no such qualms at all. "I am Darnee Al' Oryn, sent by Dallyn to provide you escort. It seems I have arrived earlier than our agreed-upon time."

"So you have," Syrie said, stepping away from him and clasping her hands behind her back. "But none too soon for us. We'll gather our belongings and be ready."

"It would seem Leala is preparing a meal for you," Darnee said, lifting her nose to the air and sniffing. "I'll await you in the woods. Feel free to take all the time you need."

Patrick didn't blame the Fae for fading into the trees. The thought of eating one more meal prepared by Leala made him want to run away, too.

"The sooner we're away from here, the safer it will be for our hostess," Syrie said.

Perhaps she'd read his mind.

"Agreed."

He'd be the first to admit to taking the coward's way out as he went directly to collect their things, leaving Syrie to make their excuses to Leala. Within minutes, they were on their way, waving their farewells to their hostess before slipping into the forest to find their guide.

Darnee waited well back out of sight within the shelter of the trees. As they approached, she once again sniffed the air, her nose wrinkling in distaste.

"I could swear I smell that woman's cooking even out here," she murmured as she turned to lead them to three horses tied in a clearing.

The Faerie captain was right. Even he could smell it.

"The odor does carry," he said.

Next to him, Syrie sighed and held up a bag she carried. "Leala insisted on sending some along," she said. "I didn't want to hurt her feelings, since she'd been working on it all morning."

"We leave it here," Darnee said, already sitting on the back of a large white horse. "We take nothing that could implicate anyone."

With a growing respect for their new companion, Patrick took the bag from Syrie's hands and tossed it into the woods before helping Syrie up onto the back of her mount.

"You ken she has the right of it," he said, forestalling any argument Syrie might be preparing. "The smell alone would leave a trail any could follow."

"I know," she said, obviously fighting the need to disagree. "It's just that she was already so disappointed. I'd hate to think of her finding this and believing that we threw it away. Which we did."

"You've a soft heart, Elesyrie Aí Byrn," Darnee said. "Not what I expected at all."

Syrie accepted the judgment without comment, something that surprised Patrick. Either her tolerance for her own kind was much higher than her tolerance for Mortals or she was beginning to learn the value of keeping her thoughts to herself.

Whichever the case, he was grateful. Should the two women disagree, he'd be forced to Syrie's defense, and, quite frankly, the idea of taking on the formidable captain was more than he was prepared for without a good night's sleep under his belt.

CHAPTER TWENTY-FOUR

Darnee's mount carried her down the trail and into the darkening gloom of the trees until, after one last wave of farewell, she seemed to simply melt into her surroundings.

One down, one to go.

Syrie maintained her outward composure as she and Patrick returned to the cabin where they would be staying, though she felt as if her insides were racing much faster than her body could ever move. The anxiety she'd hoped to eliminate with her visit to Nally had only continued to grow over the course of the day.

"The fire's gone out," Patrick said as they entered the cabin. "Do you want any more of the stew Darnee made for us before it goes completely cold?"

Syrie shook her head. Just the smell of the stuff left her feeling nauseated, without thinking of it cold and congealed.

"I take it that cooking is no' a skill that's highly valued by Faerie women," he said with a smile. "At least, that's what I'm beginning to think considering the ones I've met."

Syrie shrugged a careless response, wishing for nothing so much as for night to settle over the cottage. The sooner that Patrick took to his bed, the sooner she'd be able to sneak away for her rendezvous with Nally. She'd begun to worry that Darnee was going to spend the night watching over them, since it had taken her so long to take her leave. Slipping past Patrick was going to be challenge enough. She certainly hadn't liked the idea that she might have to evade two of them.

On top of everything, there was that damned promise she'd made to Patrick nagging away at her sanity. She'd done her best to keep the oath she gave as specific as possible when she spoke the words. True, he'd asked for, and he expected, that she wouldn't leave again without telling him. But in her oath to him, she'd been very careful to indicate that she wouldn't slip out in the early morning. Yes, it was nothing more than a technicality she clung to, but it was the only thing she could think of that would allow her to do what she needed to do and still keep him safe.

Though she needed the information only Nally could give her, the one thing she wasn't prepared to sacrifice in her quest to rescue the Goddess was Patrick. In fact, if ever she were forced to choose between the two of them—

"Syrie!"

Her head spun around to look at the man who'd called out her name, jerking her from her reverie.

"What?" she asked, trying to recover the emotional balance she'd lost as her thoughts had wandered to the possibilities of what fate might await her Patrick.

"I doona ken where you were just then, but it certainly wasn't here with me. Do you care to share what it is that's troubling you?"

"The list is too long," she muttered.

The smile slowly lifting the corner of his lips told her he'd heard her comment, whether she'd meant it for his ears or not.

"You worry yerself overmuch, *mo siobhrag,*" he said, crossing the room to pull her into his embrace. "Darnee appears a trustworthy ally. Dallyn seems a good man. A good ally, as well. When he's gathered our force, we'll determine the best plan to free yer Goddess. With her aid, we'll put an end to those who would see you harmed. Then, when we've accomplished what we've set out to do, you and I will go home and get on with our lives, aye?"

"We will," she agreed, allowing herself to relax into his arms.

Not even being called an Elf could ruin this moment with him. No more than she'd ruin it by sharing her fears that any plan they might put together had equally as much chance of failure as success. Nor was it the time to discuss a future that might well end here in Wyddecol before it had any real hope of beginning.

She wouldn't allow herself to worry over how thin a line she trod between truth and lies in going forward with her plan. She wouldn't dwell on how angry he'd be if he awoke before she returned this night. She refused to consider how she risked his trust forever with her actions, even though she followed a path designed to keep him safe.

This moment was a time meant for them. One tiny piece of time they could carve out for their very own.

She rose up onto her tiptoes, sliding her fingers up from the base of his neck, to thread into his dark, silky hair. She met no resistance as she guided his head down to her. His lips covered hers and she felt herself slipping under the lovely, dark water that was Patrick. Enchanting. Mesmerizing. All-consuming.

Her head dropped back as his mouth left hers to trail a heated path down her throat. Cold air danced over her skin as the soft cloth of her gown slipped down one shoulder, quickly replaced with the heat of Patrick's kisses.

He lifted her from her feet, to carry her to the small bed in the corner of the room. On her back, she stared up at him as he pulled his shirt over his head and tossed it to the floor before covering her body with his.

"I thought that damned Faerie was never going to leave us in peace," he murmured, heat filling his gaze as he leaned over her. "And now that we're finally alone, I intend to drive all yer worries from yer thoughts."

A warmth, comforting and exciting, filled her as his mouth covered hers once again, his tongue tickling over her lips, demanding they part to allow him inside.

His plan was working just as he'd said, stealing away any thought of what was ahead. This was their time, a moment carved out between what had been and what was to come, allowing nothing more than the pleasure they felt to fill their minds.

His hands slid from her bare shoulders to her waist, a slow, erotic movement that sent shivers of anticipation through every bit of her body. He'd just slipped his hands beneath her, to lift her hips when the pounding began.

"By Freya," Patrick growled. "Whoever it is, I'll rip his arms from his body and beat him senseless."

Syrie caught her breath, somewhere between a sob and a giggle, as he rose to stomp to the door, pausing only long enough to grab his shirt and drop it down over his head.

By the time their guests entered, she'd moved to stand by the darkened firepit, her gown adjusted into place. It had been much more difficult to eliminate all traces of emotion from her face and her mind, but she felt confident that she'd been successful.

At least, she hoped she had been.

Patrick, on the other hand, still wore the dark frown that marked his displeasure.

"You've allowed your fire to go out," Dallyn said, stepping close to stare down at the cooled embers.

"Little wonder," one of the two men accompanying him said. "There's no wood. I'm surprised Darnee would overlook such a detail."

They wouldn't have been surprised if they'd been here to see how both she and Patrick had done their best to hurry the Faerie soldier on her way.

"I'll see to it," the third responded, stepping back out into the evening chill.

"I'll help Devlin," the first said as he also made his way out the door.

"Ah well," Dallyn said with a sigh, slipping out of the heavy cloak he wore to toss it in the corner. "As they say, many feet make light work."

"What?" Patrick asked a moment after Dallyn slipped out the door. "No matter. Best I help them so we can hurry them through whatever it is they want. I've no desire to spend my night entertaining."

"Haven't you?" Syrie asked, unable to keep the smile from her lips.

"No desire to entertain that lot," he said, returning the smile before ducking out the open door.

Syrie sat in a chair, listening to the sounds of chopping wood and men's voices, enjoying the feel of the silly smile still hovering on her lips. It would be all too easy to regret the loss of the moments she'd longed to share with Patrick, but likely this interruption was for the best. The last thing she needed was to be too distracted to leave when she needed to for her meeting with Nally.

And, without a doubt, being alone with Patrick was one major distraction.

She reached for the cup on the table, surprised to see her hand shaking so noticeably as she picked it up. The damned quivering insides had returned to plague her.

She had little time to fret over the nasty, anxious feeling washing through her gut before the men returned. They each dumped an armload of freshly chopped wood onto the hearth, leaving Dallyn to busy himself building a new fire.

"Our friend Dallyn has brought the first of our new allies," Patrick said, indicating the two newcomers. "Larkin and Devlin. He thought it would be good for us to meet so we wouldn't be concerned if we should see either of them here without him."

"My pleasure," Syrie said, extending a still-shaky hand to each man in turn.

Dallyn finished with the fire and, after what seemed an eternity, the three took their leave.

A glance at the full moon outside assured Syrie she hadn't long left before she'd need to make her getaway. But before she could even hope to make that happen, Patrick would need to be soundly asleep.

After he closed the door, he turned to her, pulling her close once again.

"Now, where were we before their untimely visit?" he asked. "We are ever-plagued by unwelcome interruptions, are we no'?"

"We are," she agreed, knowing there was yet one more to come.

When he bent to kiss her, she turned her head into his chest.

"What's wrong?" he asked, as she'd known he would.

"I'm exhausted, Patrick," she said, realizing the truth of the words as she spoke. "My body is buzzing like it's filled with bees and I want nothing more than to escape into sleep. I'm sorry if I disappoint you."

Again, all true, even though sleep would be long-delayed for her this night, denied until after she'd done what she needed to do.

"I can help with that," he said, for the second time tonight sweeping her off her feet to carry her to the bed in the corner of the room.

This time, he laid her down and drew a blanket up over her, tucking it under her chin.

"Sleep well, *mo siobhrag,*" he said, before dropping a kiss on her forehead and moving away. "We've a lifetime for you to make up for any perceived disappointments, aye?"

He lay down next to her, his arm protectively wrapped around her. Any other time, she would have given every earthly treasure in her possession to spend her night exactly like this, his warm body curled around hers. Too bad she couldn't simply enjoy it now.

She forced herself to still, to relax against him, in hope of lulling him into his own slumber. She waited, unmoving, until the sound of his breathing had changed, growing slower and louder.

Once she was convinced that he slept, she carefully slipped out of bed, pausing only to stuff her pillow under his arm to take her place. Stepping back, she surveyed her handiwork. It would do. It would have to.

As quietly as possible, she made her way to the door and outside, breathing normally again only after the door was shut behind her. She sprinted across the open ground and into the trees, trying to make up for lost time. One glance back assured her that all was quiet. Patrick hadn't awakened. Her plan had worked.

Once again, luck had been on her side.

* * *

Damned stubborn woman!

Patrick sat up as the door closed, pausing only a moment to give Syrie enough of a head start that she wouldn't realize he followed. Foolish woman. Didn't she know he'd realize the minute she moved away from him? Didn't she realize he knew her too well to be fooled by her meek agreement to do as he asked of her? That was as far from the behavior he expected from Syrie as was...as was her breaking the oath she had taken not to risk her safety by sneaking away again.

Though, now that he replayed their conversation in his head, he realized that the oath he had sought from her was not the oath she'd actually given. Typical Fae wordplay, if ever he'd seen it. He'd thought it odd when she'd first agreed, but he'd let it go, wanting the issue to be settled.

So who was the foolish one now?

He was, if he allowed her to get away from him, alone, with no protection. There would be time enough to deal with the tricky wordplay after he had her safely back at his side.

Grabbing his sword and sheath, he headed for the door, shocked when it opened before he could get there.

Dallyn stood there, a puzzled expression on his face.

"Was that Elesyria I saw disappearing into the forest?" he asked.

"Aye," Patrick said, slipping the sheath onto his back. "What are you doing here?"

"I came to collect my cloak. We've an inspection tomorrow morning, and this is part of my uniform." Dallyn flashed a sheepish grin as he crossed to retrieve the forgotten item. "Where has Elesyria gone?"

"Damned if I know," Patrick said, unable to keep the irritation from his voice. "Though I've a guess. I hate to be rude, Dallyn, but I have to go now or risk losing her trail."

"And that would be where?" Dallyn asked, following him out the door. "This guess of yours as to her destination?"

"Early this morning she slipped away to meet with an old friend. Nally, I believe she called her. I suspect they didn't get to finish their conversation in the time they had. I suspect Syrie has gone back to meet with the woman again."

It might have felt like an eternity that Syrie had been missing this morning, but when he considered travel time, she really hadn't been gone very long. Certainly not long enough to have done more than pass along some superficial greetings, which wasn't at all what she wanted. She wanted information. Information that she felt she could trust.

"That would be Nalindria Re' Alyn, I assume," Dallyn said. "One of the Temple Maidens who served with Elesyria. It should be easy enough to track her, if that's the case."

Easy? Thanks to the time they'd wasted, unless Syrie was very careless in covering her tracks, following her would hardly be easy, even with a full moon. Not unless…

"You know where to find this Nalindria?"

"I told you she was a Temple Maiden," Dallyn said, pushing ahead of Patrick to lead the way. "She lives at the Temple of the Goddess."

What a boon! For the first time since the door had closed behind Syrie, Patrick felt as though he could actually fill his lungs with air.

"Though the guards the High Council placed around the Temple could well be a problem."

So much for breathing. It was a highly overrated activity, anyway.

Patrick considered himself an expert tracker, but he had to give credit to the Fae he followed. Dallyn moved silently and quickly, as surefooted as if born to the woods. They'd moved at the pace set by the Fae for almost half an hour before Dallyn abruptly stopped, holding up one hand in a silent signal.

Dallyn leaned close to whisper in his ear. "She's just through there, moving across the field to the back of the Temple."

Patrick shifted his position to see where Dallyn pointed. The building ahead was massive, surrounded by large swaths of stone staircases and columns that spanned the full height of the structure. In comparison, Syrie was but a small, furtive figure moving through the grass.

"There, do you see? Waiting in the shadows? I'd stake my commission on that being Nalindria."

Together they watched as Syrie reached the dark-haired woman waiting at the base of a small staircase set off to one side. As the two embraced, Dallyn stiffened next to him.

"Guards!" the Fae said, his hand going to his sword.

He was right—from both sides of the Temple, figures appeared, stealthily making their way toward the two women. Six, at least, by Patrick's count.

"We have to help," Dallyn said, but Patrick stopped him with a hand to his shoulder.

As much as he appreciated the sentiment, Dallyn's helping could easily jeopardize the entire operation to free the Goddess and, more important to Patrick, to stop the High Council that sought to harm Syrie.

"Not you," Patrick said. "They'll more than likely recognize you and then you'll be useless to us. Seeing me is of no matter. I'll have to do this alone."

"You are right, of course," Dallyn said, irritation flashing in his eyes. "Distract them so she can run. I will wait here to help as I can."

Keeping low, Patrick started toward the men. As it became clear to him that the guards would reach Syrie before he could reach them, he stood upright. Holding his sword high over his head, he issued a challenge in the form of a primal howl that drew the attention of everyone, stopping the guards in their tracks. For just an instant, they all froze where they stood. Not for long, to be sure, but long enough to alert Syrie to the approaching danger. As three of the guards changed direction to run toward him, Syrie took off in the opposite direction, taking the shortest route back to the cover of the forest.

Patrick would have to trust that Dallyn would make his way around the perimeter to be there waiting to protect her once she reached the trees. As for him, his hands were full with the Fae who converged on him. They were trained warriors, but so was he. Trained and tested under some of the harshest of fighting conditions. And, unlike his foes, he fought to protect the most precious thing in his world.

He had only a second's glance to assure himself that Syrie had disappeared from view. One guard slipped into the trees after her, but Dallyn should be able to handle one man easily enough. Two guards surrounded the woman Syrie had been speaking with, all but dragging her into the Temple and out of sight. That left him with three. Three were little enough challenge.

The distinctive sound of metal on metal rang out as his sword met the weapon of the nearest guard. With the strike, his opponent lost his footing in the damp grass. A second guard approached, but Patrick had lost track of the third in the shadows cast by the full moon. Another swing of his sword and he forced the newcomer backward, away from the direction Syrie had gone. Another swing and a thrust, followed by a scream of pain that split the night as his weapon sliced into the flesh of the guard's arm. The man staggered backward, holding his wound, while the first approached again.

"You've no hope of escape," he said, lifting his sword in front of him.

"You should pray yer wrong. My escape would be the best thing that could happen for you," Patrick sneered, easing toward his quarry. "You should pray for—"

His taunt ended abruptly in a burst of pain and light as something struck the back of his head.

The third guard!

Patrick thought he heard a scream as he fell, but his world faded to black before he could be sure of anything except his intent to kill Dallyn with his own two hands if the Fae had failed to protect Syrie.

CHAPTER TWENTY-FIVE

The pressure building in Syrie's chest that had come and gone for days now seemed to have become a permanent fixture. From the moment she had turned to see Patrick collapsing beneath the attack of the Faerie guards, she had felt as if she might physically explode. The pressure had filled her chest and now blossomed up her throat, pounding in her head, making concentration difficult at a time when concentration was vital.

"You can do this," Dallyn whispered at her side, giving her elbow a quick squeeze. "You must. For the Goddess. For all of us."

For Patrick.

She nodded her acknowledgment of Dallyn's encouragement, holding fast to the Magic that served as her disguise. She'd done this many times in the past, hiding her true appearance easily enough. But today, even without her inner turmoil, a disguise layered within a disguise required all the concentration she could muster.

They waited outside the impressive building where the High Council met, surrounded by what felt like every adult within the whole of Wyddecol. Normally, only festival days drew such a crowd. But times in Wyddecol could hardly be called normal, and when word came down that the Supreme Leader of the High Council intended to issue a proclamation, everyone wanted to know what new changes lurked to burden their lives.

Syrie would have preferred to avoid such crowds but, since rumor had it that the proclamation concerned an outsider who had been captured in an attempt on the Supreme Leader's life, she had as much desire to be here as anyone.

There was only one outsider she could imagine they were talking about. *Her* outsider. The only positive she could pull from any of this was that if the High Council was going to all the trouble to gather the citizens like this, it was likely that Patrick still lived.

That thought was all that kept her going.

"Damnation," Dallyn muttered. "Keep your head down."

"Dallyn?" a female voice called. "I thought that was you, my dear. We have not seen you in forever."

Keeping her head tilted down, Syrie snuck a quick glance in the direction of the voice to see a woman coming in their direction with a man trailing behind her.

"Karalina," Dallyn said with a respectful bow of his head. "Gandry. Good to see you both."

"It has been much too long," Karalina said. "Your mother? She is well?"

"She is," Dallyn confirmed.

"That is good to hear," the woman replied. "We worry about her, so far out of town, all by herself. And who is your little friend, here? Someone special? Wedding bells in your future?"

"Karalina!" Gandry barked. "Must you always?"

"It is of no consequence, my friend," Dallyn said with remarkable calm. "Wedding bells, no. But she is special, indeed. My distant cousin who's traveled from the hinterlands to spend some time with us."

"Have you a name, girl?" Gandry asked.

"Ellen," Syrie mumbled, borrowing the first name that came to mind.

"Have you a reason for hiding yourself from us?" Karalina asked. "The aura of your Magic is palpable. Here in the capital, we don't look kindly on the blatant use of disguise."

"She has good reason, indeed, Karalina," Dallyn said, placing an arm around Syrie's shoulders. "A fire on their homestead has left Ellen severely burned. She is, understandably, uncomfortable with her appearance. But, like so many of my mother's people, her grasp on the Magic is weak, so holding the disguise is tiring for her. This is why she has come to stay with us. Away from everyone, she will be able to properly rest and recover. Is that not so, Ellen?"

Syrie nodded, allowing the over layer of her disguise to shimmer and fade for just an instant, as if she struggled to hold the aura as Dallyn had claimed. Just long enough to expose the hideously burned face beneath.

Karalina gasped and quickly stepped back, bumping into the man who accompanied her.

"Exactly the reaction that drove her from her home," Dallyn said, disapproval strong in his voice.

"Our apologies, Dallyn. Please give your mother our regards," Gandry said, before steering Karalina away through the crowd.

"Well done," Dallyn murmured. "I doubt she will seek us out again this day."

Syrie might have thought to question him on how far and wide the woman's gossip of a visiting cousin would spread, but a hush fell over the crowd just then as the big doors opened and a woman stepped out onto the landing. It was not the Supreme Leader, of course, but no one had really expected that she would come. She addressed the people only from the Great Hall inside. This was one of the lesser members of the High Council.

"Know ye all present, by decree of the Supreme Leader, a Mortal has made his way into Wyddecol. He has been taken captive and will appear before the High Council in two days' time to face public questioning and to meet his fate."

A collective intake of breath flowed across the gathering and a few lone voices sprang up to demand details.

"Why is he here?"

"How did he breach our security?"

The woman on the landing held up one hand, signaling for quiet.

"He is here to conspire with the one we revered as Goddess against the High Council. More proof of her treachery against our people."

Two days' time.

Syrie turned to meet Dallyn's gaze, both of them knowing this coming event would determine the timeline for their revolt. The public appearance would be where they would confront Reynalia. With both Patrick and the Goddess present, it would be their best chance at a rescue. Perhaps their only chance, depending upon the punishment determined by the High Council.

With an arm still around Syrie's shoulders, Dallyn steered her toward the edges of the crowd as the woman on the landing disappeared inside the big doors.

Syrie let him lead her away, her mind entirely filled with the newly confirmed knowledge that Patrick lived. She should be feeling relief. Joy, even. But the consuming heaviness filling her chest seemed to prevent her feeling anything other than the anxiety that had become her permanent state. An anxiety that prodded at her emotions until she couldn't tell whether she wanted to cry or laugh.

"Quickly. Come with me."

She looked up to see that Larkin had joined them, leading the way for them to follow. They walked in silence for nearly half an hour before entering a clearing to find themselves in front of a neat white cottage.

"My home," Larkin said. "At least for the present. As you know, we will be moving soon, to take up residence in the Mortal world."

Dallyn seemed to take the comments in stride, so, obviously, he knew what their companion meant. Beyond that, it was of no matter to Syrie.

The door opened and a woman stood there waiting, a small boy in her arms. Anola, Larkin called her. One of the Fae from the south, Syrie would guess, from her dark hair and complexion. The child she held in her arms, a boy named Ian, favored her coloring.

Over the course of the next hour or so, they were served a meal Syrie couldn't enjoy while the men spoke of

Larkin's upcoming move to the Mortal world, where he would live out his days as the Guardian of a Portal. And once he was too old, the responsibility would pass to his sons, Ian and Tomas. It all seemed such a foregone conclusion that Syrie couldn't help but wonder how Anola might feel about leaving her home and everything she'd ever known for the Mortal Plain. She wanted to console the woman, to reassure her that there was much to look forward to, but she couldn't seem to work her way around the knot in her own emotions.

After Anola put her sons to bed, she led Syrie to a chamber with a small bed to sleep for the night. Sleep that she knew wouldn't come. Even without the strange anxiety roiling inside her, knowing Patrick lived but only being able to guess at how he might be made to suffer made sleep an impossibility.

No matter. She would sleep soon enough. In two days, when she had freed Patrick and had him safely by her side once again, then she would sleep.

* * *

A cold brace of water washed over Patrick. For an instant, he fought to remain in the dark oblivion where he had escaped, but the water made it impossible. Another slap of water drew him from the horrors of his dreams and cast him back into the world of the living. He licked his parched lips, his dry tongue catching up the droplets of water that trickled down his face. It was the closest he'd come to having either food or drink in the time he'd been held in this place.

The guard beside him laughed and tossed a wooden bucket to the floor, obviously the source of the water.

"Wanted you awake and coherent so that you can meet with your visitor, Mortal." Again the man laughed, but without any real emotion this time. "If you know what is best for you, you will answer the questions this time."

Patrick had never been accused of knowing what was best for him, but he found little point in sharing that with the guard. Likely would do no more than earn him another beating.

His arms ached from being stretched over his head, connected by manacles on his wrist and a chain in between. The chain had been passed across an overhead beam, so that only by standing on his tiptoes was he able to relieve the pressure on his shoulders.

"Do you know who I am, Mortal?"

His head turned more slowly than he would have liked to track the source of the voice. A woman, a Fae, tall and blond like so many he'd seen here. When he didn't answer, she spoke again.

"I am the Supreme Leader of the High Council of Wyddecol."

"The venerable Reynalia stands before you now, cur," came a voice from his left. "You should be on your knees."

"Not even if I could," Patrick managed to mumble and, at a nod from the woman in front of him, a fist smashed into his jaw.

"Consider that a reminder to remember your station here, interloper."

"How did the Goddess contact you?" Reynalia asked. "Who helped you enter Wyddecol? You need only to satisfy our curiosity and we will bring an end to your suffering."

"I ken nothing of yer Goddess," he mumbled, unable to get his lips to part properly to say the words.

"Insolence," the woman pronounced, and the fist struck him again.

Apparently the guard waited beside him for more than to awaken him with buckets of water.

"Who helped you enter Wyddecol?" she asked again. "How did you get into our world?"

"I doona know. Went to sleep by a pool of water. Woke up here. Canna remember anything else."

It was the story he had maintained from the beginning of their questions. The one he would maintain until his last breath. None that had assisted him would suffer on his account.

"Perhaps another round of lashings will improve your memory, Mortal."

Beside him, the guard unfurled a whip from his belt and cut the air with it. The cracking sound echoed loudly off the marble of the large room.

"I do not know what he is, but I can say for a fact, he is not a Mortal." A new voice. A man he had not heard before. "Any mere Mortal would have broken by now. I have seen the mark on his chest before, though I cannot recall where."

"All in good time, Orlyn," Reynalia said. "We will know all in good time."

Patrick had little time to consider who the newcomer might be or what their discussion meant. Another *crack* split the air and the sharp tip of the whip bit into the flesh of his back. He'd not taken the time to prepare, had not steeled himself in time to prevent his own cry of pain.

They'd gotten it from him once, but he'd not give them the satisfaction again.

CHAPTER TWENTY-SIX

Syrie stood at the south edge of the crowd, her fingers clenched tightly in the cloth of the robe she wore. Those who accompanied her were spread out along the edges of the gathering, the placement well planned to allow as many of the citizens to escape as possible if things went wrong.

When things went wrong. Not if. Things here were about to go very wrong.

She had no doubts about this. When they confronted the Supreme Leader of the High Council, all hell would break loose in the Great Hall. The prime task assigned to half her compatriots was to get those assembled safely away from the battle zone. Others would head straight for the Goddess. Her prime task was Patrick's rescue.

The thought of him as a prisoner had consumed her for the whole of the last two days. She'd barely been able to concentrate on anything else. Between the strange pressure inside her threatening her very sanity and the knowledge of his captivity, she'd been all but worthless in the planning for today's confrontation.

Council members began a solemn processional into the Hall from behind the dais, each one stopping behind the chair assigned to them. The members with the least power sat farthest from the center seat, itself a massive creation, more throne than chair. When all eight had taken their places, the air in the Great Hall shimmered, as if it took on a life of its own, forming a billowing curtain of silver behind the dais.

Smoke and mirrors, nothing more than a child's manipulation of the Magic. Trickery designed to impress the people gathered to witness the occasion.

A hush of reverence spread over the crowd when the Supreme Leader emerged through the curtain to take her place at the center of the table.

Reverence that should have been reserved for the Earth Mother, not so freely given to these mere men and women chosen to guide the politics of the Faerie people.

"We have called this assembly of our people to inform you all of the most serious of dangers we face. Our world is under attack," Reynalia pronounced, rising to her feet, the silver curtain behind her shimmering to form a perfectly planned backdrop. "War is coming. Our people, our very way of life are at risk. For months we have seen the tendrils of this assault creeping ever closer. Now, at last, we have the proof we needed to share knowledge of this threat with all of you. We have proof of who is responsible for this assault on the Faerie nation."

The curtain billowed open to a gasp from the crowd. There, in a glimmering cage of silver Magic, the Goddess hunkered, a band of the same silver Magic fastened around her neck.

"No!" someone cried out, but the Supreme Leader held up a hand, silencing the low murmur of the crowd.

"Yes," Reynalia said. "I'm afraid it is true. We suspected as much, but now we have our proof. Behold!"

She pointed to the back of the Great Hall just as the massive doors opened, allowing a group of guards to march in. At the center of the procession, a man stumbled along, two chains linked around his neck, held by a guard on either side.

Patrick!

Syrie's heart pounded at the sight of him, his hair dirty and tangled, his face a mass of bruises.

Once the guards forced him to his knees in front of the dais, all but the two holding his chains stepped away, giving Syrie an open view of his back, swollen and raw. An oft-applied whip, she guessed. They'd made him suffer. For her. For protecting her.

Someone was going to pay for what they had done to him.

Deep in her chest, the pressure that had been building for so long rolled itself into a tight, tiny ball, pulsing with her anger. In less than a heartbeat, the tiny ball burst forth, filling her eyes and her mind with stars. An unimaginable power surged through her body, bringing her to her knees. Her vision clouded so that she covered her eyes with her hands. Vaguely, she was aware of Dallyn reaching her side, helping her to stand, whispering, asking if she needed help.

Someone was going to need help, but it wasn't her.

When her vision cleared, everything around her seemed to sparkle, as if she viewed the world through a shimmering haze of green.

Green. The color of purest Faerie Magic. Her Magic, amplified many times over.

Slipping her arm from Dallyn's hold, Syrie pushed through the crowd. She made her way to the front of the room until she was only feet from where Patrick knelt between the guards. Once there, she let the cloak fall from her head and shoulders and dropped all pretense of the disguise she had worn, revealing herself to all those on the dais. She knew the moment she was recognized. Reynalia stopped speaking mid-sentence as their eyes met.

"It is time for your treachery to come to an end, Reynalia Ré Alyn," Syrie called out. "Release the man."

"You!" The Supreme Leader sneered. "You should have stayed where we sent you, little one."

"So that you could have me killed?" Syrie demanded. "As you tried more than once while I was there, I might add. I don't think so. Release the man."

Reynalia barked a laugh, rising to her feet. "Who do you think you are to give orders to the High Council? You are nothing. A disgraced handmaiden, returned from exile."

The other Council members were on their feet now, too, moving as a single entity toward the spot where the guards stood with Patrick, as if by their physical presence they could stop her. As they moved forward, the crowd surged back, leaving an open space between Syrie and the people she confronted.

Good. If they were to leave the Hall altogether, it would be even better. One less thing for her to worry over.

"Release the man," she said for the third time. "This is your last warning."

Three, she decided, was the magic number. She'd given them three chances to do as she asked. Three and no more.

"I have a better idea," Reynalia said as she moved to join the other members of the High Council. "What if we put you in chains with him?"

They'd had their warning.

Syrie turned her sparkling gaze on the chains that held Patrick, allowing a trickle of the fury she felt to ride the green rays of light. The band around his neck popped open and the chains slid to the floor at his feet.

"I'm not overly fond of chains," she said.

Patrick lifted his head to look at her, a smile forming on his parched lips. Her heart pounded in her chest as the power inside her pulsed in time with her heartbeat.

"What are you doing on your knees?" she asked, holding out her hand. "You belong at my side."

Patrick rose to his feet. The guards on either side of him looked first at their Supreme Leader before they stepped back to allow him to pass unchallenged.

The crowd had thinned considerably when the chains had fallen, leaving only a few bystanders mixed in with the men and women Dallyn had gathered to her support.

"Look around you, Reynalia. You are outnumbered. Release the Earth Mother," Syrie ordered, hoping this step would go as well as freeing Patrick had.

"Never!" the Supreme Leader vowed. "She'll remain as she is, chained for my entertainment, for as long as I draw breath. I am the Earth Mother now."

"You?" Syrie barked a laugh, derision and fury given life in one sound. "I don't think so. You're hardly a

Goddess. You don't even carry the blood of the royal family in your veins."

"The royal family," Reynalia sneered. "For all intents and purposes, there is no royal family anymore. I saw to their demise myself. What's left of that bloodline is little more than a self-absorbed lump of a man, confined to a glen for the rest of his pitiful life, wallowing in his own pathetic self-pity."

"There are more of the line remaining than you might imagine," Syrie said. "It was, in fact, one of their own who enabled my rescue from the hell where you'd abandoned me."

"Nevertheless, they cannot return to Wyddecol. They will never rule again." Reynalia lifted her chin, looking out over the people still gathered in the hall. "They never deserved to rule Wyddecol in the first place. They were unfit for the service. They never worked for what was right or best for the people."

It was clear that Reynalia had grown so accustomed to pandering to her audience that she continued to spout her lies even when so few of the people were left in the Great Hall to hear her.

"You expect me to believe that your High Council, this handpicked group you have assembled, is at all concerned with what is right and best for the people of Wyddecol? You think any of them believe war is best for them? War only suits your desire for power."

"You lie," Reynalia yelled.

"No, it's the truth, and we all know it. If your only desire was to do what is best for our people, you would be pleased to see me here. You would be pleased to see that I was saved from what you decreed as my fate by True

Love. If what you say is true, you should be thrilled that, in my return to Wyddecol, two souls have been set back on their proper paths. That, after all, is what is right and best, is it not? As that is the greatest desire of all our kind, is that not the task our people should devote themselves to enabling? Especially since it was the warring of our kind that was responsible for the tragedy that ripped those pairings asunder."

"Foolish child!" Reynalia shook her head, her eyes hardening. "Your priorities, the priorities of a lovesick girl, are not ours. We look to less frivolous pursuits than you suggest. You should have stayed where you were, Elesyria. You have little power here other than a few parlor tricks. You are insignificant to me, to us." She waved a hand to include the other members of the High Council stationed on either side of her. "Like a midge on a summer's night, you are but a minor annoyance. You should have remembered as much before you and these other traitors sought to rise against us."

"And you," the Earth Mother said from the cage of silver where they'd chained her, her voice hoarse and breaking. "You should have remembered more about your own history, if you ever knew it. You made a grievous error when you chose to punish my own maiden."

"We'll see about that," Reynalia snarled, extending an arm.

Jagged splinters of silver light streaked from her fingertips toward the little band of defenders, as pandemonium broke out in a cacophony of screams and barked orders.

Patrick threw himself in front of Syrie, no doubt determined to protect her. But he needn't have worried.

She lifted her hand and a net of pure light spread out around them, like a spiderweb spun of emerald shards, deflecting the bolts sent their way.

"You should have taken her powers, Reynalia." The voice of the Goddess rang out over the screams of those who had not yet escaped the battle area. "Simply sealing those powers behind a wall of forgetfulness was a poor choice on your part. Passing through the Time Flow of the All Conscious with her powers intact, like the tempering of fine steel, has made Elesyria stronger than ever. Much stronger than any of you," the Goddess intoned. "Perhaps even stronger than me."

Her? Stronger than the Goddess? Syrie didn't believe such a thing was possible. But even if it were, it didn't matter. It had nothing to do with why she'd come. She'd come to free the Goddess. She'd come to rescue Patrick. And so far, she'd only accomplished half of her goal.

"Let her go, Reynalia. Don't make this any worse than it has to be," Syrie said.

"You've already done that, girl," Reynalia snarled. "Did you not think me smart enough to realize you would come to the rescue of your man? Your Goddess? Did you not realize I would be prepared for your treachery once I knew you were in Wyddecol? I am not without my sources."

"Your spies, you mean," the Goddess said. "The ones you planted in my Temple."

"I planted nothing," Reynalia said. "I merely cultivated that which already grew wild thanks to your negligence and favoritism."

So there were spies at the Temple. A feeling of sadness filled Syrie's heart, quickly replaced with concern for her friend, Nally. The guards that had come after her, the ones who had captured Patrick, had also captured Nally.

"What have you done with Nalindria?" she demanded, dreading what she might hear but needing to know.

"I would not waste my worry on that count, if I were you," Reynalia said, moving backward to place more space between them. "She has been…" A pause, followed by an evil chuckle. "She has been appropriately rewarded for her treachery."

Poor Nally. Poor, gentle, dedicated Nally.

"You are a beast, Reynalia," Syrie said, forcing the words out through her sorrow and anger. "A beast whose time to rule has come to an end."

"I may be a beast, but you are a fool. Now!" Reynalia screamed, and her guards swarmed in from all sides of the room, streaming out from behind the draperies that lined the Great Hall.

All around Syrie, the clash and clank of metal meeting metal rose to drown out everything else. For a moment she regretted not having accepted the sword Dallyn had offered before they had come, but she knew it would do her little good. Of all the skills she possessed, use of that weapon was not one.

Beside her, Patrick laughed as he hefted a sword he'd taken from one of the guards. He swung it in an arc around his head before bringing it down in a slashing motion to stop the oncoming charge of another attacker. Around them, the battle raged, with fighters on both sides dropping. Slowly, Syrie found herself being edged toward the back of the Great Hall, forced in that direction by

Patrick's movements. It became clear to her that he fought to clear a path for their retreat.

"No," she yelled over the din of battle. "We cannot leave this place. We must free the Goddess."

Irritation flashed over his face and he exchanged words with Dallyn, who fought nearby. Together, the two of them began to move back in the direction from which they'd come, back toward the dais where the caged Goddess waited.

As soon as they were close enough, Syrie slipped around the men, darting past two approaching guards to climb onto the dais. She crawled under the long table and stayed on her hands and knees until she reached the cage. Up close, the sight of the Goddess took Syrie's breath from her. Dirty and weakened, she looked more woman than Goddess. Her hair hung in greasy clumps and her face sagged, as if the silver chain around her neck drew the very life source from her body.

"Hang on. I'll get you out of there," Syrie whispered.

"Make it so," the Goddess answered, her voice ragged, as if she had no energy left to speak.

Syrie absolutely intended to, as quickly as possible. *If* she could figure a way to open the damned cage.

There appeared to be no lock of any kind, no opening, either. Just bars of pulsing, glowing silver. After several minutes of useless examination, Syrie's frustration got the better of her. Grabbing the bars with her bare hands, she shook them violently. To her surprise, each of the bars she held ceased to glow, turning a dull gray before they crumbled to ash in her grip.

"Yes!" she exclaimed, moving her hands to the next set of bars.

She tightened her grip until those also crumbled and then moved on to the next, until a gap had formed, large enough for her to reach in to pull the Goddess toward her. When the chains pulled taut, Syrie let go of the sagging woman and fastened her hands around the chains. If it had worked for the cage, perhaps it would work for the chains in the same way.

Though it took longer, the chains ultimately gave way as well, allowing Syrie to pull the Goddess from the cage. Once she had the woman out, Syrie felt as if she were as constrained as she had been before opening the cage. The Goddess, after so long a time hunkered over in the tiny cage, was too weak to stand under her own power. She clung to Syrie as they crouched on the floor near the table.

Syrie had barely risen to her feet to search for help when she heard the ragged warning.

"Behind," the Goddess warned.

Syrie whirled to find Reynalia, knife in hand, approaching. Two cloaked figures followed closely behind her, as if to guard the Supreme Leader, but neither of these people carried weapons.

"You will not take her," Reynalia said, slowly moving forward. "We will not allow it. Neither of you will make it out of this hall."

A shout, more animal noise than words, pierced the air around them, stopping Reynalia and her escorts.

Patrick!

In one leap, he cleared the dais and landed on the table, running full speed. His sword held above his head, he threw himself toward Reynalia and those who accompanied her.

"Orlyn!" Reynalia screamed. "Now!"

In the split second before Patrick landed, the figure to Reynalia's right drew a wicked-looking sword from beneath his cloak and held it aloft, thrusting it into Patrick's chest and twisting it as Patrick fell to the ground.

"I remembered, son of Odin," Orlyn said. "Remembered the purpose of the mark you wear."

Blood pumped from the wound as the man withdrew his weapon and backed away. From across the distance between them, Patrick's eyes locked with Syrie's until they fluttered shut.

The air around Syrie pulsed, as if with an animal heartbeat of its very own. The pulse pounded against her eardrums, all but blocking the harsh sound of Reynalia's laughter when she stepped over Patrick's body, as if he were but a bump in her path to reach Syrie.

Syrie's vision clouded to a pinpoint before expanding, sharpened as if by a green crystalline lens. She felt as if she might explode until, a heartbeat later, the air exploded around her.

It took her a moment to realize that the animal scream ringing in the air came from her, ripped from her lungs as blood pumped from Patrick's wound. It took another moment to realize that the green lightning streaking across the dais came from her, too.

The filth who had thrust his sword into Patrick's chest threw himself in front of Reynalia, taking the full force of the blast Syrie sent her direction. Reynalia screamed, grabbing her face and stumbling forward. Before Orlyn's ashes finished falling, the second of Reynalia's companions grabbed hold of the Supreme Leader, dragging her to safety behind the curtains leading away from the Great Hall.

But not before betraying her own identity.

As she grabbed Reynalia's arm to hurry her away, her own cloak fell back, revealing her face.

Nalindria!

The treachery hit like a punch to the gut, staggering Syrie as she lurched toward the spot where Patrick lay. Her own best friend. The one person in Wyddecol she'd thought she could trust above all others.

Reaching Patrick's side, she dropped to her knees, her fingers searching his throat for a pulse. It was so faint and irregular, she almost missed it. Inserting her fingers into the slice in his shirt, she ripped the material apart, exposing the whole of his chest. Blood oozed up around her fingers when she laid her hand over the gaping hole, formed directly in the center of the mark on his chest. Though he still breathed, it was only shallowly, and no matter how she called to him, no matter the tears she shed, his eyes did not open.

"Help me!" she cried out, not knowing who she expected to come to her aid.

"It is too late, my lady," Dallyn said, resting a hand on her shoulder.

Too late? Impossible!

When all had been lost for her, Patrick had risked everything to find her. When her life was threatened, he'd been there to protect her. Too late, the man said? Never! She wouldn't allow it to be too late.

If she had the abilities everyone seemed to think she possessed, now was the time to call upon them.

"Can you lift him?" she asked, rising to her feet.

"Of course I can," Dallyn said, a ring of offense tinging his answer. "But to what end you ask this, I can not understand."

"You don't need to understand," she said, turning her back and starting for the door that opened onto the plaza. "You only need to bring him where I lead."

She had to act quickly. Yes, what she planned was against every rule of her people, but it was the only chance she had. It would work. It had to work. And if anyone thought to stop her? She'd incinerate them where they stood just as she had the man whose blow had taken Patrick down.

Doing her best to ignore the misery around her, she quickly threaded her way between the fallen combatants, to push open the great doors and step out into the fresh air.

"Where do you think to take—" Dallyn's question cut off with a sharp inhalation of breath when they crossed the plaza and started down the staircase, as if it had only just occurred to him what she planned to do. "You cannot take him to the Fountain. It is forbidden."

She stopped only long enough to fix him with a look. "Indeed it is. But our people have rarely been good at refraining from those things which are forbidden to them. It is for that reason that the Fountain exists in the fragile state it does now. Besides, if it makes you feel any better, we're not taking him *to* the Fountain. We're going to put him *in* the Fountain. Step lively, Captain. We've no time to waste."

"Wait," he said, holding her up once more. "You must tell me something first and you must tell me truly. Do you really believe what you said to Reynalia? That it is up to us to set straight the souls that were cleaved asunder in the War of the Long Ago?"

"Absolutely, I believe this," Syrie said. "If not us, then who should do it? It should be our life's greatest calling. Which is why you must hurry. I have finally found my other half and I don't intend that I should lose him now."

* * *

Patrick awoke, as if from a horrible nightmare, choking and spitting out water. He was drowning!

But how was such a thing possible? He was supposed to be dying. This much he knew for a fact. He'd felt the weapon used against him slide into the center of the mark on his chest, straight into his heart. Of that there could be no doubt, just as there could be no doubt that only a strike in that exact spot could be immediately lethal to him. It was as his father had always said. The Mark of the Warrior, an honor to bear. A target to wear.

And yet, once again, water filled his nose and, as he gasped for air, his mouth and throat.

"Help me pull him out."

Syrie's voice!

"Patrick? Can you hear me? Speak to me!"

He fought the exhaustion that prevented him from opening his eyes. Fought the siren call of the seductive black void that beckoned him to remain. Syrie called for him to return to her and he could do nothing but obey. For her, he would gladly give up his seat in the finest banquet hall of Valhalla.

The buzzing of a million voices filled his brain, a tingly, burning sensation that traveled into his face and down his throat. Pulsing and growing, it flowed through the whole of his body until every single part of him seemed to vibrate. When the foreign sensation reached his heart, he felt as though the sun itself were searing his skin, from the inside out.

As quickly as it had begun, the sensations ceased and, at last, he managed to open his eyes.

"There you are! You've come back to me."

Syrie's beautiful face hovered over him and, without thought, he reached for her, pulling her tightly to him in an embrace that ended in a kiss. He savored the feel of her, the scent of her, the sight of her eyes drifting shut as he held her. Had it been up to him, he would have held onto this moment, dragging it out into forever, completely satisfied to spend his afterlife in just such a manner.

But his Syrie had other ideas.

"It's done," she said, rocking back on her heels and offering a hand to help him to his feet. "The Goddess is free and our lives can return to normal."

That sounded all well and good, except for one thing. He didn't want normal. He wanted a life with her.

The question was, did she want a life with him?

"We need to talk, Syrie," he said, determined to find out once and for all how she felt about him. "We need to talk about us."

She stilled, her eyes darting to the ground in front of her. "Us?" she asked. "What about us?"

At least she hadn't claimed there was no *us* to talk about.

"Elesyria!" Darnee, the tall Faerie guard who'd loaned them her cottage in the woods, approached at a run. "The Goddess bids you come to her."

For a moment, Syrie's expression wavered, as if she might refuse. But, as he would expect of her, she turned back toward the Great Hall, accompanying Darnee.

He followed along behind the two women, back into the Great Hall where they'd battled the High Council and their army. Bodies lay everywhere, both those who had fought for the release of the Goddess and against. Off to one side he saw the body of Larkin, one of the men who'd come to the cottage with Dallyn.

As the women hurried on ahead of him, Patrick made his way through the others to pause at Larkin's side. The man's golden armor had lost its gleam, and a small, dark-haired woman leaned over him, weeping. Next to them stood two small boys, one golden like his father, the other, the elder, dark like his mother. Patrick doubted that either of the children could be more than five or six years old at most.

"You must do as I said, Anola, my love. Take the boys to Thistle Down Manor, just as we'd planned. This changes nothing of your future," Larkin rasped, a trickle of blood at the corner of his mouth.

"It changes everything," she said, her words strangled by her tears.

"And you, Ian," Larkin continued, as if determined to have his say before it was too late. "You, my son, must take my place as a Guardian. I'd have your oath, son. Your oath to devote yourself to the protection of the Fountain and of the Mortals."

"I so swear," the older of the two boys said, his dark head bending close to his mother. "I will do as you ask, Father."

This scene represented everything Patrick hated about battle. How could any amount of glory count for anything in the presence of such loss and sorrow? He turned away, uncomfortable that he should be intruding on this most private of family moments.

On the dais, the Goddess occupied a large chair with Syrie kneeling in front of her.

The sight annoyed him, that Syrie should kneel to anyone, let alone that woman, especially after all Syrie had done for this Goddess of hers. He quickened his steps until he reached Syrie, taking his place just behind her.

"What will you do next, Elesyria? What would you have of me?" the Goddess asked, her dark eyes fixed upon Syrie. "We both know I am too weak as I am now to oppose you."

"Oppose me?" Syrie echoed, her voice holding the same surprise reflected in her expression. "What makes you think you would ever have call to do that? Haven't I proved myself to you, my loyalty to you, with what I've done here today?"

The Goddess shrugged. "What you have proved is that you are indeed stronger than I am. Even at my best, I will never have the power that you have at your disposal. It would be well within your rights to challenge me."

"Challenge you?" Syrie squeaked, her head swiveling from the Goddess to Patrick and back again. "You mean challenge you so that I could be the Goddess? But...don't you have to be born special, or something?"

"This is how it has always been done. The strongest among us, the one best able to control the Magic, is the one who ascends to the position of Earth Mother. And you, my dear, were special enough by birth and even more so now by your trial of passing through the Magic."

Patrick felt his stomach tighten, like a child expecting to receive a favorite gift, only to learn at the last minute that the gift was being given to someone else. If Syrie chose to become the Earth Mother of all Wyddecol, there would be no room for him in her life.

"Right," Syrie said, rising to stand, shaking her head as she did. "All I planned to ask for was to be permanently released from service in your Temple. I want my freedom and from what I've seen, you're as much a prisoner there as you were here. Oh, there are no chains on you in the Temple, to be sure. No tiny, cramped cage, but it's a cage nonetheless. You serve the Faerie people. You live apart in a beautiful palace, but you must always be available at their beck and call. No, that's not something I ever see me wanting for myself. As far as I'm concerned, you're the Earth Mother, and welcome to it."

A flash of surprise lit the older woman's face, but it was quickly replaced with the emotionless mask she had worn before.

"You realize, of course, that if you return to the Mortals' world, you will live there in danger. Reynalia escaped, likely to join her brother, who was exiled after the last coup in Wyddecol. She will live out her days on the Mortal Plain, bereft of her Magic. That will be my official decree once all this is taken care of." The Goddess swept out an arm to indicate the devastation around them. "But, on the Mortal Plain, she will seek you out for her revenge. You and those who are important to you. It will be no different here. Though she is gone, it is likely she has followers who would be a danger to you, as well."

"Don't you worry about me," Syrie said with a bright smile. "Knowing I'm free to go anywhere I want, I think I can find a way to avoid her and all her minions."

Patrick took the hand she held out to him and led her back through the carnage out onto the plaza. Fearing what she might have to say, he knew he could delay the inevitable no longer. He had to know.

* * *

"What does the world hold for us now?" Patrick asked as they reached a quiet spot overlooking the blessed Fountain of Souls. "We've been to the future and we've been to Wyddecol. What comes next for us?"

Syrie turned to face her big warrior, moving close enough to look up into his face before she answered. "I've spent my whole life searching for two things. I've always believed that finding those two things would bring me the happiness I sought. One of things was a purpose worthy of devoting my life to and, through all of this we've faced, I've discovered that purpose at last. I know now that I'm meant to bring the souls lost to one another back together again, and I mean to spend the rest of my life doing exactly that."

True Love was, as she had told Dallyn, the most important of all causes. True Love could exist only when those souls that were meant to be together found one another and joined. For too long, that process had been burdened by the wanton loss of life and the destruction of the Fountain during the Great War. The Fountain had quickly been rebuilt, but nothing had been done to reconnect that which had been torn asunder. With her new power, she intended to be the one to do something about it.

"And the other?" he asked, his hands rigid at his side.

"The other what?" she said, biting the inside of her cheek to keep a smile from her lips as his scowl drew his eyebrows together.

Patrick was perhaps the only man she'd ever met who could look as sexy when he frowned as he did when he smiled.

"The other thing you've spent yer life searching for," he said, his exasperation clear in his voice. "You said there were two things. What is the second?"

"Why, you, of course," she said, giving up all pretext of keeping him in suspense. "And now that I've found you, I intend that you'll never get away from me, my great, scowling warrior."

No, she'd been wrong. The smile breaking over his face now was much, much sexier than the scowl had been.

"That's a good thing, then, Elf," he said, his smile playing at the corners of his mouth as he hooked his thumbs into the belt at his waist. "Since I mean to never let you get away from me again. As far as I'm concerned, it's only death what has the power to separate us now."

As much as she loved the man, he did have his aggravating habits.

"How many times must I tell you I'm not an Elf?" she began, but paused as a new thought occurred to her. "My big Valkyrie."

His brow wrinkled at her use of the name, just as she'd suspected it might.

"Valkyrie? Yer muchly mistaken in yer choice of words, my wee Elf. A Valkyrie is a female warrior. It's no' a stretch to say that I canna believe you could ever mistake me for a woman."

His stance, chin lifted, chest puffed out, would have done any strutting peacock proud.

"True. But no more so than my disbelief that you'd mistake me for an Elf," she returned.

"Ach, that one's easy enough to understand," he said with a grin. "Let me explain. You or an Elf, both have yer roots firmly planted in the world of Magic. So you can see, to an outsider like me, there's little enough difference between you."

"Really?" Syrie asked, feeling more confident in her plan by the moment. "Well, then. By that reasoning, you or a Valkyrie, both have your roots firmly planted in the legends of Asgard. There's little enough difference there, as well. To an outsider like me, that is."

Brow furrowed, Patrick stroked his chin, seemingly deep in consideration of her argument, though his eyes twinkled with humor. "I see yer point. That being the case, I suppose I'd best come up with a new name to call you by," he said.

"You might try using my actual name," she suggested, a hint of annoyance growing at his obstinate insistence on using anything else. "It's worked fairly well for any number of years."

"Granted, it's a lovely enough name. But I doona believe that will work for my purposes. It disna carry the ring to it that I seek." Again that familiar grin broke over his face. "I do have a new one in mind, though. One I've been considering for a while now, even before you pointed out the error of my ways. Might I test it on you? To see what you think of it?"

"A new name?" Syrie asked, her jaw tightening as she determined not to argue with Patrick, no matter how much he provoked her. "Oh, do tell. I can hardly wait to hear what you have come up with this time."

"Good. I've been thinking *wife* has a sound to it that pleases me. Trips right off the tongue, it does. What say you? Does that one please you more than the other?"

For one of the few times in her life, Syrie found herself close to speechless. "What are you saying?"

"I'm no' *saying* anything, my love. I'm *asking*. And I think my meaning is clear enough," he said.

"Is this your own barbaric way of proposing marriage to me?" she asked, leaning into him and placing her hand on his cheek.

"I suppose it is," he answered, at last wrapping his arms around her as she'd wanted all along. "Until death do us part."

He dipped his head, covering her lips with his, and she had only a moment to wonder if the dousing he'd taken into the Fountain of Souls just might take care of that whole death complication for them. But then, the kiss deepened and she was lost, her mind drifting in that great, soft place where only Patrick could take her.

CHAPTER TWENTY-SEVEN

"I still can't believe I'm really here." Ellen laced her hands in her lap, shaking her head. "Everyone thinks I've lost my mind in dropping everything to travel to Scotland just weeks before my wedding."

"Everyone?" Syrie sat in the backseat of the speeding car next to her friend. "Even Robert?"

"Especially him," Ellen said with a grin. "But, unlike everyone else, he told me I should do what I thought I needed to do. He even made sure my passport application was expedited."

"Good for Robert," Syrie said, grateful to hear that bit of news. "I'm so pleased that you've come. I'm just sorry Rosella decided against coming with you."

The grin faded from Ellen's face and she dropped her eyes to study her hands. "I know. But she and Clint are determined to keep their distance from all that—" She cut off what she'd been about to say, her glance darting toward the driver before she continued. "All that, you know, business."

Yes, Syrie knew what she meant. All that *Faerie* business. All that information Ellen had taken so well when Syrie had finally explained it to her.

"I understand how they must feel," Syrie said. "And I'll respect her wishes. I just hope they both realize that you can't very well keep your distance from something that is a part of you. It will be passed to her sons and her daughters. There is no escaping what you are, no matter how you might want to be something else."

"Nonetheless, they want to try and, as you say, we need to respect their wishes. It's part of the reason they decided not to wait to get married." She paused for a moment, the smile returning to her face along with a glint in her eye. "Well, that and the baby they're expecting."

"No!" Syrie exclaimed. "That's so wonderful for them. They'll be excellent parents, I've not one single doubt."

"I'm sure they will," Ellen agreed. "When Rosella shared her good news, she said it was for her child that she felt the need to bury her heritage. She asked me to let you know that she will always remember you and Patrick, but she hopes you'll understand how she and Clint feel and not try to contact her again. With a family to think of, she wants to put all those things behind her."

"I'm sure she does," Syrie agreed, her heart heavy with the knowledge that what her friend wanted was next to impossible. "Don't get me wrong. I won't make any effort to reach out to her again. I wish them all the best for success. But there are some things in life you simply can't put away from you. As I said, even if she manages to avoid the pitfalls that await someone like her, what she is will still be there. In her blood. A part of her very essence. A part of her children."

"You're probably right." Ellen shrugged, looking away and out the window at the passing countryside. "Still, at the very least, she's extraordinarily happy right now. Being a new wife and a soon-to-be mother suits her well. She's known from the first what she wanted and she's quite clearly found it. Selfishly, though, I will miss being her friend and basking in the glow of her happiness."

"With your wedding approaching in less than a month, you've your own happiness to enjoy. Right?" Syrie asked, studying her friend closely.

This was the reason she'd asked Ellen to come here. Perhaps this was the time to tell her that.

"We've arrived, Mrs. MacDowylt," the driver said, pulling off the road and into a long gravel drive.

Or perhaps that explanation would have to wait for just a bit.

"What a beautiful little house," Ellen exclaimed as she stepped out of the car.

Syrie exchanged a few words with the driver and waited silently until he'd taken Ellen's bags from the car and set them inside the front door.

"What do you think of the interior?" she asked, holding out an arm to invite her friend inside.

"Oh!" Ellen's slow release of breath and sparkling eyes held her answer better than any words. "It's exactly as I would have decorated it. All blues and yellows. It's perfect!"

"I'm glad you like it," Syrie said, unable to hold back her grin. "That's a very good thing, too, since it's yours."

"What?" Ellen stopped in her exploration of the little kitchen, her eyes wide with shock.

"Yes, yours. Not yours and Robert's. Yours. So that you'll forever have a place to come be yourself and an excuse to come see me."

No matter what choices Ellen made in the next few days, that would always be true.

"I don't know what to say," Ellen managed at last. "I don't see how I can accept something so expensive."

"Pfft," Syrie dismissed. "Let's put on a pot of water to heat and we'll have some tea. Tea, as you once told me, makes everything better."

While Syrie heated water, Ellen took her suitcase to the bedroom and, when she returned, they carried their cups to the sofa, settling in for a comfortable chat.

Well, perhaps not comfortable. What Syrie intended next would likely be anything but comfortable.

"You never answered my question, you know," she said, fixing a look on Ellen that made the other woman squirm.

"What question was that?"

"The question about your happiness, of course," Syrie said. "You told me once that you wished you could be as sure of your agreeing to wed Robert as Rosella was in her choice to wed Clint. Do you still feel that way?"

Ellen sighed, a long, shaky release of breath, as she stared into her cup of tea. "I guess. But that's only to be expected. Pre-wedding jitters, no doubt. I'm sure I told you about my parents. Danny was so much older when I was born. It was clear from the moment I was old enough to understand what was going on, maybe even earlier, that I was an accident. My parents barely tolerated each other. That's why I spent so much time with my grandparents. And that's why their home was so important to me. I just don't want to end up like my mother. Simply existing from day to day, hating every moment of my life."

"I can assure you, Ellen, that is not your path, no matter what choice you make." Syrie gave her friend's hand a pat. "But I do have one more gift for you, if you choose to accept it."

Ellen was already shaking her head before Syrie finished speaking. "I can't let you spend anything else on me. The trip here, this wonderful house. I'm already in shock with what you've done for me."

"There's no cost to this gift," Syrie assured her. "What would you say to my offering you the opportunity to make sure that Robert is the right choice for you?"

Ellen's hand froze in midair, her cup halfway to her mouth. "How could you do something like that?"

"Never you mind how," Syrie answered. "If it were possible, would you be willing to find out?"

"Absolutely," Ellen said without pause, setting her cup on the coffee table. "What do I have to do?"

This was what Syrie loved best about her friend. Ellen was absolutely fearless in her trust of her friends and family.

"My people believe in a very special Magic. The Magic of True Love, we call it. Every soul has a perfect partner." Syrie watched Ellen for any reaction, and when there was none, she continued. "The best I can explain it is that these souls are like two halves of a whole. In the ancient days of the Long Ago, those souls were perfectly matched and lived out every one of their lives together. Then came the first of battles for power in the Faerie World. It was so violent that the soul pairings were ripped asunder by those who challenged for control of Wyddecol, my home world.

Since that time, many things have changed, but what's important here, is that so many of those soul pairings are now out of sync. You might be fortunate and find your other half in your own world. Or your other half might have lived in the past so that you have no chance to be together in this lifetime."

"Soooo." Ellen stretched out the word as if she sought time for what Syrie had told her to sink in. "If I understand what you're saying, if I don't find my perfect partner in this lifetime, I'll have another chance later on?"

"Hopefully," Syrie answered, determined to be as honest as she could. "But it's a random thing now. There are no guarantees. The cycles that kept them together have been destroyed."

Ellen nodded, her brows drawing together in confusion. "If that's the case, how can you give me the opportunity to know whether or not Robert is the one for me?"

Syric chewed on the corner of her lips, reminding herself that she'd determined before she'd invited Ellen to come here that she wouldn't sugarcoat what she needed to say in any way.

"I can tell you now that Robert is not The One for you. He is not your SoulMate. Understand, that doesn't mean he isn't your best choice in this life. It simply means that he isn't the other half that completes you."

"How can you possibly know that?" Ellen asked, her hands clenching in her lap. "How can you know that, when I don't even know that?"

Finally, something with an easy answer.

"Because, if he were *The One*, you wouldn't need to question it. You'd know. Just like Rosella knew about

Clint." Before Ellen could question her more, Syrie held up a hand to forestall more questions. "I can prove it. If you're willing to try something completely out of the ordinary."

So completely out of the ordinary that she probably shouldn't even have used the word *ordinary* in speaking of it.

"Absolutely, I am," Ellen said. "What do we do to make this happen?"

No hesitation at all in her response. No need to think over the offer. More proof that Syrie was right in what she was preparing to do.

"You go to where and when your True Love lives. Spend some time with him. Decide if life with him is worth giving up everything you know here and now."

Ellen's face seemed to lose a bit of its color. Understandable, considering what it was she must decide.

"When?" she asked, her voice pitched much higher than usual. "Did you say I'd go to *when* he lives? *When*, as in a whole different time?"

"Of course," Syrie answered. "If he lived in this time, in the same time you live in, you would already have found one another. I realize this is a daunting proposition. Do you still want to do this? You don't have to, you know."

"I…" Ellen hesitated this time. "Yes, I do. The time thing be damned. If I'm ever going to be happy, I need to know for sure."

Syrie smiled at her friend. What Ellen was about to experience would be something that would change her life forever.

"It's important for you to understand before we start that there is no wrong choice for you to make. Once you find him, you can stay with him and life will proceed here as it needs to. Or you can return here, to your own time, and live out a happy life with Robert. Perhaps not as happy as you might be with your own other half, but happy enough. You simply need to understand that whatever you decide to do will have far-reaching consequences. Both for you and for your descendants."

Ellen's expression blanked as she considered what she'd heard. "You mean, if I find this perfect man and I decide to stay with him, I could be robbing my children or my grandchildren of the opportunity to find their own perfect SoulMate?"

Syrie shrugged. "There is no way to know that. You will definitely be changing who and what they are, but that change doesn't necessarily mean for the worse. Again, there is no wrong choice, only a choice. The future is riddled with paths, all the result of free choice. I can see some of those, but, without knowing each of the hundreds of choices you'll make over the years, there is no guarantee as to what things will definitely happen. There are only two guarantees I can make to you. One is that, no matter what you decide, this cottage will always be yours, to visit whenever you like."

"And the second?" Ellen asked.

"The second is that I will do my best to see to your happiness and to that of your descendants for as long as I can. I will tell you that, if you return to this place, to follow your current plans, I have seen a future path where your granddaughter will be one day faced with this same choice."

Syrie had debated sharing this bit of information, but Ellen deserved as much information as possible to make her decision.

She could have told her more. Probably should have, at least according to Orabilis. The old Faerie thought Ellen should be warned that her choice to stay with her SoulMate would cause ripples and changes all throughout the timeline.

To Syrie's way of thinking, that sort of knowledge placed too large a burden on anyone to allow them to make the choice they really wanted to make. That was the kind of knowledge that you shared to weight the scales of decision making. The kind of knowledge you shared to keep someone from doing something. Just as Orabilis had shared the knowledge with Syrie because she had hoped to prevent Syrie from making this offer to Ellen. As Orabilis had shared because she hoped to dissuade Syrie from pursuing so many of the plans she had for her own future.

No, she wouldn't tell Ellen everything. Only what she needed to know to convince her that she was free to choose whichever path would make her happier.

"If I stay there, will my granddaughter find her SoulMate in her own time?" Ellen asked, pulling Syrie from her thoughts.

"That I cannot say. I have not seen that granddaughter along any of those paths," Syrie answered honestly.

Ellen took another sip of her tea and once again set the cup on the table, a smile lighting her face when she looked up. "A lot to keep in mind when I make my decision, yes? Okay, then. Let's get the ball rolling, Syrie. I'm ready whenever you are."

Syrie stood and held out her hand, drawing Ellen to the door and outside. "Just a short hike to a lovely arbor where you'll start your journey."

A journey that might take Ellen anywhere in time.

EPILOGUE

Bield Cottage - Scotland
Present Day

"And that, my dear, is the story of everything that led up to your being here at Bield Cottage today."

Emily Evans stared at the lovely older woman sitting next to her, unable to put words together in any sort of coherent way. A Faerie world in political upheaval? Time travel to join souls intended to be together? How could that woman possibly sit there so calmly, as if she'd just spoken of the weather or some humdrum drive in the country?

Emmie had known there was something unusual about Syrie MacDowylt from the moment she'd first met the woman. Granted, something so far out of the realm of possibility as the story this woman had just told her would explain how, seven hundred years ago, the wife of the third laird of MacKillican could have had the exact same name as Annie, Emmie's cousin, who had died so mysteriously six months ago. It had been Annie's death that had led to

Emmie coming here to Bield Cottage as the caretaker of this property.

Syrie's fantastic story could indeed explain the strange coincidence if it had any basis in reality, that is. Which it didn't. It couldn't! The story Syrie had just recounted of how she'd come to know Annie and her grandmother Ellen was beyond anything Emmie could ever have imagined. Like Faeries and Magic and time-traveling adventures, the woman's story couldn't be anything other than sheer fantasy.

With a patient smile, Syrie put down her cup and rose to her feet, extending a hand down to Emmie. "Come take a walk with me, my dear. I've something I'd like to show you."

Emmie accepted Syrie's hand and stood, following along out the door and toward the woods.

"Where are we going?" Emmie asked after several moments of silence. "What is it that you want me to see?"

"We're headed toward the castle. I've something there that I think might help you to accept the truth of all the things I've told you today. And, to carry on with my plans for Bield Cottage and your staying here, it's important to me that you believe. More than important, actually. It's a necessity."

For the first time since Emmie had responded to the knock on the door this morning to find Syrie standing there, she felt a tremor of fear ripple through her stomach. Was Syrie trying to tell her that she had decided against allowing Emmie to remain as the caretaker? Even the thought of having to leave this place brought a sheen of tears to her eyes.

In the past six months she'd come to love this place as if she'd been born to live here. She'd just signed the lease on a tiny shop in the village, where she planned to display and sell the jewelry she created. Everything was finalized except the last of the paperwork, waiting only for her to choose a name for her shop. In her short time here, she'd known a sense of freedom and peace she'd never experienced anywhere else. Being forced out now would surely break her heart.

"Don't be such a silly girl," Syrie muttered before turning, that patient smile of hers once again in place. "Look ahead on the path and tell me what you see."

Though Emmie couldn't imagine how it could possibly convince her to believe Syrie's story, she did as she was asked. "We've reached the ruins of Castle MacKillican. We're standing where I imagine the gates originally stood."

"Very good," Syrie said. "Now, keep your eyes fixed in front of you."

"What is it you think—"

The question Emmie had been about to ask evaporated on her lips as the world in front of her shifted, going slightly out of focus before it hazed over, as if she viewed it through a pair of green lenses. In the next moment, much like a curtain being drawn back, everything cleared. Only, as the scene sharpened, it wasn't ruins of a castle in front of her but a fully intact, beautifully kept castle, surrounded by a lawn of green where goats wandered. A small, moat-like stream surrounded the perimeter of the castle walls, with a short bridge leading from the path, over the water, and into the massive open gate.

"What is this place? Where did it come from?" Emmie asked, finding it somewhat difficult to stand without grabbing on to something.

With a laugh that tinkled like musical bells, Syrie placed a strong arm around Emmie's shoulders, lending support. "It didn't *come* from anywhere. It's always here, in the Between. This is my home."

"The Between?" Emmie asked, lifting a hand to rub her eyes, just in case she was seeing things. "What is that?"

"The Between is…" Syrie paused and shrugged, as if searching for an answer Emmie might understand. "It is the space between the Mortal Plain, your world, and Wyddecol, the world of the Fae."

"I don't understand any of this," Emmie said. "I've walked these grounds a thousand times. I've never seen this before. I've never seen anything even remotely like this before."

"Well, of course you haven't," Syrie said, a little wrinkle on her brow. "The Between isn't a place open to visitors from either world. You can't simply wander in here. You must be invited into this place, as I have invited you."

"There were ruins here," Emmie protested. "Just minutes ago."

"They're still there," Syrie said patiently. "In your world. Do you believe now?"

Emmie didn't know what to believe now. But she did know that everything she'd thought was an absolute truth when she got out of bed this morning probably wasn't. And if she could be so wrong about everything, then what better explanation than the one Syrie had given her?"

"I do."

How could she not? The proof had flickered into reality right in front of her own two eyes.

"Wonderful," Syrie said, her voice tinged with something that sounded suspiciously like relief. "In that case, I've one more thing to show you."

Again the world shifted. This time Emmie was prepared for the change and realized it was almost like sitting in the chair taking an eye exam, with the lenses being switched quickly for you to choose the better option between A or B.

"We're back in my world, right?" she asked.

The ruins in front of her should have answered her question, but with what she'd experienced today, she wanted the confirmation.

"Yes," Syrie said. "I want to show you the guest-house."

"What guest-house?" Emmie asked before she could stop herself.

Again Syrie's laughter tinkled through the forest. "Don't worry, dearest Emmie. I should have said the location of the future guest-house. The workmen will begin arriving tomorrow. They have assured me it will take no longer than four months to complete, weather willing. The delay will give us time to work out what new duties you'll have once it's done."

"New duties?"

"Absolutely," Syrie said. "As our caretaker, you'll be indispensable in helping to make sure the people who come here to stay find their happiness. Annie was spot on in choosing you for this position before she left. I can't imagine anyone would be better to assist me."

Syrie gave her a quick hug and then rambled on about the building process, but Emmie only half listened. Her heart filled with the knowledge that she'd apparently passed Syrie's test and would be allowed to remain at Bield Cottage. In the course of the past hour, she'd gone from near heartbreak to realizing her heart's desire.

In that moment, it was as if all the tumblers fell into place and she knew what she would name her shop.

"Of course you do, dear Emmie," Syrie said, as if they'd been carrying on a conversation all along. "I think Heart's Desire is the perfect name. We'll start the advertising right away. I'm sure it will help in drawing the right people our direction."

Emmie nodded her agreement, no longer surprised at anything this strange little woman said or did. All that mattered was that she could see her life happily playing out ahead of her. And the thought of helping other people find happiness such as she knew in this moment felt like a very good way to spend her life.

* * *

Delafée Valley, Switzerland
The Present

"I know you're there, Nalindria. Whatever it is, come tell me and get it over with."

Reynalia Servans placed the tips of her fingers to her temple in a fruitless attempt to hold off the headache she felt approaching. All these centuries and that servant girl still skulked in the shadows like a timid mouse when she had unpleasant news to deliver.

"It is your brother, mistress. He insists you join him at poolside for lunch."

"You can tell my brother—"

Reynalia bit back her first response, knowing it would only irritate Reynard. Dealing with her brother's over-inflated ego was an ongoing challenge. A time would come when holding her tongue would no longer be necessary, but today was not that time.

"You can tell him I will join him as soon as I change into appropriate clothing."

Nalindria started to scurry away, but paused, turning, her eyes darting as if she had something else to say.

"Spit it out, girl."

"*She* is with him," Nalindria said, before turning to hurry out of the room.

"Of course she is," Reynalia murmured, rising to walk to her closet.

When she'd first come to this world, wounded, defeated, Reynard had taken her in. Over the years, she'd helped him consolidate power among the Nuadians until there were only a few true leaders in charge. When the time was right, she'd taken her place as one of those leaders, successfully running her own part of the organization.

Naturally, when Reynard had shown up at her door a few years back, more dead than alive, with that horrible handprint burned into his flesh, she'd had no qualms about taking him in. It was the least she could do. But after he'd healed, things had changed and one of the most annoying changes had been his bringing that trashy mistress of his into her home. Adira Ré Alyn wasn't the sort of person Reynalia had ever associated with in Wyddecol, and she had no desire to do so here.

With a sigh of irritation, she brushed the hair away from her face, catching a glimpse of herself in the mirror. Her eyes gravitated toward the scar on her cheek left there by that miserable upstart who'd been the cause of her failure. Poor Orlyn had taken the brunt of that attack, but she hadn't gone unscathed, left with this mark to remind her of all she'd lost. Once again she swore she'd one day find Elesyria Aí Byrn and make her pay for what she'd done. Her and everyone she'd ever cared about.

Slipping off the silky robe she wore, she reached for a casual sundress and let it drop over her head.

With one more glance into the mirror, she left the room, headed for the pool.

Yes, one day soon things would change around here. She'd have her revenge on Elesyria and she'd have her brother out of her home. All she needed was patience and, over the centuries, she'd cultivated patience to a fine art. She liked to think of herself as akin to the spider sitting in the center of her perfectly spun web, waiting for her prey to drop into her trap.

A few more rounds of weaving and, just like the spider, her web would be ready.

* * *

The Between
The Present

"About time you were home again," Patrick called as Syrie entered the great hall of their castle. "I'd begun to think you'd decided to abandon me in favor of your Mortal world."

"Never," Syrie promised, hurrying her steps to throw her arms around her big warrior. "As I've told you so many times, once I found you, I was never letting you get away from me. You are mine, Patrick MacDowylt. Now and forever."

"I thought that was my line," Patrick said with a laugh as he lifted her off her feet for a kiss.

"Mine now," she replied, wishing they were in their own chamber rather than in the middle of the great hall.

She had been gone for far too long.

"As it should be." Another kiss and Patrick looked down at her, his eyebrow arching in that particular way of his. "Do drop that old woman's disguise, wife. You doona wish to startle the boys, now do you?"

"That would never do," she agreed.

In less time than it took to breath in, the air shifted around her and the facade of age slipped away. She was herself again.

"Much better," Patrick said, hugging her close. "Was yer visit as you'd hoped? The girl agreed to what you asked?"

"She did," Syrie said, smiling at the memory of Emmie's day. "Though I'd say she'll be working through the shock of it all for while."

"She has my sympathies on that one," Patrick said, his lips only a hair's breadth from hers. "Once she learns to go with the flow, she'll find the going much easier."

Go with the flow?

"Have you been watching those shows on the telly again?" she asked, knowing that particular modern invention was one of her husband's weaknesses.

"Why would you even think to ask a thing like that?" he blustered, his eyes twinkling even as he pretended to deny her accusation. "It's a fair old saying I learned, long in the past. Besides, did you no' enjoy yer own share of modern conveniences while you visited Emily?"

"I did. But you say that like we live a completely primitive life here. I'd hardly call it that."

They had, in fact, made their home a combination of all the things they liked best about the variety of times in which they'd traveled. After all, it would hardly make sense to have all that power and not use a little of it for their own comfort.

"Not entirely primitive," Patrick agreed. "We do enjoy a few favorite bits and pieces, now and again."

"So we do," she said, dutifully following him as he led her to the stairs and started up. "And just where exactly do you think you are leading me, my love?"

At the top of the stairs he turned and, with a laugh, swept her off her feet and into his arms.

"You've been gone two days, love. Two days and two long nights. Where am I taking you? Why, to one of my personal favorite bits of newfangled technology, of course. If that's acceptable to you, wife mine."

"It's absolutely acceptable," she answered, her laughter mingling with his as she tightened her arms around his neck. "In fact, it's more than acceptable. It's something I'd have insisted upon myself, husband mine, if I'd thought of it first."

This, this giddy feeling of happiness and excitement, this was what she wanted for everyone. This was what she was determined to give to as many people as she could. Their own personal happily ever afters. As soon as the guest-house was complete, she'd begin her search for those people she could help.

But for right now, with Patrick's plaid hitting the floor to pool around his feet, it was her own happily ever after she was most interested in. Because there were, after all, few things in life that made her happier than a rousing afternoon romp in the shower with the man of her dreams.

Dear Reader ~

Thank you so much for reading ANYWHERE IN TIME I do hope you enjoyed spending time with Syrie and Patrick and learning more about them and how their story will change their world — both past and future..

Next up in the series will be TIME TO SPARE, due out in late 2016. If you'd like to be notified when the next book will be released, you can sign up for my New Release Newsletter by going to my website at www.MelissaMayhue.com.

Have a comment or a question? You can find me on Facebook at www.Facebook.com/Melissa.Mayhue.Author. Or, contact me directly at Melissa@MelissaMayhue.com. I'd love to hear from you! We even have a special Facebook group just for the readers of this series and lovers of all time travel romance. We'd love to have you join us - www.Facebook.com/groups/Magic.of.Time/.

If you enjoyed this book, please consider leaving a review at your favorite online retailer or at Goodreads.com to help other readers find it.

~ Melissa

ABOUT THE AUTHOR

MELISSA MAYHUE, married and the mother of three sons, lives at the foot of the Rockies in beautiful Northern Colorado with her family and one very spoiled Boston Terrier. In addition to writing *The Magic of Time* Series, she has also written two additional paranormal historical series, *The Daughters of the Glen* Series and *The Warriors* series. She is also writing *The Chance, Colorado* Series, contemporary feel-good romances set in a small mountain town.

Want to be notified when the next book is due out? Sign up for Melissa's new release newsletter at her website, www.MelissaMayhue.com.